"Are you saying I told you I like turkey and grilled onions?"

Sam demanded.

"Not exactly," Jennifer answered. "But I can tell all sorts of things about you." Feeling bold, she dared to grin at him. "You like just about any movie Clint Eastwood ever made, and your favorite color is blue. You like to fish but not hunt, and—"

"Shut up."

But she'd come too far to be intimidated now. "You like your toast nearly burnt, your steaks medium rare. You played football in high school, hate baseball and—"

"Dammit, I'm warning you—" Sam began.

"What's the matter, Detective? Am I hitting a nerve? Shall I tell you about your ex-wife?"

Just then Sam moved to close the distance between them. "Watch it, sweetheart," he growled softly. "If you're so smart, tell me something about myself that's not common knowledge. Tell me what I *really* like."

Dear Reader,

A new year has begun, and in its honor we bring you six new—and wonderful!—Intimate Moments novels. First up is *A Marriage-Minded Man?* Linda Turner returns to THE LONE STAR SOCIAL CLUB for this scintillating tale of a cop faced with a gorgeous witness who's offering him lots of evidence—about a crime that has yet to be committed! What's her game? Is she involved? Is she completely crazy? Or is she totally on the level—and also the perfect woman for him?

Then there's Beverly Barton's *Gabriel Hawk's Lady,* the newest of THE PROTECTORS. Rorie Dean needs help rescuing her young nephew from the jungles of San Miguel, and Gabriel is the only man with the know-how to help. But what neither of them has counted on is the attraction that simmers between them, making their already dangerous mission a threat on not just one level but two!

Welcome Suzanne Brockmann back with *Love with the Proper Stranger,* a steamy tale of deceptions, false identities and overwhelming passion. In *Ryan's Rescue,* Karen Leabo matches a socialite on the run with a reporter hot on the trail of a story that starts looking very much like a romance. *Wife on Demand* is an intensely emotional marriage-of-convenience story from the pen of Alexandra Sellers. And finally, welcome historical author Barbara Ankrum, who debuts in the line with *To Love a Cowboy.*

Enjoy them all, then come back next month for more excitement and passion—right here in Silhouette Intimate Moments.

Yours,

[signature]

Leslie J. Wainger
Senior Editor and Editorial Coordinator

Please address questions and book requests to:
Silhouette Reader Service
U.S.: 3010 Walden Ave., P.O. Box 1325, Buffalo, NY 14269
Canadian: P.O. Box 609, Fort Erie, Ont. L2A 5X3

Linda Turner

A Marriage-Minded Man?

Silhouette®
INTIMATE™MOMENTS®

Published by Silhouette Books

America's Publisher of Contemporary Romance

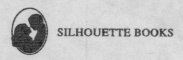 SILHOUETTE BOOKS

ISBN 0-373-07829-3

A MARRIAGE-MINDED MAN?

Copyright © 1998 by Linda Turner

This edition published by arrangement with Harlequin Books S.A.

Printed in U.S.A.

LINDA TURNER

began reading romances in high school and began writing them one night when she had nothing else to read. She's been writing ever since. Single, and living in Texas, she travels every chance she gets, scouting locales for her books.

I'd like to extend a special thanks to Francine Maness, friend and psychic, for her contribution to this story, and her tips over the years on what I can expect in the future. You were right, Francine, about the car wreck. Now, if the movie deal will just come through! Thanks for your help and friendship.

Prologue

It was the howling of a norther ripping through the caverns of downtown San Antonio, and not her alarm clock, that woke Jennifer three hours before dawn. Shivering, she reached for the patchwork quilt her grandmother had made when she was a girl and pulled it up until only her nose peeked out, like a beacon in the night. Outside in the alley, trash cans rattled and rolled, pushed along by the wind, and even though she knew she would have to chase them down later, she couldn't help but grin. She loved fall, especially the first cold front and the bite it put in the air. The north wind always put a sparkle in people's eyes and stirred their appetites for comfort food.

She'd have to change the lunch special, she decided. And make sure there was oatmeal for the regulars who came into her café for breakfast every morning like clockwork. They'd want plenty of coffee. And it went without saying that she'd have to double up on the cinnamon rolls.

The smell of cinnamon always put a smile on the grumpiest face on a cold morning.

Suddenly realizing she was lying there wasting time, grinning like an idiot while the clock ticked off precious moments, she threw off the covers and headed for the bathroom. If she was going to be ready for the morning rush, she had to get a move on.

She got only as far as the bathroom door when the vision came out of nowhere to engulf her. One second she was fumbling for the light switch in the dark, and the next a scene unfolded in her mind, consuming her, sucking her into it. There was no time to brace herself, no time to fight the powerful pull of the vision. Not that it would have done any good to resist. She'd learned a long time ago that the experience was much less traumatic if she didn't fight the image that for some God-given reason she was supposed to see.

Frozen, standing as still as death, she found herself staring through the open door of a room she'd never seen before. Decorated in chintz and lace and furnished with expensive antiques, it was obviously the bedroom of a wealthy woman. A wealthy *older* woman. Faded sepia photographs from a bygone era were prominently displayed on the dressing table and nightstands, and lingering on the air was a loneliness that Jennifer could almost reach out and touch it was so palpable.

The elderly lady who suddenly sat up in the ornate poster bed in the corner and clutched the covers to her thin bosom ached for the loved ones she had lost, but it wasn't her pain that caused Jennifer's heart to suddenly beat jerkily in her breast. It was fear. The kind that crept out of the shadows of the night and chilled the blood. Shivering, Jennifer wanted to believe that it was just the rustling of a branch against the eaves that had alarmed the old lady, but she knew better. The visions that had haunted her for as long as she could remember were never concerned with the mundane. Where there was fear, there was almost always danger, and there was nothing she could do to warn the old lady. She was only an observer, fated to stand and watch as events beyond her control unfolded.

Braced for God knew what, she gasped when a giant of a man rose up out of the darkness like the devil himself emerging from the smoky gates of hell. Easily six foot four or more, he was steeped in the foul odor that only clung to the really wicked. Instinctively Jennifer slammed her eyes shut, but the nightmare was there, in her head, inescapable. With her mind's eye, she saw the man, his features horribly distorted by a stocking mask, lunge for the old lady and grab her around the throat. Shrunken and frail, she never stood a chance. Her screams silenced by his powerful hands, she went limp and didn't make so much as a whimper when he tossed her aside like an old rag doll. Before she hit the floor, he was stepping over her, reaching for the jewelry case on the dresser.

Chapter 1

The bar was nothing but a sleazy dive on the west side, an old gas station that went bust during the oil embargo of the 1970s and sat empty until the present owner bought the building and turned it into a "private club." The place was no more a club than the Alamo was an amusement park, but it did have a membership that was notorious. Drug pushers, pimps and ex-cons from all over the city patronized the joint, and it wasn't just the cheap liquor that drew them there. According to rumor, on any given night you could buy or sell anything from young boys to the finest grade of china white.

Sam Kelly had raided the place more times than he cared to remember, usually without success, thanks to the eagle eye of Jason, the bouncer who stood guard outside the front door till all hours of the night, regardless of the weather. An ex-wrestler with hands the size of hams, he could spot an undercover cop half a mile down the road in the time it took to blink.

Tonight, however, Jason was in the hospital recovering from an emergency appendectomy. It was four o'clock in the morning, and the guard substituting for Jason had nodded off more than thirty minutes ago. Parked in the dark down the block, Sam could see that the bouncer was snoozing like a baby.

"This is it," he told his partner, Tanner Bennigan, as he drew his service revolver. "If we wait much longer, the jerk's going to wake himself up with his own snoring."

Tanner, relishing the thought of waking the thug himself, grinned in the dark. "Poor baby, this'll be the last time he sleeps on the job." Drawing his own gun, he gave a quiet command in his radio, signaling the team of uniformed officers waiting patiently in the shadows for the word to move in. "Let's go, men. It's party time."

It should have been a piece of cake. Another well-organized bust that went down without a hitch. But right from the second they rushed the front door, Sam knew something was wrong. When Tanner jolted the goon on guard duty awake, he didn't so much as sputter in alarm. Instead, he gave them a smug smile and invited them in for a drink at the bar. The second they hustled him inside, they knew why. The lowlife who patronized the place were wide-eyed and innocent and there wasn't an illegal substance in sight.

Swearing, Sam watched in growing frustration as first one, then another customer was patted down and searched without success. When the only damning evidence they came up with was an unpaid parking ticket, it didn't take a Ph.D. to figure out that they'd been made by someone. His jaw clenched on an oath, Sam just barely resisted snarling. Weeks, he thought in disgust. The raid had been planned for weeks, and all they had to show for it was a damn parking ticket! No wonder the jerk guarding the door had nodded off like a baby.

It was not, needless to say, the ideal way to end his shift, and by the time Sam arrived back at the police station downtown, he was in a bear of a mood. It was going on six in the morning, and it would be at least another hour or more before he finished typing up his report and explaining to the lieutenant what went wrong with a bust that should have gone down like clockwork. It wasn't an explanation he was looking forward to, especially when he still didn't know what the hell had gone wrong.

Going over the details again in his mind as he began the tedious task of writing his report, he never noticed the woman who stepped into the detective-squad room and headed straight for his desk until she spoke. "Excuse me, I'm sorry to interrupt you, but I'm looking for Detective Sam Kelly."

Scowling at his half-written report, he didn't even glance up, but simply pushed the nameplate on his desk to the front. "You found him," he said curtly. "Give me a second and I'll be right with you. I've got to finish this while it still makes some kind of sense. Have a seat."

Without a word she took the chair in front of his desk and sank into it. She didn't fidget or fiddle with her hair; she just sat there and waited patiently for him to look up from his work. Sam shouldn't have been distracted. He never had trouble concentrating, not even when the squad room was at its craziest. But he could feel the woman's steady gaze on him, studying him, and he didn't like it. Determinedly he dragged his attention back to the report, only to misspell two words in one sentence.

Irritated, he sat back in his chair and lifted a jaundiced eye to his visitor. She was young—mid-twenties—and pretty, in spite of the haunted look in her green eyes.

Small-boned and fragile, with a cloud of honey blond hair that fell in loose curls about her shoulders, she had an air of vulnerability that another man might have found impossible to resist. Sam, on the other hand, had no such trouble. As far as he was concerned, young, pretty and vulnerable was a combination he wanted nothing to do with.

His angular face set in hard lines, he growled, "What can I do for you?"

"I want to report a crime," she replied. "Robbery and assault."

All business, Sam immediately reached for pen and paper. "Your name and address?"

"Jennifer Hart. I live at 205 West Commerce, but —"

"Were you the victim or a witness?"

"A witness, but—"

"Where and when did the crime take place? Was the assailant armed? Did you get a look at his face?"

"Yes. I mean, no! Yes, he's armed—at least I feel like he was—but I couldn't see his face." Flustered by his rapid-fire questions, the images still so vivid in her mind she couldn't stop shaking in reaction, Jennifer said, "Please, you've got to do something! An old lady could be seriously hurt—"

"You didn't call an ambulance?" Swearing, he snatched up the phone and immediately punched in 911. "Where is she? What was her condition when you left her?"

"I didn't leave her," she blurted, stung that he thought she would just walk away from someone in trouble. "She hasn't been hurt yet, but she will be if you don't do something."

His midnight blue eyes suddenly dark with suspicion, he carefully replaced the phone in its cradle. "What do you mean, she hasn't been hurt *yet?* When exactly did this robbery take place?''

It was a logical question, one Jennifer had been dreading from the moment she walked in the door. Reluctantly she admitted, ''It hasn't happened yet. At least I don't think it has. I just had the vision this morning, so in all likelihood, it won't take place for a couple of days.''

''A vision,'' he repeated flatly. Tossing down his pen, he leaned back in his chair and all but rolled his eyes. ''You're psychic.''

From his tone, that made her lower than a snake and not much better than a con artist. Once she would have flinched just at the idea of anyone thinking so poorly of her, but she'd learned the hard way that she couldn't be concerned about what people thought. She had to do what was right. If other people had a problem with that, they'd just have to deal with it.

Lifting her chin, she looked Sam Kelly right in the eye and dared him to mock her. ''Yes, Detective Kelly, I'm a psychic. Obviously you don't have much use for people like me, but I'm not here to ask you to join my fan club. Just take a few minutes to listen to me, then check out my story.''

If she'd expected him to be suitably chastised, she might as well have saved her breath. Making no effort to hide his skepticism, he retorted, ''*If* there's a story, it will be checked out. Where does this woman live?''

''On the northeast side.''

That was all she could tell him, and not surprisingly, he jumped on that like a duck on a Junebug. ''The northeast side, huh? That covers a little less than a half a million people. Where would you suggest I start knocking on doors?''

He was so smug Jennifer wanted to smack him. Why,

out of all the detectives she could have dealt with, had she been handed an insufferable one with a smart mouth? Giving him a too-sweet smile, her green eyes sparking fire, she confided softly, "I think you must have me confused with God, detective. I'm not omniscient, just psychic. Believe me, if I knew which door to knock on, I'd do it myself, but I was only given a limited amount of information."

"Isn't that convenient?" he drawled. "You don't know who the old lady is, where she lives, or when some monster's going to try to choke the life out of her and rob her, but *I'm* supposed to find her beforehand and prevent it. And just how would you suggest I do that, Ms. Hart? With a crystal ball? Or maybe I should call 1-800-psychic. Just give me a clue about where to begin and I'll be happy to get started."

Oh, she'd give him a clue, all right, she fumed. A clue about just what he could do with a crystal ball, and she hoped he choked on it!

But even as the words hovered on her tongue, she knew the dangers of giving free rein to her temper. It left her vulnerable to others psychically, and that was the last thing she wanted to experience with the cynical Detective Kelly.

Clamping her teeth on a sharp retort, she struggled for control, only to find to her dismay that it was already too late. With no warning his emotions hit her like a blast of hot air. Anger. Disappointment. Frustration.

Caught up in the vortex before she could draw a steadying breath, she instinctively tried to slam the door shut on her own intuitiveness. She didn't intrude on anyone's privacy without an invitation—ever. But the barriers she usually threw up with ease evaded her grasp, and between one heartbeat and another, she found herself inundated with images from his most private thoughts and emotions.

His aura was dark and cloudy, his mood foul. He'd had a bad night, a case that hadn't turned out the way he'd expected, and he blamed himself. A less conscientious man would have shrugged off the foul-up as just one of those things that happens and let it go, but that clearly wasn't Sam Kelly's way. He didn't like mistakes, especially his own, and he took his responsibilities seriously. It was his duty to keep the bad guys off the street, and tonight he'd failed to do that. And although others had been involved, he blamed himself completely.

He had a John Wayne complex, she decided. Normally she found that admirable. There was just something about a tall, rawboned man fighting the injustices of the world that appealed to her. And like it or not, Sam Kelly fit that description to a T. He had a jaw like granite, piercing eyes that missed little and a toughness that no doubt could be incredibly reassuring when trouble loomed on the horizon.

But she wasn't trouble, and she didn't appreciate him looking at her like she was.

"Ms. Hart? I'm waiting. Are you having another vision or just coming up with another outrageous story?"

His mocking drawl snapped her back to attention and irritated her no end. Flushing, she clenched her teeth and counted to ten. It didn't help. "This isn't a story, Detective. Outrageous or otherwise. The victim is wealthy and appears to live by herself in a fieldstone house on a large tree-covered lot. Her husband may have died recently—she's very lonely. The attack isn't a random one—the robber has been watching her and other senior citizens who are vulnerable. He's already picked out his next victim."

Far from impressed, the detective lounged back in his chair, not even bothering to take notes as she gave him further details. "You can see all that," he said dubiously, "but you can't see the thug who half kills this old lady. Tell me something, Ms. Hart. Just what kind of psychic are you?"

"Actually, a damn frustrated one," she confessed. "After the night you've had, I would think you could sympathize with that, but I guess that's too much to ask." As regal as a queen, she rose to her feet and handed him her business card. "You will find the little old lady, Detective Kelly, hopefully in time to save her. When you do, I'm sure you'll want to talk to me."

She turned and walked away with an unconscious grace that no man with any blood in his veins could fail to appreciate. Sam was no exception. With his eyes locked on the gentle sway of her hips, he was forced to grudgingly acknowledge that the lady was a looker. And a few bricks shy of a load. The loonies always came out when the moon was full—every law-enforcement officer and emergency-room nurse in the city could attest to that— and the moon had been at its zenith for most of the night. Last month, he'd had to deal with a jumper on the Tower of Americas who thought he could fly like an eagle. If Ms. Hart wanted to prove she could really tell the future, she could give him Saturday's lottery numbers—then they'd talk! Until then, he had better things to do with his time.

Turning his attention back to the report he had to finish before he could go home, he deliberately tried to push the too-young, too-off-the-wall Jennifer Hart out of his mind, but one thought kept needling him, refusing to be ignored.

What the hell did *she* know about the kind of night he'd had?

Still steaming when she arrived back at Heavenly Scents, the small bakery and café she owned a block from the River Walk, she couldn't help but feel a surge of pride at the sight of the place. It was hers, bought and paid for, thanks to the generosity and farsightedness of her grandparents. They'd always wanted more for her than the whispers, finger-pointing and distrust of the closed-minded people she'd had to deal with in the small town of Sandy Bluff, where they'd raised her after her mother died of breast cancer when she was seven. In their will, they had instructed her to sell their bakery so she could start over somewhere else. For that, and their love, she would always be grateful.

All she'd wanted was to live a normal life...*be* normal. So when she'd moved to San Antonio, she'd kept her psychic abilities to herself, and for the first time in her life, she'd lived just like everyone else.

Until that morning.

Shivering, she hugged herself and tried to push back the horrifying scenes from the vision, but the images were too strong, too brutal. The elderly woman, alone and scared. Strong fingers squeezing her throat, cutting off her air until she tumbled unconscious to the floor. As much as Jennifer treasured the normal life she'd been able to create for herself, she'd known she couldn't keep what she'd seen to herself. Not after she'd felt the victim's terror and her attacker's total lack of conscience.

But she couldn't think about that now. Not when the café was overflowing with the usual morning rush. Later she knew she would worry and lose sleep over what awaited an old woman she didn't even know, but for now, all she could do was send up a silent prayer and go to work.

Pulling open the door, she stepped inside. Every table was full, and at the door customers stood three deep, waiting for a seat. At the grill, Molly, her cook, was frying bacon and eggs and sausage and cracking jokes for the crowd. For the first time that morning, Jennifer grinned.

White-haired and well past seventy, Molly had worked everything from hamburger stands to high-dollar restaurants and could cook just about anything. When she'd showed up at the café looking for a job two days after Jennifer bought it, she hadn't lied about her age or her arthritis. She readily admitted that she couldn't move as fast as she once had, but she'd tried retirement and didn't like it. Sitting around all day was for old geezers, and she had a good ten or fifteen years to go before she'd consider herself old. If Jennifer would just hire her, she promised she'd never regret it.

Liking her immediately, Jennifer had had no qualms about her age, not when she'd seen her own grandparents work long after they could have retired. They'd taught her the baking business, but she'd never run a restaurant on her own, and Molly's unexpected arrival was like a gift from heaven. She'd hired her on the spot and had thanked God for her every day since. Molly did the cooking, she did the baking and waited tables, and together they'd made Heavenly Scents a hit.

"Sorry I'm late," Jennifer told her as she hurriedly grabbed an apron and tied it on. "It looks like you've got your hands full. Who gets the pancakes?"

"Table three. Hang on—you can take these cacklers to four since you're headed that way."

Orders were backing up because of the size of the crowd, but the two women worked well together and soon had things straightened out. At the first lull Molly blurted, "You going to tell me what happened at the police station? Or do I have to hog-tie you to a chair and make you talk? I've been waiting all morning to find out what's going on, and it's killing me.''

Her green eyes twinkling, Jennifer almost laughed. There was only one thing Molly liked to do more than cook, and that was gossip. She'd arrived at work that morning just as Jennifer was leaving and was startled to learn she was going to the police station. She'd thrown one question after another at her, but there'd been no time for explanations. The morning baking was already in the oven, the first customer's arrival less than an hour away. Forced to stay behind, Molly had still been grumbling when she'd left. She'd probably been watching the door ever since.

Jennifer had every intention of telling her about her vision, but it was hardly something she could do in a couple of minutes, especially when Molly didn't have a clue that she was psychic. ''You can put the rubber hose away—I'll talk,'' she promised, chuckling. ''But after the rush. This is going to take some time.''

The food on the grill forgotten, the older woman whirled on her in alarm. ''Why? Are you in some kind of trouble? Darn it, Jennifer—''

''No, it's nothing like that,'' she assured her. ''It's just…complicated.'' There was no time to say more—there were empty coffee cups to fill, dirty tables to clean, orders to take. Grabbing the coffeepot, she went to work.

An hour and a half later, the crowd thinned and the café began to clear out. The lunch crowd wouldn't be in for several more hours, but she and Molly already had the day's soup on and had begun work on the blue-plate special. With only a handful of customers to wait on, they had plenty of time to talk.

Finding the right words, however, wasn't nearly as easy as Jennifer had hoped. People always reacted in different ways when they found out about her psychic abilities. Some immediately wanted to know about their futures while others accused her of being in league with the devil. Molly was the closest thing she had to family now—if she *was* judgmental, Jennifer didn't know what she would do.

Refilling her coffee cup, she didn't realize Molly was watching her struggle for words until she said quietly, "Whatever it is, it can't be that bad. Just spit it out and get it over with."

Jennifer laughed, but the sound didn't hold much humor. "That's easy for you to say—you don't know what I have to tell you."

Unperturbed, the older woman only shrugged and shoved three meat loaves into the oven. "How bad can it be? Unless you murdered your grandparents, of course I might have a problem with that. You didn't, did you?"

"Of course not!"

"Then there's nothing you can't tell me," she said simply. "If you're in some kind of trouble, I want to help."

There'd been a time in Sandy Bluff when Jennifer would have given anything to hear those words from people, other than her grandparents, she'd known and trusted all her life, but they'd withheld them and turned their backs on her, rejecting her for something she could no more help than they could control the color of their eyes. Molly, on the other hand, offered her support without even knowing what the problem was.

Hot tears stinging her eyes, she gave her a quick hug and a watery smile. "I'm not in any trouble. Really," she insisted when the older woman still looked skeptical. "I'm just...psychic."

Whatever Molly was expecting, it obviously wasn't that. Shocked, she exclaimed, "You mean you can read palms and all that stuff? Just like Jeanne Dixon? Can you read mine?''

She couldn't have been more excited if Jennifer had told her she was Frank Sinatra's granddaughter, and with her acceptance, a burden of silence was lifted off Jennifer's shoulders. Leaving her past behind hadn't been as simple as moving to a new town and starting over. There'd been times over the past six months when she'd literally ached to tell someone, anyone, about her grandparents and, by doing so, bring them back to life. But she couldn't do that without opening herself up to questions of why she'd left Sandy Bluff, and up until now, that hadn't been something she'd been willing to chance.

''Actually I can see more if I close my eyes and just concentrate on you. And sometimes I have visions.'' Images from that morning once again stirred in her mind, haunting her. ''That's why I went to the police this morning. I saw an old lady being assaulted and robbed and had to do something to try to stop it.''

''You're kidding! What are the police going to do?''

''Nothing,'' she said flatly. ''The detective I spoke to thought I was some kind of wacko.''

''He said that to your face?''

''Not in those words, but he didn't have to. It was pretty obvious he didn't take me seriously.''

Bristling indignantly, Molly marched over to the phone and snatched it up. ''What's his name? I'm calling him right now and giving him a piece of my mind! The man obviously needs a stern talking-to.''

''Oh, no, you don't!'' Grabbing the phone, Jennifer quickly returned it to its cradle. ''It won't do any good, Molly,'' she said quietly when her friend opened her mouth to protest. ''Believe me, I know. I've been dealing with people—men—like Detective Kelly all my life. He doesn't believe in what he can't see, and all the talking in the world won't change that.''

''But there's an old lady out there who's going to get hurt,'' she protested, outraged. ''Are you saying we can't do *anything?*''

Her eyes anguished, Jennifer nodded. ''Nothing but wait.''

Two evenings later an elderly widow who lived alone in an exclusive neighborhood on the northeast side of town was in bed when she was surprised by an intruder. He choked her, nearly strangling her to death, then robbed her of a small fortune in jewelry. Unconscious, she might have lain there all night if her son hadn't called and become worried when she didn't answer the phone.

When Sam and Tanner arrived on the scene, the evidence team was inside and an ambulance was just leaving with Agatha Elliot, the eighty-three-year-old victim. Michael Hawkins, the uniformed officer who answered the 911 call, was sober-faced as he met them on the lawn and gave them the details. ''The perp broke in through a kitchen window while the old lady was upstairs in bed,'' he told them. ''Apparently she didn't hear anything until he stepped into her bedroom.''

''Did she get a look at him?'' Sam asked.

The younger man shook his head. ''Not really The only light was a night-light and she didn't have her glasses on. He had something on his face, so she couldn't see his features at all. She blacked out when he choked her, so what she does remember is a little hazy. She thought he had a ponytail and he seemed pretty tall to her. But she's a little bitty thing, barely five feet, so she'd have to look up to just about anybody over five-six.''

''And that's it?'' Tanner asked incredulously, frowning.

"None of the neighbors heard or saw anything? It's barely eleven o'clock!"

"The neighbors on the left aren't home, and the ones on the right were in their den at the back of the house watching TV," the officer replied. "They didn't know anything was wrong until they heard the ambulance drive up."

His angular face etched in harsh lines, Sam studied the victim's fieldstone house, with its servants' quarters and four-car garage and heard a soft feminine voice describe the layout in his head. *The neighborhood is old and refined, the homes large and stately and set well back from the road. Instead of fences, most of the homes are separated by thick trees and foliage, so it's very private. The old lady's attacker will walk right out the front door with a sackful of jewelry and no one will see a thing.*

With a will of their own, his eyes moved over the landscaped yard that was now illuminated by floodlights, noting the spaciousness of the lots, the lack of fences, the forestlike setting right in the middle of the city. Just as Jennifer Hart said she had seen in her so-called vision.

"Do we know how the perp exited the house?" he asked Michael Hawkins curtly. "Or what he took?"

He nodded. "The front door was standing wide open when Mrs. Elliot's son arrived. He took a quick look around before he left with the ambulance. The only thing he noticed missing was the jewelry. Apparently his mother had an extensive collection she refused to keep locked up."

It was all there—the house, the old lady, the jewelry, the crime. He'd already told Tanner all about Jennifer Hart, and he only had to exchange a look with him to know they were on the same wavelength. The robbery and attack on Mrs. Elliot hadn't been a random act of violence, but a well-thought-out crime. And only one person had prior knowledge of it—Jennifer Hart. Sam didn't think for a minute it was because she was psychic.

Chapter 2

"Looks like the place is locked up tight," Tanner said as they pulled up in front of Heavenly Scents Café. Located in a small two-story building that had been built at the turn of the century, the café took up the entire lower floor. "You sure this is the right place? I thought you said the lady was a psychic."

Sam checked the address on Jennifer Hart's business card again, then frowned at the darkened windows of the café. The card just said "Heavenly Scents," and he'd assumed, like Tanner, that she had one of those hokey shops where they sold scented oils and tarot cards, and told fortunes in the back behind a beaded curtain. So much for stereotypes.

"That's what *she* said," Sam corrected him. "Evidently she's not too good at it or she wouldn't have to sling hash for a living. C'mon. There's a light on in the back—it looks like someone's moving around. Let's check it out."

Circling the block, Sam pulled into the back alley and

braked to a stop behind the café's delivery entrance. Before they'd even climbed from the car, the light over the back door flared on. "Who's out there?" a female voice demanded suspiciously.

The door remained stubbornly shut and no doubt locked, but Sam didn't have to see the woman to know that she was not Jennifer Hart. Her voice had the gruffness of age, which the psychic's had lacked. Flashing his badge, he held it up to the small barred security window in the steel door. "Sorry to disturb you, ma'am, but I'm Detective Sam Kelly and this is Detective Bennigan, SAPD. We're looking for Jennifer Hart."

The door swung open with a creak to reveal a tall plump woman with white hair and sharp brown eyes that raked over him without mercy. "You're the one who gave Jennifer such a hard time the other morning at the police station."

She had him nailed—he couldn't deny it. One corner of his mouth turning up into a rueful smile, he said, "Guilty as charged, Mrs...."

"Tucker," she supplied shortly. "Molly Tucker. I'm the cook here at the café." Refusing to be distracted, she gave him a steely-eyed look that would have had a lesser man shaking in his shoes. "You should be ashamed of yourself for treating that girl that way you did," she scolded. "She was just trying to help an old lady, and all she got for it was a slap in the face."

Wound up, she didn't give him a chance to defend himself, but lit into him like a mother hen protecting her young. And there was nothing Sam could do but take it with good grace. Which wasn't easy. He could almost feel his partner's glee at the turn of events. By this time tomorrow, everyone from the lowest rookie to the commissioner would be splitting a gut over the story.

Silently groaning at the thought, he was wondering what it would take to pacify the old lady when Tanner stepped in and drew the line of fire. The minute the old lady paused for a breath, he drawled, "In Sam's defense, we do encounter our fair share of wackos, Mrs. Tucker. Just last week, Jimmy Hoffa and Jesus Christ both came into the station to file complaints."

"Jesus Christ!" she sputtered, wide-eyed. "But—"

"He wasn't happy with the state of the world and wanted us to do something about it," he continued with a straight face. "Granted, compared to that, Ms. Hart appeared downright normal, but most people don't walk around claiming they can predict the future, either."

"But Jennifer's not like that!" she argued hotly. "She doesn't talk about being psychic. Why, I didn't even know she was until the other day when she came back from talking to Detective Kelly."

Surprised, Sam frowned. "How long have you known Ms. Hart?"

"Six months," she replied promptly. "She hired me right after she moved to San Antonio from Sandy Bluff."

"And all this time, she never once predicted the future, even jokingly? Or teased the customers about telling their fortunes?"

Adamant, she shook her head. "No. Never. She's friendly with the customers, but she's not one of those people who likes to be the center of attention. I don't think she would have said anything about her vision at all if she hadn't been worried sick about that old lady."

Unless she was trying to establish a story to explain how she had prior knowledge of the robbery, Sam thought cynically. Keeping that thought to himself, he looked past Mrs. Tucker's shoulder to the café kitchen and baking area. "We'd like to talk to her about that if she's here," he said. "I have some questions I need to ask her."

"Now?" Molly asked, hesitating. "That could be a problem. She wasn't feeling well earlier and went upstairs to her apartment. She may not feel like seeing anyone tonight. Couldn't you come back in the morning?"

Turner and Sam both followed her gaze to the exterior metal stairway that led to the apartment over the café. "It's really important that we talk to her now," Tanner insisted. "What time did she go upstairs?"

Molly frowned, trying to remember. "Oh, I don't know. About three hours ago. We had another hour to go before we closed up, and suddenly she turned white as a sheet and said she had to go upstairs and lie down."

Three hours ago, Sam thought, exchanging a telling look with Tanner. She'd had plenty of time to sneak out and play lookout for whoever robbed Mrs. Elliot. "Have you checked on her lately?" he asked Molly. "Her lights are still on. She must be feeling better or she'd have gone to bed."

"We'll just go up and see," Tanner added easily, heading for the stairs with Sam right behind him. "If she doesn't feel like talking to us, we'll come back tomorrow."

Molly snorted. "I may be forty years older than you, young man, but I still know bull when I hear it. You know you're going to badger that girl until you get the answers you want, so why don't you just say so, instead of beating around the bush?"

Fighting a smile at her bluntness, Sam tried to placate her. "We're only doing our job, ma'am. We're not going to badger anyone."

"Then you won't mind me listening in on your questions,'' she concluded triumphantly. Huffing and puffing, she followed them up the stairs.

Short of arresting her for interfering with a police investigation, there was little they could do but grit their teeth and allow her to accompany them. Making room for her on the second-floor landing, Sam graciously motioned for her to take the lead. ''After you, Mrs. Tucker.''

Her chin high and her spine ramrod straight, she pounded on the locked door and called loudly, ''Jennifer? I'm sorry to disturb you, but Detective Kelly is here with his partner to talk to you. Can we come in?''

For what seemed like a good minute, there wasn't so much as a whisper of sound from the apartment. Then, in the tense expectant silence, the dead bolt clanged free. A split second later the door was pulled open and Jennifer Hart stood before them.

She'd told him there'd come a time when he'd need to talk to her again, and it galled him to admit that she'd been right. He didn't like *I told you so's* and was prepared to tell her that when he got a good look at her face and the words died on his tongue.

Haunted. He could think of no other way to describe the look in her shadowed eyes. Deep pools of pain in her colorless face, they were the eyes of a tortured soul. And they were latched unblinkingly on him.

''It's happened, hasn't it?'' she whispered hoarsely. ''I felt it the second he grabbed her by the throat.''

His face set, he nodded. ''About an hour and a half ago.''

Suddenly remembering her manners, she pulled the door wider and motioned them inside. ''I'm sorry, I didn't mean to keep you standing outside! It's just been such a horrible evening. Please...come in.''

She introduced herself to Tanner and was about to get

both him and Sam something to drink, but Molly would have none of it. "This isn't a party, and you're in no shape to be playing hostess. If anybody wants anything, I'll get it. You sit down—you're as white as a ghost." Clicking her tongue reprovingly, she grabbed an afghan from the end of the couch and draped it around Jennifer's shoulders as she sank into an easy chair. "You should be in bed. You look like you're coming down with the flu."

Ashen, still dressed in the bakery whites she'd worked in that day, she hugged herself and grimaced ruefully. "I wish it was something that simple, Moll, but it's not. Anyway, I'm not the one who's hurt." Her eyes pleading, she turned back to Sam, who had, along with his partner, remained standing at the entrance to the living room. "How is she? Is she going to be okay?" When he hesitated, she blanched. "Oh, God, he killed her, didn't he?"

"No," Tanner said quickly. "At least, not that we know of."

"He roughed her up pretty badly," Sam added. "An ambulance had to be called to take her to the hospital. We haven't gotten a report yet on her condition."

"Oh, God, oh, God! I can't stand this!" Unable to sit still, she threw off the afghan and jumped to her feet. "I have to go to the hospital and see her." Flustered, she looked around for her keys. "Where did I put my purse?"

Tears spilling over her thick lashes, she looked small, fragile, breakable. Watching her, Sam felt something shift in the region of his heart, something he would have sworn was as hard as stone and immovable as Gibraltar. He'd always had a weakness for a woman's tears, but this was different, stronger. He had this crazy need to reach for her, to wipe her cheeks and enfold her in his arms. Just this once.

Then he remembered why he was there, and it wasn't to give her a hanky and console her.

Stiffening, he bit off a furious curse. He was losing his mind—he had to be! Why else would he be thinking such ridiculous thoughts about a woman who'd had prior knowledge of a vicious robbery? She was a suspect, for God's sake, who'd greeted him at the door with the announcement that she'd known the crime had already taken place! Just because she could shed a few tears on cue didn't make her an innocent. This entire act was no doubt for his benefit, and he'd do well to remember that.

His jaw rigid, he moved to block her path when she suddenly spied her purse on the small table by the front door. "That'll have to wait," he said coldly. "Right now we need you to answer some questions for us."

Confused, she blinked up at him. "Answer some questions? What kind of questions?"

"Where were you between seven-thirty and nine tonight?"

"Right here," she said, surprised. "Why?"

"Because they think you had something to do with that old lady getting nearly strangled to death!" Molly deducted shrewdly, glaring at the two men. "You ought to be ashamed of yourselves! She hasn't done anything but try to warn you that this was going to happen and you ignored her. Now someone's been hurt and you want to hang it on Jennifer. How dare you!"

"We're not accusing Ms. Hart of anything," Tanner said calmly. "But she did have prior knowledge of the crime, so we have to question her about what she knows. It's just standard procedure."

Molly eyed him and Sam as if they'd both just crawled out from under a rock. "I should have shown the two of you the door the second you flashed your badges. She doesn't have to tell you jack squat, you know. Or even let you speak to her without having a lawyer present. I know—I watch 'NYPD Blue.'''

Tanner, struggling with a smile, agreed. "You're absolutely right, ma'am. She can call her lawyer if she'd feel more comfortable. And she can, of course, refuse to talk to us. But the only reason I can think of why she'd do either one of those things is because she has something to hide."

"If I had something to hide, Detective, I would never have gone to the police in the first place," Jennifer pointed out coolly. "Now that we've got that settled, why don't you put some coffee on while I answer the detectives' questions, Molly? I imagine this will take a while."

Retreating to the kitchen just when things were heating up would have been difficult for anyone, but for Molly, who loved being in the thick of things, it was darn near impossible. She wanted to stay and help defend Jennifer, but she also despised interfering busybodies who didn't know when to hold their tongues.

Torn, she finally gave in. "Okay, I know when to make myself scarce. But I don't have to like it!"

She stormed off to the kitchen, grumbling under her breath all the way. If the situation hadn't been so grim, Jennifer would have laughed. But her eyes were dead serious when she turned back to face her accusers. "Now, gentlemen, please sit down and let's get this over with. What else did you want to know?"

They each took seats, but they didn't relax. All business, Sam trapped her in the unyielding hardness of his eyes and began. "You said you've been in your apartment all evening. Was the café closed?"

"No. We don't close until eight, but I felt sick and came upstairs early."

"And that's when you claim you knew the robber attacked the old lady in your vision? When you felt sick?"

Her stomach churning at the memory, Jennifer nodded. She could still taste the inexplicable terror that had come out of nowhere to seize her by the throat. One second she'd been perfectly fine, and the next she'd wanted to run for her life and couldn't say why. "I knew he had to be after her," she said thickly, "and there was nothing I could do. I didn't know who she was or where, but I could feel how scared she was, and it literally made me sick to my stomach. I tried to lie down, but I just couldn't."

"Did you talk to anyone during that time on the phone?" Tanner asked, jotting notes in a small notepad he'd pulled from the pocket of his jacket. "See anyone who would be willing to confirm that you were in your apartment for the past three hours?"

"No. All my friends know I'm usually working at that time, and Molly was busy downstairs closing up."

"You claim you've had these visions before," Sam said tersely. "Do you usually get nauseated?"

"Sometimes. It just depends if the scene is a particularly violent one."

"And when was the last time you were sick like this?"

"I don't know. Maybe a year ago."

"So of all nights," he concluded, "you pick tonight, when you're up here all by yourself, to claim you were sick. And you don't think that's odd?"

"It's not a claim," she said hotly. "It's the truth."

"Is it? The stairs to the apartment are outside the café, instead of inside. You could have left, met with your accomplice to stand guard, then hurried back here with no one being the wiser."

"That's ridiculous!"

"Who is he?" he pressed. "Your boyfriend? Did you

have a fight? Is that why you really came to the station the other morning? You had a lovers' spat and you wanted to get back at him? But you changed your mind, didn't you? You were with him tonight—''

"No! There's no one. I was here all evening—"

"If that old lady dies," he promised silkily, "I'm going to make your life a living hell, Ms. Hart. So if I were you, I'd spend the rest of the night on my knees." Rising abruptly to his feet, he turned away as if he couldn't stand the sight of her. "C'mon, Tanner, let's get the hell out of here."

Shaken, feeling as if she'd stepped back in time into a nightmare, Jennifer watched them leave and told herself this couldn't be happening. Not again. When she was eighteen and still living with her grandparents in Sandy Bluff, she'd had a vision of the local mayor embezzling money from the town coffers. Young and idealistic and knowing it was her civic duty, she'd gone to the police. Only to live to regret it.

Six years had passed since then, but it still seemed like yesterday. Her grandparents had supported her decision, but they'd also warned her that people didn't always want to hear the truth. And oh, how right they'd been! The mayor had always been well liked and respected, and no one had wanted to hear that he was stealing tax money like a common thief. Instead, they'd wanted to lynch the messenger.

Sick to her stomach, she tried to force the old memory back into the past where she'd thought she'd buried it, but it clung like a burr. With no effort whatsoever she could still feel the shock she'd felt when the focus of the investigation had turned on her. *She* was the oddball in town with few friends, the one whose grandfather had had a running feud with the mayor for the past thirty years. She was mocked and openly accused of lying and became the brunt of more jokes than she cared to remember. And when the mayor left town three years later, taking sixty thousand dollars of the taxpayers' money with him, she wasn't vindicated but blamed for not making people believe her when she had the chance.

Never again, she'd sworn. Never again would she open herself up to that kind of humiliation. The police didn't want or need her help, and she didn't care what kind of vision she had, she was keeping it to herself and minding her own business. It might be the coward's way out, but she'd rather be called a coward than a liar.

Or so she'd thought until she'd had the vision of that poor old woman being choked by a fiend.

Shivering, she hugged herself and knew in her heart she'd had no choice but to go to the police. The road to hell might be paved with good intentions, but she never would have been able to live with herself if she'd kept the vision to herself. If Sam Kelly had a problem with that, that was his tough luck. He was just looking for someone to blame. Because he had to know that if he'd taken her warning seriously and done something, no one would have gotten hurt. As it was, an innocent person was in the hospital fighting for her life, and only God knew if she was going to make it.

The robbery made headlines the next morning and was the main topic of conversation for most of the day. Not only was the victim, Mrs. Agatha Elliot, one of an increasing number of senior citizens targeted by the lowlifes of the city, she was also the matriarch of one of the oldest families in the city. If she, with all her money, could be attacked and robbed in her own home, a newspaper columnist speculated, then the rest of the city's elderly population didn't stand a chance.

Winding her way through the café's tables refilling iced tea glasses and coffee mugs as the lunch crowd began to thin, Jennifer unabashedly eavesdropped as customers repeated the latest conflicting gossip about Mrs. Elliot. Someone said she had brain damage from the near strangulation and didn't remember her own name, while at another table a bank teller confided to her companion that old lady Elliot was as sharp as a tack and had identified her attacker as the son of her gardener. On the radio her condition was reported as critical, on the TV as greatly improved. One gossip had her planning her next big charity event, while according to another, she had one foot in the grave.

Forcing a smile as she chatted with customers, Jennifer tried to convince herself that the old woman was fine. Mrs. Elliot wasn't her responsibility and she'd done all for her that she could. But she couldn't shake the feeling that something wasn't right. By two in the afternoon, she knew the feeling wasn't going to go away until she saw the woman for herself. Untying her apron, she went to the back of the café to find Molly, who was taking her lunch break.

"This is a joke, isn't it?" her friend said when she told her where she was going. "You can't be serious!"

"The papers said she's at the Methodist. I won't be gone long. Just an hour or so. Rosa will be in soon to help you if things get busy before I get back—"

"It's not me I'm worried about," Molly retorted. "For God's sake, Jennifer, the police were here last night! That Detective Kelly was just itching to arrest you. What do you think he's going to say when he hears you went looking for the same woman he thinks you robbed?"

"How will he know?" she argued. "I'm not going to stay the rest of the day with her—just make sure she's okay. It'll take all of five minutes. What can it hurt?"

Molly could think of a whole lot of ways it could hurt, but Jennifer had made up her mind. Promising her friend she'd be back before she knew it, Jennifer grabbed a jacket and rushed out the back door to where she kept her grandfather's old 1968 Jeepster behind the building. Seconds later she was headed for the Methodist Hospital.

Agatha Elliot's son had hired a guard to watch over his mother while she was in the hospital, and no visitors were allowed in the old lady's private room without his say-so. Taking a chance, Jennifer told him she was working with Detective Kelly on the case, and the name-dropping did the trick.

Breathing a sigh of relief, Jennifer stepped into the open doorway and felt her heart constrict at the sight of the old lady. Her attacker had not only choked her, he had punched her a couple of times, blackening her eye and splitting her lip. In spite of that, she was still a beautiful woman, with wavy white hair and flawless skin that Jennifer could only pray she would be blessed with at eighty-three.

It was her spirit, rather than her body, however, that was really battered. From halfway across the room, Jennifer could sense the older woman's despondency and actually feel her heartache. She was hurting, and not just from the abuse she'd taken. And just that quickly Jennifer knew why she'd needed to see her.

Knocking softly on the doorjamb, she said, "Mrs. Elliot? My name is Jennifer Hart. I wonder if I might speak with you for a moment?"

Caught off guard, Agatha Elliot looked up, then glanced away and made a hasty swipe at the tears that dampened her cheeks. In the second it took her to turn and face her visitor, she'd gathered her dignity around her like a cloak and was once again the proud matriarch of one of the oldest, wealthiest families in the state. "If you're another reporter, I'm afraid you're too late to get an exclusive. I've already spoken to a man from the *Daily News.*"

Smiling, Jennifer stepped farther into the room. "No, I'm not a reporter. I..." She hesitated, reluctant to admit she was a psychic after dealing with Sam Kelly's skepticism. But her gut told her Agatha Elliot was much more trusting than Kelly. Which was probably why she was in her present position, she thought ruefully. "Actually I'm a psychic," she admitted as she approached the bed. "I've been working on your case with the police."

"Oh, really?" Intrigued, Agatha Elliot sat up straighter in bed, her eyes lighting with interest. "I've never met a psychic before. How does that work, dear? Can you really predict the future? What can you tell me about this terrible mess I seem to have gotten myself into without even trying?"

Grinning, Jennifer couldn't help but like her style. "I can't tell you how it works—I don't know. I just seem to know things that other people don't. Like your jewelry. You're very worried about the older pieces—"

"You know where my jewelry is?" the woman cut in, relieved. "Thank God!" She motioned to the chair next to the bed. "Please—sit down. You have no idea how worried I've been!" Suddenly realizing what she'd said, she chuckled. "Well, maybe you do. It's just that the heirloom pieces mean so much to me." Sobering, she admitted, "I know I should have kept them locked up in the safe, but I liked to have them around me. They're all I have left of my parents, and I always feel closer to them when I wear them."

Jennifer empathized completely. Her memories of her parents were sketchy—her father was killed by a drunk driver when she was four, and cancer took her mother three years later—but she had their things and her grandparents' scattered around her apartment so she could touch them when she needed to and remind herself she hadn't always been so alone in the world.

"I can't promise that everything will be recovered," she told her. "But the pieces you care the most about are at a pawnshop on the south side. Sometime within the next twenty-four hours, you'll get news that they've been recovered. The rest, I'm sorry to say, may be lost forever."

Unconcerned, Agatha shrugged that off. "The insurance will cover the loss—it's the others that can't be replaced. So the heart locket my father gave my mother when I was born will be found? And the brooch that's been handed down to the women in my family for over a hundred years? That will also be recovered?"

"If those are the pieces that hold the most sentimental value for you, then, yes, they should be returned to you. I wish I could be more specific, but I can only tell you what I see."

Thrilled, Agatha couldn't have been more excited if Jennifer had told her the police already had not only the jewelry in hand, but the man who'd attacked her. Tears glistening in her eyes, she gave Jennifer a watery smile. "Please don't apologize. You have no idea what this news has done for me. I've just been lying here feeling sorry for myself and thinking nobody in the world cared what happened to me. If my husband, James, were here, God rest his soul, he'd say I was acting like a spoiled little girl who'd lost her toys. He always did tease me unmercifully, but he was usually right. But there I go, rambling like an old woman."

Agatha grimaced at the thought, drawing a chuckle from Jennifer. "I'm glad I could help," Jennifer said. "After everything you've been through, I just wanted to let you know you're worrying needlessly. Now all you have to do is get better so you can get out of here."

"You must come and see me when I do," the old woman said promptly. "You've just brightened my whole day."

When the phone on his desk rang, Sam barely had time to identify himself before Agatha Elliot gushed, "Detective Kelly? This is Agatha Elliot. I've had the most wonderful news! I know where my jewelry is! Can you believe it? Just when I thought I'd lost it forever, it turns up in a pawnshop on the south side. You have to send a squad car over there immediately of course. Before someone comes in and buys it."

In a bear of a mood after spending the morning in court testifying against a bully who'd beat up and robbed a tourist from Canada three months ago, Sam frowned, shifting gears. "Whoa, whoa, Mrs. Elliot. What do you mean your jewelry's in a pawnshop? How do you know?"

"It's the most incredible thing!" she laughed. "I was so depressed I couldn't do anything but cry about it, then this angel walked into my hospital room just a few minutes ago and told me right where it was."

"An angel," he repeated dryly. He should have figured. He had a fender bender on the way to work, he'd been late to court, and the defense attorney had tried to make him look like an incompetent fool on the stand. Now angels. At least that was better than little green men from Mars. The old lady's brain must have been deprived of more oxygen than he'd thought.

Jotting down a note to call her doctor, he tried to humor

her. "Well, hey, that's great, Mrs. Elliot. Personally I've never seen one myself, but if somebody upstairs wants to help us with this case, you won't hear me complaining. So what's this angel look like? Did she have wings and a halo and the whole nine yards?"

"Of course not!" Laughing gaily, Agatha said, "She wasn't a *real* angel, silly! At least I don't think she was—though come to think of it, she was dressed all in white. But she was so sweet and helpful and she knew I was worried. That's why she told me to check out the pawnshops on the south side. That's where we'll find the family pieces I'd just hate to lose."

"I see." His jaw clenched on an oath, Sam saw, all right, and he didn't like what he saw. Agatha Elliot was an old lady, hurt and vulnerable and rich. And just that morning she'd been front-page news. That made her ripe pickings for any con artist out there just looking for someone to scam. Like any other city, San Antonio was full of them, and it sickened him. What the hell was the world coming to?

"And what did this *angel* charge you for this information, Mrs. Elliot?" he asked tersely. "You should have let me talk to her. Did she give you her name? It was probably an alias, but we still might be able to track her down. What did she look like?"

"Young, pretty, with green eyes and this beautiful wavy golden hair that fell to her shoulders," she supplied promptly. "She said she was a psychic, but she didn't charge me anything. She just wanted me to quit worrying so I could get well and get out of the hospital."

Just that quickly the pieces fell together. Swearing under his breath, Sam tossed down the pen he'd used to scribble notes. "This psychic's name wouldn't happen to be Jennifer Hart, would it, Mrs. Elliot?"

"Why, yes, it is," she replied, pleased. "She was the sweetest girl. And so helpful! Just talking to her made me feel better."

"I'm glad to hear it, but I wouldn't put too much stock in what she says if I were you," he warned. "I'd bet money the lady's not any more psychic than I am."

Stunned, the old lady sputtered, "B-but she knew things about me, how worried I've been, how much the family pieces mean to me."

Anyone with a smidgen of perception would have known the same thing, but that was something Agatha Elliot wasn't prepared to hear. And after all she'd been through, Sam wasn't prepared to push the point. "You may be right. Mrs. E. For your sake, I hope you are. But if Jennifer Hart is psychic, she hasn't given us a whole heck of a lot to work with. Do you know how many pawn-shops there are on the south side?"

"I haven't got a clue, but I know you'll find the right one," she said confidently. "Jennifer promised me you would."

Faced with that logic, there was nothing he could say but, "My partner and I'll get on it this afternoon."

When he hung up, he looked up to find Tanner balefully watching him from his own desk, which was directly across from his. "Tell me I didn't hear you right. You didn't just promise that old lady we'd check out every two-bit pawnshop on the south side."

"Stop your crying," he growled. "You're the one who's always telling me a lead is a lead is a lead. And like it or not, Jennifer Hart is the only lead we've got right now."

It was nothing less than the truth and they both knew it. Groaning in defeat, Tanner pushed to his feet. "God, I hate it when you're right."

"Hell, Bennigan, I thought you got used to that years ago."

Far from being offended, his friend only snorted and led the way to the door. "Stuff it, Kelly. You're getting delusional on me again. I'm telling you, you should really get some help for that. The last time you were right about anything, Reagan was in office. I can even tell you what day it was...."

An hour later, they were still jawing good-naturedly at each other when they walked into a pawnshop that was hardly bigger than a closet on Southwest Military Highway. The owner, a tall skinny ex-con by the name of Benny, had a bad habit of stuttering whenever he was nervous. The second they stepped through the front door, his tongue started tripping all over itself.

"Hey, S-Sam! T-Tanner! What's g-going down?"

"We were hoping you could tell us that, Benny," Tanner drawled with a lazy grin. "How's business?"

"Er...not s-so bad. C-could be better." Tearing his gaze from Tanner, he blanched at the sight of Sam heading for the jewelry display case. "Hey, Sam, you still s-seeing that pretty b-blonde? I've got something i-in the other d-day she m-might like. C'mon in the b-back and I'll sh-show you."

His eyes hard, his smile easy, Sam said, "You talking about Tina? We split up months ago, right after that hot-shot lawyer of hers got her child support doubled. But that's okay. I've been seeing this redhead now, and she likes diamonds. Whatcha got over here?"

"N-nothing y-you'd be interested i-in," he said hurriedly, only to groan as Sam headed stubbornly for the display case. "Aw, c'mon, g-guys. G-give me a b-break!"

"You seem awful jumpy about this case, Benny," Tanner said as he followed Sam across the room. His smile abruptly fading, he gave him a look guaranteed to make a guilty man squirm. "You wouldn't be trying to pull a fast one on us again like you did last month, when you tried to hide that hot watch in plain sight, would you?"

"No! H-honest!"

It was a poor choice of words—Benny had a reputation on the streets for avoiding the truth like the plague—and he only had to see Tanner arch a brow at him to blush crimson. "I mean I—I wouldn't d-deliberately do s-something like that. Last t-time was just a f-fluke."

"Of course it was," Sam said agreeably, easily sliding into the game of good cop/bad cop. "Quit giving the man a hard time, Bennigan. It could happen to anyone. A piece of sleaze comes in to hock a ten-thousand-dollar watch, tells you his dead granny left it to him, and you buy it. Only a fool would turn something like that down, and Benny's no fool. Right, Benny?"

Benny hesitated, obviously not quite sure what he was admitting to. "Well...yeah. I mean...no!"

Struggling to hold back a smile, Sam nodded solemnly. "I knew it was something like that. Old Benny's a good guy just trying to make a living. You can't condemn him for one lousy mistake."

Benny fairly glowed at the praise, just as Sam knew he would. He might be as crooked as the San Antonio River, but secretly he longed to be buddies with the cops. All he needed was a few verbal pats on the back, and he'd tell you anything you wanted to know.

"I was just telling Tanner on the way over here that we could really count on you to help us with this case we're working on," he continued, idly scanning the display case. "Somebody knocked this rich old lady about and—"

He broke off abruptly, drawing a quick look from Tanner. "What is it? Did you find something?"

His jaw rigid, Sam nodded. "See for yourself."

He stepped back, giving Tanner a clear view of the contents of the glass case. And there, lying on a bed of dirty cream-colored satin like a lady in a whorehouse, was an antique heart-shaped locket that exactly matched the description of the one that just yesterday had been stolen from Agatha Elliot.

Chapter 3

This couldn't be happening.

Stomach jumping, knees trembling, Jennifer preceded
Sam Kelly and his partner into the interrogation room,
only to stop dead in her tracks at the sight of her own
image, pale and wide-eyed, in the mirror covering the far
wall. Oh, God, she thought shakily. A two-way mirror. It
had to be. Someone was sitting on the other side. She
could feel their eyes on her, watching her, studying her,
waiting for her to crack and to admit God knows what.
Merciful heavens, what was she doing here?

Instinctively she turned to flee, but there was no way
out. The two detectives had followed her into the tiny box
of a room and blocked the only way out. It was then that
the panic she'd been trying to keep a firm grip on ever
since they'd showed up on her doorstep to take her in for
questioning slipped its leash. Hating herself for the weakness, she begged them to listen, to understand, to believe
her.

"Please...this is all just some horrible misunderstanding. I don't know anything about the break-in at Mrs. Elliot's. You have to believe me! I've told you everything I know."

"Oh, really?" Sam taunted. "Then maybe you'll explain how you knew where to find this." Reaching into his pocket, he mockingly dangled Agatha Elliot's heart necklace in front of her nose. "Look familiar, Ms. Hart?"

It didn't, not in the least. She'd never seen it before in her life, but she only had to reach out and touch it to know that Agatha Elliot's vibrations were all over it. "My God, you found Mrs. Elliot's jewelry! Does she know yet? She'll be thrilled!"

Relieved, she started to close her fingers around the locket, which was, to anyone sensitive enough to feel it, still warm from generations of loving care. But the detective never gave her a chance. Lightning quick, he snatched it back, his blue eyes icy with reluctant admiration as they raked over her. "You're one cool customer, lady. If I didn't know better, I'd swear you really cared about that old lady."

"But I do!"

"Oh, please," he groaned. "You're breaking my heart."

What heart? She almost spit the words at him, only to quickly bite them back. Dear God, what was she doing? Trying to antagonize the man and get herself locked up? Struggling for control, she dragged a calming breath and slowly released it. "I do care about Mrs. Elliot," she said quietly. "That's why I went to the hospital to see her. All this worry about the loss of her jewelry has sent her blood pressure through the roof. I wanted to make her feel better."

His mouth curled contemptuously. "You're just a regular Mother Teresa, aren't you? A real do-gooder."

She knew he was deliberately needling her, but she couldn't help but snap back. "I'd rather be that than a cynic who wouldn't recognize the truth if it bit him on the nose!"

Struggling with what sounded suspiciously like a laugh, Tanner coughed. "Why don't you sit down and tell us about your visit with Mrs. Elliot at the hospital, Ms. Hart? Why did you feel the need to talk to her?"

She didn't want to sit—or explain herself to either man. Bennigan might at least do her the courtesy of listening to her, but although he hid them well, his suspicions were there, just beneath the surface. And Kelly, well, it went without saying that he wasn't a man to hide his emotions. The walls of the small room fairly vibrated with his distrust.

God, she hated this! She'd had to deal with negativism and distrust all her life, and it never got any easier. She'd thought when she moved to San Antonio she'd finally put that behind her. Wishful thinking. If she didn't convince both men she was really what she said she was, she was going to be in serious trouble. Left with no choice, she sighed tiredly and sat—facing *away* from that awful mirror.

"I know you don't believe me, but I really was concerned about her. I could tell she was worrying herself to death about her jewelry, and there was really no need to."

"Because you knew where it was," Tanner concluded as he took the chair across from her at the scarred table while Sam prowled like a caged lion. "Isn't that right?"

"Well, I didn't know the exact location of course. But I had a general idea—"

"Because your boyfriend told you he was hocking it

on the south side," Sam cut in ruthlessly, scowling at her. "Isn't that what you're really saying, Ms. Hart? He didn't give you all the details so you could plead ignorance if you were questioned, but he told you enough. We only found two pieces. So where's the rest of it? He must have told you."

"No, that's not what I'm saying!"

With a muttered curse he slapped both hands on the table and leaned toward her intimidatingly. "Dammit, we know there's a man involved! Who is he? Your lover? Some piece of trash who had you scout out rich little old ladies at the mall and follow them home? Did he threaten you? Is that how he got you to go along with him? Give us his name and I swear he'll never come near you again."

"How can I give you a name when I don't know who did this? There's no lover. No man, period!"

"Oh, c'mon," he scoffed. "There's got to be somebody. You're a good-looking woman. You probably meet a lot of men in that café of yours."

"There's no one, damn you!" Pushed to the limit, she surged to her feet and leaned across the table to stand nose to nose with him, her green eyes flashing fire, every line of her body stiff with defiance. "I'm not seeing anyone, dating anyone, sleeping with anyone! How many times do I have to say it to get it through your thick head, Detective? *There is no man!*"

Caught in the heat of her eyes, Sam found that hard to believe. He hadn't been stringing her along when he'd said she was a good-looking woman. She was damn easy on the eyes. Even when those green eyes of hers were snapping with fury and she appeared to want to slug him. Her chin up, she faced him unflinchingly, in spite of the fact that he was a hell of a lot bigger than she was, and suddenly all he could think about was tasting the fire in her. With all her pent-up passion, she'd burn a man up in bed.

The unwanted thought brought him up short as nothing else could. What the hell was he doing? he wondered angrily, jerking back like he'd been stung. She was a suspect, and he'd damn well better remember that. What she did in bed was none of his business. Uncomfortable, he glanced up to find Tanner watching him with narrowed eyes. With a subtle jerk of his head toward the door, he suggested they talk outside.

"Sit down and cool your jets," he told Jennifer coldly, then followed Tanner out into the hall.

The door had hardly shut behind them when his friend turned on him. "You want to tell me what the hell you're doing in there?" he demanded in a low voice that wouldn't carry to the other room. "We brought the girl in to question her about the jewelry, not rake her over the coals about her love life. If you keep going the way you are, she'll either call her lawyer or refuse to cooperate, and then where'll we be?"

"Dammit, I'm just trying to get the truth out of her!"

"Has it crossed your mind that maybe you already have?"

Caught off guard, Sam blinked. "What are you saying? You think she's really psychic? C'mon! Next, you'll be telling me you believe in Santa and the tooth fairy."

He expected a denial. He didn't get it. "There's a lot of things in the world that can't be explained," Tanner said simply. "In your world there's no such thing as St. Nick, but my three-year-old would swear by all that's holy that he exists. Jennifer Hart thinks she can see things days before they happen. If she believes strongly enough…who knows?" he said with a shrug. "Maybe she can."

"Like hell," Sam growled. "She's scamming us, and

I'm going to prove it. All I have to do is push her hard enough and she'll crack.''

His jaw set at a rigid angle, he stormed back into the interrogation room determined to break her. He asked her about Benny and his pawnshop and the man who hocked the jewelry and gave the name John Donovan for the claim ticket. She didn't know any of them. Frustrated, he had her go over her story again, then again, picking it apart each time, but the lady, despite her air of fragility, proved as tough as an old boot. She stood strong, never wavering, not even when she was so close to tears he could see them clinging to her lashes. Without a single word of reproach, she managed to make him feel lower than dirt. Riddled with guilt and furious with himself because of it, he finally had no choice but to let her go. She'd been there three hours.

Exhausted, angry, her feelings hurt and bruised, she wouldn't even let them take her home. ''No, thank you. I don't need your help.''

''Don't be that way, Ms. Hart,'' Detective Bennigan said soothingly. ''It's getting late and you really shouldn't be walking the streets by yourself. After everything we've put you through, at least let us take you home.''

She would have rather taken her chances with a stranger on the street than accept a single favor from Sam Kelly, but she couldn't bring herself to say that to his partner, not when *he* had tried to be civil to her. ''I appreciate the offer, Detective Bennigan, but it's only six blocks. I'd rather walk, thank you.''

''Don't be ridiculous,'' Sam snapped. ''A woman walking the streets alone is just a mugging waiting to happen. We can have you home in five minutes.''

Standing proudly before him, the tilt of her head disdainful, she managed to look down her nose at him even though he towered over her by a foot or more. "I'm not going to get mugged—I'm a psychic, remember?" Giving him a faint smile that was guaranteed to set his teeth on edge, she turned and sailed regally out the door.

She'd thought that would end it—it should have—but she hadn't counted on Sam Kelly's persistence. Obviously the man couldn't take no for an answer. Muttering and swearing under his breath, he followed her downstairs and out the front door of the police station, chastising her all the way. "You're being ridiculous. You may not give a damn about your personal safety, but it happens to be my job. Dammit, woman, wait up!"

He was right behind her, practically breathing down her neck. She felt her heart lurch and told herself it was only because she'd never been angrier with a man in her life. Stubbornly staring straight ahead, she kept walking. "Go away, Detective. I've seen how you do your job and I don't care for it."

"You would if you were the one who'd lost thousands of dollars of jewelry," he retorted. "Sometimes the only way to get to the truth is to ask hard questions."

"You heard the truth," she tossed back. "You weren't willing to accept it."

"What I heard was a fairy tale—"

"Why? Because you can't explain it?" Stopping abruptly in the middle of the sidewalk, she whirled to face him and grabbed him by the tie. "If the only things you believe in are the things you can explain, then explain this. Up until a week ago, I'd never seen you before in my life. But I know you're divorced, your first car was a 1964 Ford Falcon, and you were born in a little town south of here. If I'm not psychic, how do I know all that?"

He couldn't answer because there *was* no answer. Smiling mockingly, she released his tie and stepped back. "I rest my case. Good night, Detective."

Turning her back on him, she started down the street again, but this time he didn't follow her. She didn't have to turn around to know that he still stood where she'd left him, staring after her, and she took no small measure of satisfaction in knowing that she'd left him speechless.

"Hey, Hart!"

His call caught her two steps away from the corner. Half-tempted to ignore him and continue on her way, she made the mistake of looking over her shoulder. He still stood right where she'd left him, but he suddenly looked mighty pleased with himself. Suspicious, she hesitated. "What?"

"You really had me going there for a minute," he yelled. "You're sharp, lady. Real sharp. But next time you want to convince someone you're psychic, try telling them something that's not a matter of public record."

He was so smug she would have thrown something at that handsome head of his if she'd had anything at hand. Instead, she had to be content with a rude hand gesture, which only drew a laugh from him. Fuming, she turned and disappeared around the corner.

At three in the morning she was still thinking about him. Disgusted with herself, she punched her pillow into a more comfortable shape and told herself the man didn't deserve a second thought. He was suspicious, quick to judge and positively infuriating. How did his partner put up with him?

But even as she closed her eyes and courted sleep, honesty forced her to admit she was condemning the man unfairly. He might be maddening, but her instincts told her he was an excellent cop who took his responsibilities seriously. If he had a problem with her special talents, well, so did most of the rest of the world. People instinctively distrusted what they couldn't explain; it was human nature. She couldn't fault him for that when she didn't anyone else.

If she didn't like him, she decided, it had nothing to do with the fact that he thought she was a flake who didn't make a move without consulting her crystal ball. There was just something about him that rubbed her the wrong way. Every time their eyes met, her hackles rose and she didn't know why. She just knew she wanted nothing further to do with the man.

But even as she tried to banish him from her thoughts, the memory of his rare smile flashed before her closed eyes, and a restlessness she couldn't explain stirred in her. Muttering curses, she flipped her pillow over and willed her too-active brain to shut down for the night. But an hour later, when she was finally able to fall back asleep, Sam Kelly was there, waiting for her in her dreams.

When the alarm went off at four-thirty, she felt as if she'd hardly slept at all. Her head thick, her eyes sandy, she wanted nothing more than to go back to sleep, but she couldn't. It was Saturday, and the café was closed except for supper so that she could bake bread and pastries for several of the homeless shelters around town. Her grandparents had instilled in her the importance of giving something back to the community, and she'd started the practice the first week she'd opened the café. The day always reminded her of her childhood and she loved it.

With no customers to worry about facing until much later in the afternoon, she didn't bother with her appearance, but simply dragged on jeans and an old T-shirt and stumbled downstairs to the café kitchen. Switching on the lights, she'd just tied on an apron when there was a soft knock at the back door and Rosa swept in like a small whirlwind.

"Good morning!" she said breathlessly. "I'm sorry I'm late. The car was stubborn this morning and wouldn't start. I think it needs a new starter."

Just sixteen and always seeming to move at the speed of light, the teenager had come into the café six weeks ago in search of a full-time job. She'd been desperate and defiant, and when Jennifer asked about her age, she'd lied through her teeth and claimed she was twenty-three. Anyone with eyes could see she was little more than a child. Afraid she was a runaway, Jennifer finally got her to admit that her widowed father had been hurt in a car accident and lost his job. Unless she could find work to help support him and her three younger brothers and sisters, they would all be out on the street by the end of the month.

Instantly sympathetic, Jennifer sat her down, fed her and learned that the girl had quit high school earlier that week because she didn't think she had any other choice. She'd spent every day since looking for work, but she had no skills or training, and no one had been willing to take a chance on a dropout. She'd been at the end of her rope and near tears when she'd seen the Help Wanted sign in the café's front window.

Jennifer hadn't had the heart to tell her she was a far cry from the type of help she was looking for. She'd expected to hire someone older and more responsible, another senior citizen like Molly who wanted to work instead of sit around and wait to die. But fate had sent her Rosa, and she knew what it was like to feel you had nowhere to turn. If her grandparents hadn't taken her after her mother died, there was no telling where she would have ended up.

So she'd struck a deal with Rosa. She would hire her

to work three afternoons a week and all day Saturday, and in the process, teach her how to bake—with one stipulation. She had to go back to school. Tears welling in her eyes, Rosa had thrown herself into her arms and promised her she'd never regret it. Hiring her had turned out to be one of the best decisions Jennifer had ever made.

"You didn't walk, did you?" she asked in alarm as the girl shrugged out of her jacket and tied on an apron. "At this hour of the morning! You should have called me. You know I would have come for you."

"But that would have put you behind with the morning baking and we'd have been playing catch-up all day," Rosa replied with a logic she couldn't argue with. "Anyway, I'd already promised Carlos I'd call him the next time the car gave me trouble. You know how he worries about me. He really doesn't even like the idea of me driving by myself, so he was happy to give me a ride."

Jennifer just bet he was. Carlos Santos, Rosa's nineteen-year-old boyfriend, was a subject they would never agree on. An arrogant macho thug as far as Jennifer was concerned, he treated Rosa like a little girl who couldn't cross the street without his help. Not only did he discourage her from driving, he didn't care for the idea of her working, either. He pretended to be concerned and protective, but the first time Jennifer had met him, she'd seen the way he manipulated the girl, and she hadn't liked it at all. She'd tried to drop a hint in Rosa's ear by suggesting that any man who tried to wrap a woman in cotton and make her dependent on him might have a controlling personality; but so far, where Carlos was concerned, Rosa wore blinders.

Knowing better than to criticize him outright, Jennifer said, "That was very thoughtful of him. But I thought he worked the night shift somewhere. Did he have to take off early to come and get you?''

"Well, no. Not exactly.'' Rosa hesitated. "He was working as a security guard at a nursing home, but he couldn't handle being around sick people all the time.''

"So he quit.''

Looking decidedly uncomfortable, Rosa nodded. "But he's looking for something else,'' she added quickly. "A day job so we can spend more time together. Before, we hardly ever got to see each other.''

That wasn't necessarily a bad thing, but Jennifer wisely kept the thought to herself as she began to assemble ingredients for the day's first batch of bread. "I'm sure he'll find something,'' she said dryly. "He always does.''

Carlos had, in fact, had three jobs in the past six weeks, proving that finding work wasn't the problem. Keeping it was. According to Rosa, he always found some reason to quit—either the boss was a SOB who didn't pay him what he was worth, or he needed something more challenging. And every time he was out of work, he convinced Rosa to lend him money. He rarely paid her back.

"He has a lot of talents,'' the girl agreed seriously. "Last night we watched this show on TV about how to build a house yourself from the ground up, and Carlos already knew how to do it. If he had the money, he could start his own construction company.''

Helping Jennifer without having to be told what to do next, she rattled happily on, too infatuated to notice that the only hopes and dreams she talked about were Carlos's. *He* was going to do something great one day. *He* was going to make a lot of money. It was all Carlos, Carlos, Carlos. Just listening to her made Jennifer want to grab her by the ears and shake some sense into her. The jerk was nothing but a big talker who didn't like to work and would probably never amount to anything unless he found a smart, hardworking woman to support him. But she couldn't tell Rosa that, not without putting her in the position of defending him. So she bit her tongue and prayed that one day soon the girl would see the light on her own.

They'd punched down the first batch of bread and set it aside for a second rising when Rosa thought to ask her about her own evening. "I'm sorry! I've been rambling and forgot to ask you about last night. You and Molly went to the movies, didn't you? What'd you go see?"

The last thing Jennifer wanted to talk about was last night, but Rosa would find out about it soon enough, and it would be better if she heard the story from her. "Actually we never made it to the theater," she admitted reluctantly. "I spent the evening at the police station, instead."

"Is that detective bothering you again?" Rosa demanded indignantly. "The one who doesn't believe you're psychic?"

Surprised, Jennifer sank onto a nearby stool. "You know about that?"

"Sure," she said with a shrug. "Molly told me. She thought I should know in case the cops come back asking questions. What's this Kelly dude's problem, anyway? Is he blind or what? You'd never do anything to hurt anyone. Especially a senior citizen. You gave Molly a job when nobody else would, and the only reason old lady Winston around the corner is still kicking is that you make sure she gets a hot meal delivered to her doorstep three times a day. Does that sound like someone who's going to have anything to do with choking an old lady?"

Wound up, Rosa spent the rest of the morning working herself into a lather about the detective, making Jennifer laugh at her indignation. Then, just after lunch, when they were bagging the dozens of loaves of French bread they'd baked for the homeless, the devil himself knocked at the back door.

He was the last person in the world Jennifer expected. After his heated three-hour interrogation of her, she'd thought they had nothing more to say to each other. But there he was, dressed in jeans and a faded navy blue sweatshirt that had SAPD boldly printed across the front, looking far too good for her peace of mind. When her heart lurched at the sight of him, she told herself it was a natural enough reaction to a cop who seemed determined to pin a crime on her she hadn't committed. If her pulse had a tendency to skip, too, well, that was nobody's business but her own.

Frowning, she stopped him in the doorway with just a look. "What are you doing here, Detective?"

It was a legitimate question. One he wished like hell he had an answer for. It was his day off, and he'd have sworn Jennifer Hart was the furthest thing from his mind. But when he'd gone out for a walk, his feet had led him straight to her, and he didn't for the life of him know why.

"I smelled bread," he said, grabbing at the first explanation that made sense. "It smells good."

"We're closed," the girl at her side said coldly. "And even if we weren't, no one's allowed in the kitchen but employees."

Surveying the angry teenager with narrowed eyes, Sam didn't have to ask who she was. He'd already gotten a list of the café employees, and there was only one other employee he'd yet to meet. "You must be Rosa Martinez."

She nodded stiffly and made no effort to conceal her dislike. "And you're the detective who's trying to pin a rap on Jennifer."

"Rosa!"

Ignoring Jennifer's gasp, Sam grinned down at the girl. He liked a kid with guts. And loyalty, even if it was misplaced, was a rare commodity these days. "I'm not the bad guy here—I'm just trying to do my job and get at the truth."

"She told you the truth, but you won't believe her. She doesn't lie."

"Sweetheart, I've never met a suspect yet who did," he drawled. "They're all God-fearing clean-living citizens who'd die before they'd do anything dishonest."

His gentle mockery stung. Color climbing into her cheeks, Rosa said stubbornly, "But Jennifer's not like that. She's not!" she insisted when he only shrugged, unconvinced. "If you don't believe me, look around. All this bread is going to be donated to homeless shelters. Would a thief do that?"

"A smart one would," he tossed back. "Appearances can fool a lot of people. Take this setup your boss lady has here. It looks legit. She seems like a hardworking, charitable lady who pays her bills and doesn't bother anybody. But how do I know what she's hiding upstairs? Even a good-looking apple can be rotten to the core. For all I know, she could be selling dope out of there after she closes up at night. Or hiding loot from a robbery. I don't know what's in her closets. Of course, if she'd let me look around, that might go a long way toward clearing up any misunderstandings I have about her."

Outmaneuvered, Rosa looked uncertainly at Jennifer. "Uh...Jennifer?"

No! Every instinct Jennifer possessed screamed at her not to be a fool. Kelly didn't have a search warrant. She didn't have to let him anywhere near her things.

But if she didn't, it would seem as if she had something to hide.

Seething, she shot him a look that should have slayed him where he stood. The fact that it didn't only served to infuriate her more. "You think you're pretty clever, don't you, Kelly?"

"One can only try," he said modestly, grinning. "So what's your answer? Yes or no?"

What could she say? "Yes," she said through her teeth, "*if* my attorney says it's all right."

She didn't have an attorney, but that was none of Sam Kelly's business. Leaving him to cool his heels in the kitchen she hurried into her small office, shut the door and tried not to panic. It was Saturday—most people weren't working, especially at this hour. Dear God, what was she going to do? Then she remembered the attorney who came into the café just about every morning for Danish and coffee. Praying the woman had a listed number, Jennifer reached for the phone book.

Brenda Ferguson was cleaning house and thankful for any interruption that took her away from it for a few minutes. When Jennifer identified herself and apologized for disturbing her, she laughed. "Are you kidding? You're a godsend. What can I do for you?"

"I hate to call you at home and on a Saturday, but it's sort of an emergency and I need a lawyer. I didn't know anyone else to call."

Instantly alert, the other woman shrugged off the apology and said, "What's the problem?"

Quickly and succinctly, Jennifer told her everything. "Detective Kelly is here now and wants to look around. I didn't know how to tell him no without looking guilty."

"No!" Brenda said immediately. "If he wants to look around, he can damn well get a warrant. And don't talk to him! If he doesn't like it, I'll explain the facts of life to him when I get there.''

"You're coming over?" Jennifer asked in surprise.

"Just as soon as I turn off the vacuum cleaner," she assured her grimly. Without another word, she hung up.

Chapter 4

If she was going to have a lawyer, she should have followed her advice to the letter. Logically, she knew that, but when she returned to the kitchen to inform Sam that she couldn't, on the advice of her attorney, allow him upstairs, he gave her that look. The one that made her want to squirm and rush to offer an explanation. The next thing she knew, she was instructing Rosa to watch the bread, then leading Sam outside and up the stairs to her apartment. Giving him carte blanche to dig into any drawer or closet he liked, she just dared him to find a single piece of physical evidence that linked her to the burglary and attack on Mrs. Elliot.

He wouldn't of course. There was nothing *to* find. Confident, she followed him from room to room, watching him like a hawk when he put his hands on her things and all but crowing when he found nothing the least bit suspicious. Then he stepped into her bedroom and went right to her dresser and the silver-plated antique jewelry box sitting on top of it. She'd played with it as a little girl and loved it all her life. It was the one item above all others that she treasured the most, and at the sight of it in Kelly's strong, lean hands, her heart lurched.

"That was my grandmother's," she said sharply. "All the jewelry in there belonged to her, and I'd just as soon you didn't handle it. Some of the pieces are quite old and in need of repair."

"I'll be careful," he promised, and flipped open the lid. At the sight of the diamonds sparkling there, he whistled softly. "Well, well, well. What have we here? And you said you had nothing to hide."

"I don't!" she snapped. Alarmed by the glint of satisfaction in his eyes, it was all she could do not to snatch the case out of his hands. "Those were my grand-mother's!"

"So you said. Can you prove it?"

Taken aback, she paled. "No, but—"

"Then how do I know these aren't Mrs. Elliot's? We've only recovered two pieces so far."

"Because they're not. They don't even fit the description."

"She said they were old diamond pins and bracelets." Dipping his fingers into the jewelry box, he pulled out a handful of old diamond pins and bracelets. His smile smug, he arched a brow at her. "I'm not much of an expert at jewelry, but these look like a match to me. What do you think?" And without so much as a by-your-leave, he dumped the entire contents of the jewelry box into an evidence bag he pulled from his pocket.

"No! Dammit, you can't do that!"

"Watch me, sweetheart."

"You have no right! Every one of those pieces was left

to me in my grandmother's will. Give them back right now, or I swear I'll—''

"Would someone like to tell me what the hell is going on here?"

Whirling, Jennifer sighed in relief at the sight of Brenda Ferguson standing in the open doorway with a frown of displeasure lining her brow. "Brenda! Thank God!"

Dressed in a red suit that had power written all over it, the attorney stepped into the bedroom like she was walking into court. Less than twenty minutes had passed since Jennifer's call had caught her cleaning house, but she was as put together as if she'd had hours to dress. Her iron gray hair hung to her shoulders in a sleek pageboy, and somehow she'd found the time to meticulously apply makeup. Her sharp blue eyes shifting from the evidence bag in Sam's hand to Jennifer's flushed indignant face, she summed up the situation in a single glance.

"If you're Sam Kelly and that bag is what I think it is, you're in a whole lot of trouble, Detective," she told him after crossing the room to introduce herself. "You have no right to search this property without a warrant."

Not the least bit perturbed, he tucked the evidence bag into the pocket of his jacket with a maddening lack of haste. "Sorry to disappoint you, Counselor, but I don't need a warrant. Your client gave me permission to conduct a search."

Glancing at her, the other woman arched a brow. "Jennifer?"

"I know you told me to tell him no, but I didn't think it would hurt since I don't have anything to hide," she said defensively. "How was I supposed to know the man was totally unreasonable? He expects me to prove my grandmother's jewelry is mine! Tell me how I'm supposed to do that. They don't exactly come with a deed of trust, you know.''

"There was a will, wasn't there?'' he replied. "If she left this stuff to you, it'll be in her will. Drag it out and let's see what it says.''

"There's no point—she didn't list the individual pieces. All the will says is that she wanted me to have the contents of her jewelry box.''

"So you could put anything you wanted in there and claim Granny left it to you, couldn't you? Sorry, sweetheart, but that's not going to wash.''

"Be careful, Detective,'' Brenda Ferguson warned quietly. "You don't have anything against my client and you know it. You're just blowing smoke.''

Unperturbed, he replied confidently, "I wouldn't be too sure of that if I were you. Ms. Hart has prior knowledge of the crime and jewelry that fits the description given by the victim. She's new to San Antonio and may, for all we know, have a rap sheet a mile long in that little town in West Texas where she claims she grew up. I'm going to check out her background and show these pieces to the victim. If I find something I shouldn't, you'll be the first to know.''

He turned on his heel and walked out, leaving behind a silence thick with apprehension. Staring after him, Jennifer wondered how she'd ever thought the man the least bit attractive.

Standing at her side, Brenda said dryly, "Please tell me you don't have a record a mile long in West Texas.''

Jennifer laughed shakily and obediently repeated, "I don't have a record a mile long in West Texas. But,'' she added, sobering, "I did develop something of a reputation there.''

"As what?''

"An oddball psychic. And the woman who accused the mayor of embezzling city funds after I had a vision about it."

Interested, Brenda lifted a brow. "Did he do it?"

That period in her life wasn't something Jennifer liked to talk about, but after Brenda had dropped everything to rush over there to help her, the least she owed her was an explanation. "He did it," she said stiffly, "but not many people thanked me for exposing him."

She had, in fact, been ostracized and treated like a leper by people she'd known her entire life. She'd only been eighteen at the time, but she still felt the hurt as if it were yesterday. "He was well liked and I was a nobody who everyone thought was a little strange."

"But surely the local authorities did something to him," the older woman said incredulously. "He embezzled public funds, for God's sake! At the very least he should have been run out of office."

"He was—eventually. By that time there wasn't much anyone could do to him, though. Last I heard, he'd run off to Puerto Rico and was living like a king."

"But there were some discrepancies in the books? Just as you told the police? That's a matter of public record?"

"Actually I went to the sheriff, but yes, I suppose it's in the case records somewhere. It would have to be. No one even suspected anything was wrong until I came forward."

Brenda couldn't have been more thrilled if Jennifer had just predicted she was going to be appointed to the Supreme Court.

"Yes!" she crowed, shooting a triumphant fist into the air. At Jennifer's look of surprise, she laughed and slung a friendly arm over her shoulder. "Don't you get it? Detective Kelly is hoping you've got a record, and you do, but not the kind he wants. It's on record that you assisted the police and exposed a criminal. God, I wish I could see Kelly's face when he finds out!''

First thing Monday morning Sam called the sheriff of Sandy Bluff. He was named Homer, for God's sake. Homer Winslow. He was a slow-talking good ol' boy who either had too much time on his hands or didn't take his duties all that seriously. When Sam told him he was a detective with SAPD and calling on official business about Jennifer Hart, all the man could talk about was the cherry Danish Jennifer's grandmother, God rest her soul, used to make. It was the best he'd ever put his mouth to.

Struggling to hold on to his patience, Sam said, "That's great, Sheriff. But about Ms. Hart—"

"I always said it was a shame about that girl," he confided. "She comes from good people, you know. And she lost them all by the time she was twenty-two. But she handled that just like she handled everything else life threw at her."

"And what was that?" Sam asked curiously. "What exactly has life thrown at her besides the loss of her family?"

"Well, you know, she never had many friends when she was growing up. She was different, and a lot of parents didn't want their kids associating with someone who always seemed to know what was going to happen tomorrow. And then there was that mess with Mayor Denton."

Alarm bells clanging in his head, Sam sat up straighter and grabbed pencil and paper to take notes. "What mess?"

"The jerk was helping himself to city funds." Disgust flattened the sheriff's voice. "Even when she came to me and told me what was going on, I'm sorry to say I didn't believe her. I liked the guy, you know. So did everybody else. But he was nothing but a two-bit thief and no one could see it but Jennifer.''

"How did she know it?"

"How does Jennifer know anything?" he asked ruefully. "She just did. And people didn't like her for it, either. In fact, it got pretty ugly. Some even accused her of framing the mayor because her grandparents didn't agree with his politics. I had to check her out of course, but she was clean, just like I knew she'd be. That didn't stop people from talking, though. Then when old Denton destroyed most of the records and slipped away in the dead of night, the holier-than-thou types blamed Jennifer because he got away. Nobody was too surprised when she sold their business after her grandparents died and left town. She wasn't real happy here.''

He rattled on about her grandparents and how the bakery just hadn't been the same since it had changed ownership, but all Sam heard was the case he was trying to build against Jennifer going down the drain. And he couldn't even say he was surprised. On the way into work, he'd stopped by Agatha Elliot's to show her pictures of the jewelry he'd confiscated from Jennifer. The old lady had loved them, but none of the old-fashioned pins and bracelets were hers. He'd still needed to check out her background just to be sure, but he'd already figured he wasn't going to find anything.

That didn't, however, mean he was willing to concede that Jennifer was in any way, shape or form, psychic. She just had good instincts.

She wasn't real happy here.

Long after he thanked the sheriff for his help and hung up, Winslow's words echoed in his ears. The sheriff had painted a grim picture of a young girl who'd grown up alone and lonely, all because she had the misfortune to be different. Just thinking about it made Sam furious.

"Problems?" Tanner asked, pushing in on his troubled thoughts with the arrogance of an old friend.

"It looks like we may be back to square one with the Elliot case," Sam said in disgust. "The sheriff in Sandy Bluff verified that Jennifer Hart worked with him on a case a few years back. She had a hunch about the mayor embezzling money, and it turned out she was right."

Amusement glittered in Tanner's eyes. "So she *is* psychic. Ain't that damn interesting?"

"Stuff it, Bennigan. She just got lucky, all right? If she was really psychic, she should have known we'd suspect she was somehow involved. So why didn't she take steps to prevent that from happening? Tell me that, hotshot. One phone call from the sheriff in Sandy Bluff and she would have saved herself a lot of grief."

"Maybe," Tanner said with a shrug. "Maybe not. The sheriff just verified that she's psychic and you still don't want to believe it, so what's the point of verifying her story? You still wouldn't have believed her."

"Because there's no such thing as psychics!"

Amused by his vehemence, Tanner grinned. "Isn't there? The lady looks pretty damn real to me. And I think that's what's got you all in a stew. You'd rather not notice, but she's kind of hard to ignore."

He was right. Deep in his gut Sam knew it, but he was damned if he'd admit it. "Don't start with that crap that I need a woman. I date."

"When?"

"A couple of months ago. I went out with Tom Saboda's sister. We went to that new Harrison Ford movie."

"And you left early with the excuse that you were

catching the flu," Tanner retorted. "You had to take two days' sick leave just so Tom wouldn't guess you'd lied to his sister. You haven't been out since."

"So I'm busy," he growled. "And I just got busier. In case you haven't noticed, we've now lost our one and only suspect. Unless you want to be the one to tell that to the lieutenant, I suggest we find us another one."

They spent the rest of the day running down leads, but they had little to work with. There were no fingerprints at the Elliot estate or on the two pieces of jewelry hocked at Benny's and no description of the perp. Agatha could testify that the man was big and strong, but that was all; and Benny conveniently had a memory that wasn't good with details. If he got a good look at the character who'd brought in the jewelry, he wasn't talking, and the name and address the man had left had, not surprisingly, turned out to be bogus.

All Sam wanted to do at the end of his shift was go home and forget the whole damn thing. But first he had to return Jennifer's jewelry to her and concede that she'd been telling the truth, at least about that. He wasn't looking forward to it.

He didn't like to think he was one of those men who couldn't admit he'd made a mistake, but he damn sure wasn't taking a witness along to record the event for posterity. So when he dropped by Heavenly Scents on the way home, he was alone.

Keep it simple, he told himself. Get it over with and get out. But the second he stepped through the front door of the café, he knew that wasn't going to be possible. It was the middle of the supper rush and the place was packed. The only available table, in fact, was wedged back in a corner. Reluctantly he took it and sat back to wait.

Molly was running the grill while Rosa and Jennifer waited tables, and Sam didn't doubt for a second that they saw him the minute he walked through the door. Molly got this tight, persimmon set to her mouth, and Rosa shot him dirty looks whenever the opportunity presented itself. Jennifer, on the other hand, ignored him completely. At first Sam was willing to give her the benefit of the doubt. Considering how crowded the place was, it was entirely possible that she just hadn't seen him. But she was too good a waitress to leave a customer alone for long, and as he watched, she deliberately avoided the corner where he sat. Humor suddenly glinting in his eyes, he sat back to wait, wondering how long it would take for her to acknowledge him.

Exactly ten minutes later she put in an appearance at his table. "If you're here to harass me again, Detective, I'd appreciate if you'd do it at another time," she said stiffly. "I've got people waiting and could use the table."

Far from being insulted, he only grinned. "The name's Sam. And if this is the way you treat all your customers, it's a wonder you have any at all. What's today's special?"

Stunned, she nearly dropped her order pad. "You're going to eat?"

"I thought I might. You got a problem with that?"

"No, of course not." Color stinging her cheeks, she handed him a menu. "I'll be back in a minute to take your order."

"Just give me the special and iced tea."

"I haven't told you what it is yet."

"Is it liver?"

"No!"

"Then I'll eat it," he said, and handed the menu back to her.

She took it absently, her brows knit in a puzzled frown, and it didn't take a psychic to know she was trying to figure out what the hell he was doing there. He was wondering the same thing. When he'd walked through the front door, his only thought had been to get the deed done and leave. But Tanner was right, damn his hide. She was hard to ignore. She walked away to turn his order in, then refill iced-tea glasses at several tables, and he couldn't take his eyes off of her.

It had to be the way she moved, he decided broodingly. She just seemed to glide from table to table with unhurried grace, even when she was laden down with trays of food. And then there was the way she treated her customers. She greeted a lot of them by name and asked about their jobs and families as though she really cared, chatting with them as if she had all the time in the world. With just a word, a touch, a smile, she made everyone she spoke to feel special.

Except him. He might as well not have been there for all the attention she paid his corner. She even had Rosa bring his food to him when it was ready, along with the check, thereby avoiding any further need to speak to him.

From the sassy swing of her hips as she walked past his table without sparing him a glance, she obviously thought she'd outmaneuvered him. She'd thought wrong, however. He was a patient man, who'd learned as a rookie cop how to wait. If she wanted to play games until she closed up for the night, he was more than happy to accommodate her. Picking up his fork, he dug into the special, which turned out to be chicken and dumplings, one of his favorites. And all the time, he watched every move the lady made.

What was he still doing there? Irritated, Jennifer kept her eyes firmly averted from the corner table and wondered when the dratted man was going to leave. He'd cleaned his plate, then lingered over a slice of Molly's famous banana-cream pie like a man who'd died and gone to heaven. The supper rush had come and gone, and just when she thought he was finally finished, he'd signaled Rosa for a cup of coffee. He'd been nursing it ever since. That was fifteen minutes ago, and whatever he had left in the bottom of his cup had to be stone cold. Yet there he sat, his long legs stretched out in front of him as if he didn't have a care in the world, watching her with those wicked blue eyes of his. It was enough to make a sane woman pull out her hair!

And he wasn't going to get away with it! she decided abruptly. This was her café, her territory, and he'd rattled her long enough. It was time she took control of the situation and booted him out the door. Grabbing the coffee-pot, she made a beeline for his table.

Without asking him if he wanted more coffee, she filled his cup to the brim, then set the pot on the table with a thump. "All right, Detective," she said curtly. "You've had your fun and games. Playtime's over. I'm closing up in twenty minutes. If you don't want to be locked in here for the night, I suggest you pay your bill and head for home."

With maddening calm, he lifted an inquiring brow. "Are you throwing me out?"

"In a heartbeat." Whipping out her hand, she said, "That'll be $8.54, please—not counting tip of course."

"Of course," he said dryly. Digging his wallet out of his back pocket, he pulled out a ten and dropped it into her hand. "Keep the change."

"I'm sure your waitress will appreciate it," she said just as dryly.

She would have pulled her hand back then, but before she could so much as move, his fingers closed like a sprung trap around her wrist.

"Not so fast, Ms. Hart," he murmured. "I have something for you."

She could have pulled free. Somewhere deep inside, a quiet voice whispered that his grip was gentle and hardly unbreakable, but she couldn't hear anything but the unexpected thundering of her own heart. Transfixed, she stared down at the fingers encircling her wrist and was swamped with the oddest feelings. She hardly knew the man, but his touch felt so familiar. So... *right*. As if he'd touched her this way a thousand times before.

Suddenly afraid, she jerked her eyes up to his and found him frowning at the hold he had on her wrist, too. When his eyes lifted to hers, they were dark and turbulent with an emotion that seemed to steal the air right out of her lungs. Her heart stumbled. What was going on here? Torn between the urge to run and the need to stand her ground with this man, she tugged against his hold. Without a word he released her.

In the blink of an eye, his expression was shuttered, and suddenly she couldn't be sure she hadn't imagined the whole thing. It mortified her to admit it, but she had no experience with men. None. She hadn't been lying when she told him there was no man in her life—there never had been. The boys in Sandy Bluff had all been scared off by the idea that she knew what they were going to try before they did, and they'd avoided her like the plague. So while other girls had learned the flirting game in high school and how to read the signs of male interest, she never had. And nothing had changed since. Prince Charming himself could have shown up on her doorstep, and she never would have known it unless he came right out and told her.

Not that she thought Sam was her prince, charming or otherwise, she hastily assured herself. Horrified at the direction of her thoughts, she felt color spill into her cheeks and was helpless to stop it. Did he know what she was thinking? Had he guessed that she was mooning over him after nothing more than a touch?

Feeling like a gauche teenager suffering from her first crush, it was all she could do not to run. Instead, she forced herself to stand her ground and look him in the eye. "I can't imagine anything you could possibly have for me, Detective," she said in a voice she hardly recognized as her own. "Now if you'll excuse me, I have work to do."

When she would have turned and walked away, he reached into his pocket and pulled out the plastic bag that held her grandmother's jewelry. "The story about your grandmother appears to check out," he said stiffly, "so you can have these back."

"I think my ears are playing tricks on me," she said, stunned. "Would you repeat that?"

A smile, a faint one, curled the edges of his mouth. "So you want your pound of flesh, do you? I guess you're entitled. You were telling the truth. Maybe I should have believed you at the time, but Mrs. Elliot has a lot of connections in this town, and there's a lot of pressure on the department to solve the case. I couldn't take any chances." His gaze still steady on hers, he pushed the bag across the table. "If you're going to keep them in your apartment, you need to get a safe. They're too valuable to leave lying around on a dresser."

Surprised, a tremulous smile whispering over her mouth, she reached for the bag and clutched it close. She knew he was right. She did need a safe. But locked away out of sight in some vault, the jewelry wouldn't mean nearly as much to her as it did when it was on her dresser within easy reach.

That, however, was something a practical man like Sam Kelly would never understand. "I'll think about it," she conceded softly. "Thank you for returning them so quickly."

Unable to stop his eyes from drifting to her mouth, Sam felt something hot and swift kick him in the gut. She had the most amazing smile—soft and vulnerable and sexy enough to tempt the devil himself. And the crazy thing was, she didn't seem to know it. If she'd been the type of woman he wanted to believe she was, the type who would ruthlessly plot with some lowlife to rob an old lady blind, she would have used any advantage to get to him. But she flirted so unconsciously she didn't even seem aware of what she could do to a man—to him, dammit!—with just a smile.

Annoyed with himself for letting her get to him, furious with her for being totally unaware of it, he pushed abruptly to his feet. "I was just doing my job," he said gruffly, and headed for the door. He could feel her eyes on him, but he'd be damned if he'd look back. He didn't dare.

Deliberately he tried to put her out of his mind, but he could still feel the softness of her skin under his fingertips when he walked into the Lone Star Social Club a few minutes later. The old Victorian home, right on the river in the middle of downtown, had once been a place where cowboys met decent women when they came in from the cattle drives. Long after such social clubs had gone out of fashion and the house was converted into eight elegant apartments, the name still stuck.

His apartment was on the second floor at the back, away from the noise of the street, and he made a habit of never taking work home with him if he could help it. He had a feeling he wasn't going to be able to do that today, though, and it was all because of Jennifer Hart's touchable skin. It was enough to drive a man to drink.

Wondering if he had any beer in the refrigerator, he started up the central staircase, which looked like something straight out of *Gone with the Wind,* and was halfway up when a door opened below and familiar voice called happily, "Sam! There you are! I've been looking for you all over the place. What are they doing to you over at the police station? Working you to death? It seems like I never see you anymore."

He didn't have to force an affectionate smile as he turned to face his landlady. A small spry lady who could have been anywhere from her late sixties to early eighties, Alice Truelove was a sweetheart who managed the Lone Star Social Club as if all the tenants were members of her family. She fussed over them, shared their joy when they were happy and worried about them when their lives got a little bumpy. He couldn't have been any fonder of her if she'd been his own mother, but if she had one trait that sometimes set his teeth on edge, it was her love of matchmaking. She firmly believed that no one could find true happiness without a spouse to share it with, and she'd been trying to find him a wife ever since his divorce became final six months ago.

"I had the weekend off, but somebody said you'd gone out of town."

"Oh, yes!" She beamed, her blue eyes sparkling as he turned and headed back down the stairs toward her. "I had the most marvelous time! You should have been there."

Already guessing where this was heading, he quickly moved to cut her off. "That's great, Alice. I'm glad you had a good time. So why have you been looking for me? If it's a police matter, you should have called me at the station."

"Oh, no, dear! Nothing like that," she assured him easily. "I was just talking to Melanie the other day. You know Melanie, don't you? My niece? Well, she's got a good friend whose daughter is thinking about going into law enforcement, and I told her she should talk to you. She's a really sweet girl—and gorgeous, from what Melanie says—and I thought you might want to call her."

"Then ask her out, fall in love with her and marry her," he finished with a teasing grin. "I don't think so, sweetheart. I tried that once and it didn't work. That was enough for me."

"Oh, pooh!" she scoffed. "You're a young good-looking man, and there's no way you're going to spend the rest of your life alone. Not living in this house."

"Don't start, Alice," he groaned. "You know I don't believe in all that malarkey about the house having some kind of matchmaking magic."

"But it's true! Anyone who lives here will meet the love of their life within a year. I've seen it happen over and over again."

"Then what happened to me and Patricia? We lived here three years and ended up divorced. Where was the magic then?"

"But you were married before you ever moved in, so it didn't apply to that relationship," she said logically. "Anyone with eyes could see that you two had nothing in common but the bed you shared. Patricia was spoiled and self-centered and—"

"Too young," he finished for her. "If she'd been older, we might have had a chance."

"That girl was a holy terror then, and she'll still be when she's fifty-three. You're well rid of her. Next time things will be different."

"There isn't going to be a next time," he said, scowling at her persistence. "Trust me on this, Alice. I know what I'm talking about."

"That's what everyone says after a divorce." She reached out to pat him consolingly on the arm. "But you'll forget all that heartache just as soon as you meet someone new." Flashing her dimples at him, she teased, "I'll dance at your next wedding, so don't forget to invite me."

In her own way, the old gal was as stubborn as a mule. Amused in spite of himself, Sam laughed and hugged her. "I wouldn't dream of getting married without you. If I even think about getting hitched again, you'll be the first person I'll call."

With the return of her grandmother's jewelry, Jennifer assumed the police no longer considered her a suspect. But the next day when she left right before the lunch rush to take a hot meal to Mrs. Winston around the corner, the first thing she saw as she stepped outside was Sam Kelly's unmarked car across the street. Startled, she felt her heart skip a beat, and she was chagrined to admit it wasn't with fear. For hours after he'd left last night, she hadn't been able to think of anything but the heat that had flared in his eyes when he'd grabbed her wrist. She could still feel the warmth of it in her blood, which was crazy. The man didn't even like her. So what was he doing there?

He was gone by the time she returned, but he was back the next evening, parked in the same spot during the supper rush. By the third day, when she found herself watching for him, she knew she had to do something. The second she saw him pull up across the street, she reached for the phone and called her lawyer.

"I know it's frustrating," Brenda told her, "but there's not a lot I can do but call his captain and complain. Not that it'll do any good," she warned. "He'll just claim that Detective Kelly is in the middle of an ongoing investigation and has the right to observe any and all suspects. That includes you."

"But how can I still be a suspect? There's no evidence linking me to the man who robbed that old lady," she argued. "Can't we accuse Detective Kelly of harassment or something?"

"I'm afraid not. Not unless he does something a lot more serious than occasionally dropping by to watch you from across the street. I know that's not what you want to hear, but you might as well know where you stand— the man's just pushing your buttons and there's not a heck of a lot you can do about it. Sorry."

Glaring at the nondescript, unmarked beige police car through the café's large plate-glass window, Jennifer was half-tempted to storm out there and tell him and his partner exactly what she thought of them. But just then, a spark of mischief flared in her and she turned back to the grill to quickly assemble two sandwiches. In record time she had them wrapped and bagged. Once she had two large paper cups filled with soda and secured in a carrier, she motioned Rosa over to the counter.

"Take this out to Detective Kelly and his partner," she said, unable to stop grinning. "They're parked across the street in the beige sedan. Make sure Kelly gets the turkey and Dr. Pepper."

Still resentful of the way the detective had treated Jennifer, Rosa grudgingly agreed. "All right, if you insist. But I don't know why you're being nice to him after the way he treated you. Where's the bill?"

"There isn't one—this is a freebie. They can give you a tip if they want to, but don't let them give you any money for the food, okay? And don't forget who gets what. That's very important."

"I got it," the girl assured her. "Kelly gets the turkey and DP, and it's on the house."

Tempted to follow her to the front door and watch her all the way across the street, Jennifer had to make herself stand behind the counter and observe from a distance as Rosa waited until the traffic was clear to approach the two detectives. Both men sat up straighter as she drew near and, from their frowns, seemed to deny that they'd ordered anything. But Rosa had had the foresight to approach Bennigan on the passenger side, and he wasn't nearly as argumentative as Kelly. Once he learned that the food was on the house, he was all smiles, despite the frowning objections of his partner. Taking the food through the open car window, he dug a tip out of his wallet for Rosa, and within seconds she was hurrying back across the street with a big grin on her face and a five-dollar bill clutched in her fist.

So Kelly thought he could push her buttons, did he? Well, two could play at that. Taking a rare break, she grabbed a stool behind the counter and sat down to watch.

"Hey, man, look what she sent you!" Tanner said, surprised. "Turkey on whole wheat with grilled onions and mustard. I don't know anybody else who eats grilled onions on turkey. How'd she know that was your favorite?"

"It's just coincidence," Sam muttered, scowling at the sandwich Tanner held out to him. "She probably just threw something together and got lucky." Reluctantly he took it. "What's yours? Peanut butter and jelly with bananas?"

It was an old joke between them, one that went back to their days as rookie detectives. Tanner had walked into the squad room their first day with two peanut-butter-and-jelly-with-banana sandwiches and been needled unmercifully by the older detectives. In self-defense, he switched to something more sophisticated just to regain his self-respect with his coworkers, but he still loved PBJ and bananas.

"I wish," he said with a rueful grin. "But she'd never guess I'd like something like that."

But when he unwrapped the white butcher paper Jennifer had wrapped his sandwich in, he took one look and started to laugh. "I don't know how she does it, but you gotta admit she's good, man. No wonder you can't stay away from her."

Sam took one look at the PBJ sandwich with bananas and swore. For the past few days Tanner had done nothing but needle him every time he pulled up across the street from the café. He'd claimed he was just keeping an eye on the lady while they took a break, but Tanner knew him too well. "She could have talked to someone at the station…or one of the cops on this beat. Just about everybody knows you'll do cartwheels for peanut butter and jelly."

"Yeah, but that doesn't explain your grilled onions. Nobody at the station knows about that, and I haven't said anything to the lady. So how do you explain it?"

He couldn't. Not then or the next evening when he impulsively stopped by the café on the way home from work and she had a piece of coconut-cream pie and a hot cup of coffee set out for him. The place was empty, Molly had already left for the night, and only the lights over the grill were on. The place was obviously closed, but the front door was still unlocked. When he stepped inside, Jennifer turned from where she was cleaning the grill and didn't appear the least surprised to see him. And there on the counter sat that damn pie and steaming coffee, waiting for him.

It was, Sam decided, the last straw. A man could only take so much sass from a woman, and he'd had enough. Stalking toward her, he ignored the pie and coffee and stepped around the counter to confront her. "You think you're real clever, don't you, lady? Sending out sandwiches and stuff to me and Tanner without asking us what we like. I guess we're supposed to be real impressed with what a great psychic you are, aren't we? Think again, sweetheart. I don't know how you found out what my favorite foods are or how you knew when my shift ended tonight, but my bet is you've become pretty chummy with someone at the station. I want to know who it is. You hear me? I'm not leaving until you give me a name!"

Chapter 5

Jaw rigid, blue eyes fierce, he was the picture of a man pushed to the edge. A wise woman would have gotten out of his way till he cooled off, but after running headlong into his cynicism day after day for what seemed like weeks now, Jennifer couldn't resist needling him. "Then I guess you're staying a while because I haven't talked to anyone at the station but you."

"Are you saying *I* told you I like turkey and grilled onions? When, dammit?"

"Not verbally, no. But there are other ways to communicate, and your psyche has told me all sorts of things about you." Feeling cocky, she dared to grin at him and taunt, "You like just about every movie Clint Eastwood has ever made, and your favorite color is blue. You like to fish but not hunt, and one of these days you'll own a place in the country and—"

"Shut up."

Scowling, he took a step toward her, but she'd come

too far to be intimidated now. "And you like your steaks medium rare, your toast nearly burnt and your eggs scrambled. You played football in high school, hate baseball and see a Spurs game whenever you get the chance—"

"Dammit, I'm warning you..."

"What's the matter, Detective? Am I hitting a nerve? Shall I tell you about your ex-wife? Your marriage? The woman was a fool. She hurt you—"

Muttering a curse, he moved like lightning, closing the distance between them to grab her by the arms and snatch her up on her toes. His eyes, dark with fury, glared down into hers from only inches away. "Watch it, sweetheart," he growled softly. "We're talking about me, not Patricia. If you're so smart, tell me something about myself that's not common knowledge among my friends. Tell me what I *really* like."

She didn't pretend to misunderstand. He was asking about sex, just daring her to make the conversation intimate. Shaken, caught in the trap of his eyes, she told herself to end this craziness right now. Before she made a complete fool of herself. Before she opened her mouth and he realized that what she *didn't* know about pleasing a man in the bedroom could fill the Gulf of Mexico.

But he seemed able to push her buttons as easily as she pushed his, and the devil had a hold of her tongue. With the spicy scent of his aftershave surrounding her, seducing her, she leaned close, closed her eyes and imagined what would turn a man like Sam Kelly on. The images that sprang to mind came surprisingly easy.

"You like a woman who enjoys touching as much as you do," she whispered huskily. "One who isn't afraid to drive you wild with her hands and mouth and tease you until you're so crazy for her that you lose control..."

Her breath was warm and moist against his ear, her

breasts just touching his chest in an intimate caress, as she told him private, personal things that only a woman who had been to bed with him could possibly know. It was unnerving. And damn seductive. His heart slamming against his ribs, Sam told himself not to listen, but it was too late. In ten seconds flat she had him hot and hard and aching.

Torn between fury and need, he should have gotten the hell out of there right then and there. But instead of releasing her, his fingers tightened around her arms, dragging her closer until her breasts pressed more fully against his chest and her hips nudged his. He saw her eyes widen with surprise, felt her breath catch and couldn't for the life of him remember why he shouldn't do this. Swooping down, he took her mouth in a hot fierce kiss.

She'd been driving him crazy for longer than he cared to admit, and at the first touch of her lips, something in him seemed to snap. His hands tangling in her hair, holding her captive, he crushed her close, groaning at the taste of her. Madness pulled at him, clouding his senses. He was rough and hungry and couldn't seem to help himself. More, dammit! He wanted, *needed* more!

Lost to everything but the passion clawing at his gut, he didn't realize anything was wrong until he heard her whimper. The sound washed over him like a bucket of ice water. What the hell was he doing?

Muttering a curse, he jerked back and stared down in self-directed fury at her swollen mouth. He'd never been rough with a woman in his life, and it left a sick feeling in his stomach. "God, I can't believe I did that!"

"I shouldn't have pushed you..."

"That didn't give me the right to hurt you. I'm sorry. I'm usually not such a bastard."

Still caught close, they both spoke at once in hushed

whispers, stumbling over each other's words like a couple of awkward teenagers. His heart still slamming against his ribs, Sam knew he should let her go, but he couldn't seem to stop touching her. With a will of their own, his fingers traced the curve of her delicately arched brow, the slant of her pert nose, the swollen softness of the mouth he'd so thoughtlessly bruised.

"Sam, please..."

"Let me," he whispered thickly when she winced and would have pulled back. "Let me make it feel better."

She should have slugged him—he wouldn't have blamed her. But when he leaned down and carefully brushed his mouth, whisper soft, over hers, once, twice, then a third time, the wariness slowly drained out of her. With a sigh that could have been his name, she leaned into him trustingly and shyly opened her mouth to him. Groaning, he knew he was in trouble when he had to remind himself to keep it light. Still, he couldn't bring himself to ignore the invitation she so sweetly offered. With a tenderness he hadn't known he was capable of, he took the kiss deeper.

At the first touch of his tongue Jennifer jolted as if she'd touched a live wire. Heat streaked through her, lighting little fires one by one all over her body, melting her bones. Moaning, she clung to him as the strength in her legs seemed to give way. Every touch of his hands seduced, burned. Shuddering, her senses humming, she tasted passion for the first time in her life, and she loved it.

She wanted to sink into the pleasure of it and never come up for air, but she'd never been so stripped of defenses before, so emotionally at the mercy of another human being. She didn't know what he wanted, what to expect of him. To him a kiss was probably just a kiss, but when you could count the ones you'd been given on fewer than half the fingers of one hand, every one meant something. And this one meant he could hurt her in a way no one ever had.

Suddenly afraid, she tried to pull back, but she never got a chance. A vision bore down on her like a freight train from out of nowhere, and before she could do anything but gasp, she was hurled right into the middle of it.

"Jennifer? What is it? What's wrong?"

Caught up in the images that flashed against the back of her eyelids, she hardly heard Sam's worried voice. Unaware of the cold stiffness of her body, she stood frozen as an old man stepped into his house and found himself face-to-face with a masked man with a gun. His fear hit her like a fist in the throat, choking her, but even as she watched, he faced the bandit defiantly.

Don't! she wanted to cry out. *Don't be brave—he'll only hurt you.*

But he couldn't hear her, and there was no one there to warn him that he was dealing with someone who thrived on other people's fear and pain. A hard fist to the mouth knocked all the fight out of the old man, and before he knew what hit him, he was standing in front of the safe in his own library, fumbling for the combination while his assailant held a gun to his head. The second he had the safe open, the intruder shot him.

"No!"

Her painful cry startled Sam out of ten years' growth. "What the hell?" He felt the fine hairs at the back of his neck rise as she stared sightlessly past him out the front window of the café. She didn't seem to have a clue that she was standing stiff as a board in his arms.

"Jennifer? C'mon, sweetheart, snap out of it! This isn't funny."

She didn't answer, didn't even blink. He wanted to be-

lieve she was playing some kind of a trick on him, but
then, with no warning, she turned white as a sheet and her
eyes rolled back in her head. If he hadn't been watching
her so closely, she would have fallen. Lightning quick, he
caught her—right before she would have hit the floor.

"Dammit, Jennifer, this has gone on long enough!" he
muttered, only to feel his heart stop as her head lolled
back on his shoulder.

He almost called for an ambulance, but she was
breathing all right and didn't seem to be in any physical
distress. There was, he figured, a good possibility she'd
just fainted, though he had yet to figure out why. If she
regained consciousness to find herself surrounded by paramedics, she'd not only be embarrassed, she'd probably
want to kill him. He'd give her a few minutes, he decided
as he cradled her in his arms and made his way through
the kitchen to the back door. But if she didn't wake up
pretty damn soon, to hell with embarrassment. He'd call
911.

He found the keys to her apartment hanging on a hook
near the back door to the café kitchen. Seconds later he
was letting himself into her apartment and carrying her
through to her bedroom. Taking time only to switch on a
light, he laid her gently on the bed. She didn't move so
much as a muscle.

Staring down at her, he swore softly. She was too pale,
too still. He was worried and not afraid to admit it. He'd
dealt with a few fainting women in his time, but never
anything like this. She should have been conscious by
now. Muttering curses under his breath, he stalked into
the bathroom and wet a washcloth. "This is your last
chance, sweetheart," he told her as he returned to her
bedside. "If this doesn't do the trick, then you're just
going to have to risk being embarrassed."

With a gentleness that belied his gruff tone, he slowly ran the damp cloth over her face and arms and throat. And all the while he watched her. One more minute, he promised himself. That was all he was giving her.

One second she was out cold, and the next she stirred and her eyes fluttered open. Confused, she looked from him to the washcloth in his hand and back again. Without an ounce of color in her face, her eyes looked huge. "What happened?"

Her voice was weak, barely above a whisper, and did nothing to reassure him. "I was hoping you could tell me that," he said quietly as he reached out to brush her hair back from her face. "You passed out down in the café and I carried you upstairs. How did you feel?"

"Like I just got run over by a truck." She sighed tiredly. Still dazed, she tried to remember what happened as a particularly nasty headache started to throb at her temples. "I can't believe I just passed out like that," she muttered to herself. "The last time I fainted, I—"

Before she could complete the thought, the fog clouding her brain abruptly lifted and her memory came flooding back, shooting a hot tide of color into her cheeks. Sam had been kissing her as if he'd never let her go. And she'd loved it—until she'd realized how easily he could hurt her. And then...and then...

"Oh, God!" Horrified, she sat bolt upright on the bed and clutched at him. "A vision! Oh, God, Sam, I had another vision! We've got to do something!"

Her head pounding like a jackhammer, the beat of her heart frantic, she started to swing her legs off the bed, only to find herself flat on her back. Sam was leaning over her, his eyes fierce and his strong hands pressing her into the mattress. Startled, she squeaked, "What are you doing?"

"Keeping you still until I find out what the hell is going on," he growled. "In case you haven't noticed, you've got about as much strength as a day-old kitten. You're not getting out of this bed until I'm sure you won't fall flat on your face."

"But I've got to get up!" she cried, frantic, struggling against his hold. "The man who attacked Mrs. Elliot— he's going to strike again. Tonight! And I know where!"

Scowling, he let her sit up, but that was it. With the bed up against the wall on one side and him blocking the other, there was no way she was getting up without going through him. "How?" he demanded, his narrowed eyes searching hers. "I thought you said you didn't pick up those kind of details."

"I don't usually. But I've been to this house on a catering job. In the vision I saw a library with floor-to-ceiling bookcases and a secret door that hides the safe. Mr. Stubbings has one just like it. He had to get into the safe to pay me when I catered his granddaughter's engagement party."

Unconvinced, Sam frowned. "There must be dozens of other houses in the city that fit that description. How do you know that particular house is going to get hit tonight? Last time you couldn't be sure when the perp was going to strike."

"I don't know!" she cried. "I just know it. I *feel* it. Mr. Stubbings is going to be shot tonight, and if he doesn't get help, he'll bleed to death." When Sam just sat there, doubt clearly visible in his midnight blue eyes, she snapped, "Dammit, Sam, if you're not going to call someone and have it checked out, then get out of my way and let me do it! I'm not letting Mr. Stubbings die just because you doubt me."

She would have shoved her way past him, but he was

already rising to his feet. "There's no need to call anyone—I'll check it out myself."

"But you're off duty, aren't you?" she began, only then
putting two and two together. Hurt squeezing her heart,
she looked at him reproachfully. "You still don't believe
me, do you? You don't want to call in the police until you
get a chance to check out the scene for yourself, because
you think this is some kind of trick."

"I didn't say that."

"You didn't have to," she retorted. "You just kissed
me silly, but you don't trust me as far as you can throw
me. I'm surprised you don't want me to go along so you
can keep an eye on me. Who knows? I might call the perp
once you leave and warn him you're on your way."

"Don't be ridiculous. I'm taking you along in case
you're wrong. Then *you* can explain to Mr. Stubbings
what we're doing on his doorstep at ten o'clock at night."

She gave him an address in Monte Vista, one of the
older, more affluent areas of the city, then didn't say another word until they pulled up in front of the Tudor-style
house that sat well back from the road. Half-hidden by
trees, the house was dark, not a single light shining.

Jennifer shivered. "Something's wrong," she said huskily, hugging herself. "Mr. Stubbings isn't one of those
old people who goes to bed with the chickens. He loves
Letterman. He wouldn't be in bed yet unless he was sick."

"Maybe he's visiting friends," Sam suggested as he
pulled into the drive. "Or out of town. Just because the
house is dark doesn't necessarily mean he's in trouble."

"No," she said in a hollow tone that set Sam's nerves
on edge. "He's been here already."

"Who?" he asked sharply. "The perp?"

Her eyes never leaving the darkened house, she nodded. "Can't you feel it?"

What he felt was the hairs rising on the back of his neck again, and he didn't like it one little bit. Swearing, he switched on the spotlight that was mounted on the driver's door and turned the bright beam toward the front door. It was standing wide open.

"Damn!"

"Oh, God, I knew it!"

Already on his radio, Sam called for backup and asked the dispatcher to put a call in to Tanner. But when Jennifer urged him to request an ambulance, he couldn't. "Not until I know for sure someone's hurt." Drawing his gun, he pushed open his door. "Stay here."

"Not on your life," she retorted. "If you're not waiting for backup, neither am I. Anyway, the intruder's already gone."

She was out the passenger door before he could stop her, and short of cuffing her to the car, there wasn't a damn thing he could do about it. If her friend Mr. Stubbings really had been shot, he didn't have time to reason with her. "You stay outside until I signal that it's okay for you to come inside," he said in a low curt whisper as they slowly approached the front door. "And don't touch anything! If we're lucky, the bastard left some fingerprints this time."

Right on his heels, Jennifer nodded. "I won't touch a thing, just Mr. Stubbings. Hurry."

His instinct warning him there was no time to waste, he motioned for Jennifer to wait, then slipped soundlessly through the front door. Engulfed in darkness, he was four steps into the foyer when he suddenly realized that Jennifer was right behind him. Dammit to hell, didn't the woman have any sense of self-preservation? Swearing softly under his breath, he turned to confront her—and heard a noise somewhere in the back of the house.

"What was that?"

Her startled whisper hardly carried to his ears, but he pressed a finger to her lips anyway, silencing her. Then they both heard it again—a low moan. All his senses on alert, he turned and searched the dark, dangerous shadows before them for some sign of motion. Nothing moved. Reaching back, he found Jennifer's hand and pulled her behind him as he glided through the darkness toward the moans in the distance.

They found Frank Stubbings in the library just as Jennifer had predicted. He'd been shot in the shoulder and was lying in a pool of blood beside an open door, disguised as a bookcase, that cleverly hid an old Wells Fargo safe. He wasn't dead, but he'd lost a lot of blood and his pulse was weak. While Jennifer fought to staunch the seeping wound and keep him from going into shock, Sam called for an ambulance. He'd just hung up when the first police backup unit arrived with sirens blazing. Tanner was right behind them. Within seconds, the place was crawling with cops.

Still woozy, the old man cried weakly, "My coins! He took my coins!"

"Please, Mr. Stubbings," Jennifer pleaded. "You've got to lie still until the ambulance gets here, or your shoulder's going to start bleeding again."

"But you don't understand," he argued, clutching at her hand. "I started collecting those coins when I was a boy! I've had them all my life. And now they're gone. All of them!"

"We'll do what we can to get them back for you, sir,"

Sam said quietly as he went down on a knee behind the old gentleman. "Can you tell me what happened?"

"He was already here when I got home from the Elks Lodge. I go every Wednesday night, and there he was, standing in the damn foyer like he owned the place when I came through the front door." He coughed, his strength ebbing as he tried to get the words out while he still could. "He was big and tall and dressed all in black. He wore a mask, one of those weird rubber ones that distorts the features. It made him look like he was smiling all the time. And he had a gun. He told me he wouldn't hurt me if I cooperated. All he wanted was the coins."

Jotting down notes, Tanner frowned. "He knew you had a coin collection, sir?"

The old man nodded miserably, pain etching his pale, wrinkled face. "It was worth half a million dollars, and he said he was willing to kill me to get it. I believed him, so I opened the safe. When he had what he wanted, he shot me."

Outside, the ambulance Sam had called for roared up the driveway, the scream of its siren cut off in midwail as it braked to a screeching halt right in front of the mansion. Knowing he was running out of time, Sam asked hurriedly, "Does your house have a security system, Mr. Stubbings? Was it on tonight while you were gone?"

"Yes, of course. I never leave the house without activating it."

"Then why didn't it go off when the intruder broke in?"

He could see by the old man's face that that was a question he'd already worried himself sick over. "I don't know," he gasped as the paramedics rushed in. "I don't know."

The place was chaos after that. While the paramedics applied emergency first aid and prepared Mr. Stubbings for transport to the hospital, Sam and Tanner went over the entire house with the evidence team. Not wanting to be in the way, Jennifer quietly slipped outside.

It was a cold night, fireplace weather, and the pounding in her head that always followed one of her visions was vicious. Hugging herself, she told herself she could relax now that Mr. Stubbings was in the paramedics' hands. He was going to be all right. She dragged in a deep breath, hoping the fresh air would ease her headache. It didn't. Her nerves were strung tight and brittle. The silently flashing light bars on the patrol cars parked haphazardly at the curb brought tears to her eyes, and she could still smell blood on her hands. Her stomach turned over, and it was all she could do not to gag. Home. She just wanted to go home now. But it would probably be at least another hour before Sam would be able to leave.

No one would have said anything if she'd gone back inside and found a bed to lie down on while she waited for Sam. Leaning tiredly against a tree, she was seriously considering doing just that when news crews from the city's three major television stations arrived. Within seconds they had lights and television cameras up and running and were throwing questions at anyone who would talk to them.

Turning her back on them, Jennifer never saw a reporter conferring with one of the uniformed officers guarding the front door of the mansion. Without warning a light was trained on her, a microphone thrust under her nose, and she found herself confronting a tall, hawk-faced reporter. "Ms. Hart? I'm Jonathan Lake, KSTA TV. I was just told by the police that you're a psychic who's been working with them on this case. What can you tell me about it?" he demanded aggressively.

Caught off guard, she never thought to deny it. "I contacted them, yes."

"And told them what? That Mr. Stubbings was going to be robbed and shot tonight? How did you know that? Did you try to warn him?"

He threw questions at her like darts, not giving her time to even think of an answer for one before he came up with another. Alarmed, hating the idea of her face being plastered across TV screens all over town, Jennifer tried to step back, only to slam into the tree behind her. Trapped, her heart pounding, she said stiffly, "You'll have to direct your questions to Detective Kelly—he's in charge of the case."

She skirted around the reporter and headed for the house at a good clip, but Jonathan Lake wasn't one to take no for an answer when he smelled a story. Right behind her, his cameraman recording her hasty retreat, he yelled out questions at her and invariably drew the attention of every other reporter scrounging around in the dark for a story. Fifty feet from Mr. Stubbings's front door, she was surrounded.

She couldn't move, couldn't draw a breath without drawing in the scent of her tormentors' bloodthirst. They were hungry, and she was fresh meat. More microphones were waved in front of her face; the lights that blinded her intensified as frenzied questions were barked at her. Panicking, she tried to fight her way through the crowd, but she was much smaller than the men who towered over her, and no one gave so much as an inch. Cornered, she broke out into a cold sweat. "Please," she cried, "let me pass!"

"If you knew this was going to happen, why didn't you stop it beforehand?"

"Just how good a psychic are you, anyway?"

"Have you worked on other cases with the police? Why haven't we ever heard of you before?"

"What the hell's going on here?"

Sam's furious roar cut through the barrage of questions, stunning the shouting reporters into instant silence. They fell away, and there in the middle stood Jennifer. Small and pale, she was trapped and outnumbered and her eyes filled with panic, but her chin was lifted defiantly and her hands were knotted into fists. She looked ready to deck somebody, and Sam couldn't blame her. He felt the same way.

"The lady said to let her pass," he said silkily. "That means get out of her way. Now."

"We were just asking her some questions," Jonathan Lake said belligerently. "We've got a job to do, too, Kelly."

Protectiveness stirring in his gut, he strode forward, forcing Lake to step back or get run over. "Then go do it somewhere else," he snarled. "She has nothing to say to any of you."

He didn't give them time to protest, but simply took Jennifer by the elbow and escorted her out of the circle of reporters. A few of them grumbled and shot him looks that should have killed him on the spot, but no one dared try to stop them.

"Officer Dean will take you home," he said quietly as he led her over to a patrol car and introduced her to the uniformed officer there. "If those bozos follow you and try to harass you, tell them to get off your property or you'll call the police. That should get rid of them, at least for tonight. Are you all right?"

She nodded, shivering as a brisk wind swirled around them. "I don't know where they all came from. One minute I was trying to get away from that awful Mr. Lake, and the next I was surrounded."

"I should have warned you that the police radio is usually pretty well monitored by the press. Anytime a call for backup and an ambulance is made in this kind of neighborhood, you can guarantee you're going to get flooded with reporters."

He hesitated, the apology he owed her for doggedly doubting her psychic abilities hovering on the tip of his tongue. He'd made a whale of a mistake with her—he knew that now and didn't intend to make excuses for it. But what he had to say would take time, and that was something he didn't have right now.

Knowing she was going to make him eat crow and it was no more than he deserved didn't make it any easier to walk away from her. She might have been ready to punch out the lights of every one of those pushy reporters, but there was still something in the shadow of her eyes that made him want to wrap his arms around her and just hold her.

His need a tight painful knot in his gut, he started to reach for her, only to have one of the evidence-team members call his name. Remembering he still had a job to do, he gritted his teeth on an oath and stepped away from the temptation she presented just by breathing. "I've got to get back to work," he said. "Dean'll take you home now if you're ready." Turning on his heel, he walked away while he still could.

She couldn't sleep. An hour after Officer Dean had escorted her to her apartment door, she lay flat on her back in bed and stared up at the shadowy ceiling, her head still pounding. She desperately needed to sleep, but every time she closed her eyes the events of the evening came flying at her in a dizzying rush, a bombardment of images and emotions. Mr. Stubbings, the fear that they wouldn't get to him in time, the relief of knowing that he was going to be okay, the scent of his blood that she couldn't seem to wash away.

And then there was Sam. And a kiss that felt as though it'd happened in another lifetime. She could still taste it. Her body ached in places it never had before, yearned for something it had no knowledge of, and she didn't know what to do about it. *He* had made her feel this way. *He* had shown her a side of herself she hadn't even known existed.

Restless, she tossed and turned and couldn't find a comfortable spot anywhere on the bed. Outside, the rain that had been threatening all evening started to fall. Sighing, she closed her eyes in relief. Maybe now she'd be able to sleep. She loved the sound of rain at night.

At first she didn't hear the footfall on the outside stairs that led to her apartment. But then a whisper of sound, a mere vibration, disturbed the silence of the night as someone started up the stairs. She should have been alarmed. She lived in the business district of downtown, and the closest neighbor was two blocks away. The police patrolled the area intermittently through the night, but if someone timed a break-in just right and came after her, there'd be no one to hear her screams.

But with a knowledge that came from within, she knew it wasn't just anyone on the stairs. It was Sam. And she hadn't been able to sleep because she'd been unconsciously waiting for him. Her heart starting to pound, she didn't question why he was there, but just grabbed her robe at his quiet knock and hurried to the door, switching on lights as she went. Without even checking the peephole, she flicked on the outside light and pulled open the door.

Standing on the small landing, he looked like something out of one of her dreams. His hair was damp and windswept, his shoulders impossibly broad in his dark brown leather jacket. Rain pelted him from behind, but he didn't seem to notice. The second he saw her old chenille robe and the faded flannel gown peeking out from beneath, something flared in his eyes, something hot and dangerous that made her achingly aware she was naked beneath her nightclothes.

"You were asleep," he said roughly. "I shouldn't have come."

"Actually I was just lying in bed staring at the ceiling," she admitted with a grimace. "I guess I'm too wired from what happened to Mr. Stubbings to sleep. Would you like to come in?"

A wise man would have stood right where he was, spoken his piece, then gotten the hell out of there. But her feet were bare and the robe and gown she wore did little to protect her against the cold wet night. She shivered, hugging herself, and took the decision out of his hands. He never remembered moving, but suddenly he was inside, with the door at his back and Jennifer standing right in front of him. All he had to do to touch her was reach out.

Stuffing his hands into the pockets of his jacket to resist temptation, he said, "I just came by to make sure you got home all right and see that you were okay."

"I'm fine," she assured him softly. "Or at least I will be after my mind winds down and I get some sleep."

That was his cue to leave; he should have taken it. But his feet were glued to the floor and his eyes to her. She looked tired—and soft. The kind of touchable womanly soft that a man could sink into and gladly lose himself in after a long hard day. But that wasn't why he was there.

Squaring his shoulders, he brought his gaze back to hers. "I owe you an apology," he said stiffly. "I've been called a stubborn jackass a few times in my life, but I like to think I'm not a complete fool. The only reason Mr. Stubbings is alive now is because of you, and there's no way to explain how you knew he was in trouble. Unless you really are psychic.

"I know I should have believed you when you first came to me about Mrs. Elliot," he said quickly when her eyes widened in surprise. "But I'm a logical man, and there was nothing logical about your story—unless you were somehow involved. I was rough on you. I'm sorry."

He expected an *I told you so* or at the very least a grudging acceptance of his apology. After the way he'd treated her, it was no more than he deserved. Instead, she gazed up at him with wide green eyes that filled with tears even as he watched. If she'd wanted to make him sweat, she couldn't have found a better way.

Swearing, he had her in his arms in the time it took to blink. "Don't," he groaned. "Call me every name in the book if you want to—you can even punch me if it'll make you feel better—but please don't cry."

"I'm not." She sniffed, swiping at her streaming eyes. "But it's been such a long day and I didn't think you were ever going to believe me. I guess I'm just tired."

The tears still didn't stop, and it tore him apart. "I know, honey. I'm sorry. I've been a real jerk."

Murmuring to her soothingly, he trailed slow kisses across her damp face. He only meant to comfort her, to stop her tears and make her smile, but suddenly his mouth was on hers. Memories from earlier in the evening stirred, heating his blood, and all too easily, he could hear her husky whisper in his ear as she told him what he liked a woman to do to him in bed. Hot, already hard for her, he tightened his arms around her and took the kiss deeper.

Her tongue met his eagerly, her womanly curves melted against him, and he was seduced. Wildly, tantalizingly seduced. He wanted her naked, his hands on her breasts, her hips, between her thighs, his mouth tasting her, loving her until she screamed. Now. Right here on the floor of her small entrance hall.

Unable to wait another second, he blindly tore at the tie of her robe and jerked it free. A split second later he found the buttons at the neck of her gown. He had the first two undone and was reaching for the third when sanity hit him like a bolt of lightning.

This was Jennifer he was about to take like a madman. The psychic who could see things he couldn't, including his future. He didn't want her in his head, and she was too young to be in his bed, dammit! She probably still believed in fairy tales and happily-ever-afters and making love when he knew damn well there was no such thing. She needed someone her own age, a fresh-faced kid who still thought he could slay dragons for her and love her the rest of his life. That wasn't him.

His jaw rigid, he put her from him abruptly and tried not to notice the stunned, painful confusion in her eyes. "It's late," he rasped. "And I still have paperwork to do at the station. I've got to go."

Turning before she could protest, he shut the apartment door behind him and hurried down the stairs like a man running scared.

Chapter 6

News of the latest robbery and attack of a senior citizen was all over the front page of the newspaper the next morning, not to mention the main topic of conversation on all the local news shows, but Jennifer never noticed. Her every thought focused on Sam's scorching kisses and the abrupt way he'd left her last night, she walked around in a daze that lasted all the way through the lunch rush. She mixed up orders, forgot the names of customers she saw every week and stared off into space like a smitten teenager when she had people waiting three deep for tables. Molly was ready to kill her, and it was all Sam's fault.

For the first time in her life, she wished she had more experience with men. She had so many questions. Why did a man kiss a woman like he was starving for the taste of her, then find an excuse to leave the very next second? Was he really interested, or could he summon up passion for any female he found reasonably attractive? How was she supposed to know?

Molly would tell her if she asked—she'd married and buried two husbands, and she certainly knew what made the male of the species tick. But she felt like such a fool for needing to ask. And what she'd shared with Sam last night had been so private. How could she possibly discuss what happened between them with anyone but him?

"Jennifer? Can I talk to you for a minute?"

Glancing up from inadvertently serving chicken salad to a customer who'd ordered tuna, she frowned at the sight of Rosa hovering uncertainly a few feet away. Her dark eyes black with distress, she was all but twisting her hands and looked ready to bolt any second. Immediately concerned, Jennifer motioned to Molly that she was taking a quick break, then preceded Rosa to her office.

"What's wrong?" she asked the minute the door was shut behind them. "Shouldn't you be in school? Something's happened, hasn't it?"

"No...not exactly." Unhappiness clouding her eyes, Rosa blurted, "I have to quit my job."

Braced for some teenage catastrophe, Jennifer couldn't have been more surprised if the girl had slapped her. "Quit? But why? I thought you loved working here!"

"I do," Rosa said miserably. "But Carlos thinks it would be better if I found a job somewhere else. He thinks you're a bad influence on me."

The charge was so ludicrous Jennifer would have laughed if she hadn't been so indignant. She should have known this was Carlos's idea. Macho and domineering, with a chip on his shoulder the size of Texas, he had never pretended to like Jennifer or the idea of Rosa working for her. Rosa had never been able to understand why, but Jennifer had known the second she laid eyes on him what his problem was with her. *She* had insisted that Rosa stay in school, then not only given her a job, but started teaching her a trade that could, in the future, make her a good living. And every chance she got, she encouraged the girl to be strong and independent. To a man like Carlos, who liked having a woman under his thumb so that he could control her, she was nothing but a threat.

Rosa, however, was too young to see that. She saw Carlos's possessiveness as protectiveness and was thrilled that he cared so much about her. As much as Jennifer wanted to tell her that he really just wanted to control her, she knew it wouldn't do any good. Not when Rosa was still so infatuated with him.

But she couldn't just let her walk out without giving her something to think about. "I can't stop you if you really want to quit," she told her quietly. "Just be sure you're doing it because it's something *you* want to do. I know you're crazy about Carlos, but a man who really cared about you wouldn't be threatened by your job or your friendship with me."

"But Carlos isn't *making* me quit," she said quickly, defending him just as Jennifer had known she would. "He left the decision totally up to me...."

"So you're quitting because you agree with him? You think I'm a bad influence on you?"

"Oh, no!" Rosa cried, horrified. "He didn't mean... *bad*, exactly. Just that all the time I spend here keeps me away from my family."

"And him."

"Well, yes," she was forced to admit. "But he's right. I haven't got to see a lot of him lately. Or my family. So I thought I should find something that at least leaves my weekends free."

She'd found a way to justify giving in to Carlos's demands before she'd ever walked into the café, and nothing Jennifer could say at this point was going to change her mind. Forcing a smile, she gracefully accepted the inevitable. "Make sure you put me down for a reference, sweetie. I'll do whatever I can to help you."

Mature up till that point, Rosa ducked her head to hide the tears welling in her eyes, and suddenly she looked like the sixteen-year-old girl that she was. "Please don't be mad at me," she said, and threw herself into Jennifer's arms for a fierce hug. A second later, she was gone.

Watching the door close behind her, Jennifer tried to tell herself Rosa would be back. She was a good kid. And smarter than most. She'd come to her senses soon and realize that not only was everyone at the café like family to her, but that by quitting, she'd walked away from an incredible opportunity most kids her age didn't get. During the six short weeks she'd worked there, she'd already learned a great deal about baking. If she stuck with it, she'd be a full-fledged baker by the time she graduated from high school, while her classmates were still trying to figure out what they wanted to do with their lives.

But as much as she wanted to believe it, the inner voice that never failed Jennifer told her it wasn't going to happen. Not as long as Carlos was a part of Rosa's life. He would make sure of it.

Hurt, she squared her shoulders and went to tell Molly the news. But she never got the opportunity. The moment she stepped out of her office, Jonathan Lake, complete with camera crew, walked through the café's front door, and it didn't take an Einstein to figure out why he was there. He planned to take up where he'd left off last night.

Molly, who had seen the segment on the morning news where Jennifer was surrounded by the snapping jaws of the press last night, had been fuming about it ever since.

She took one look at the reporter and stiffened like a watchdog.

"Hold it right there!" she growled. "This is a respectable establishment—we don't serve your kind in here. So you and the rest of your bullies just turn around right now and get out. You're not welcome here!"

"This is a public restaurant," he reminded her smugly. "We've got as much right to be here as anyone else."

"You think so?" she challenged, moving to the phone. "We'll see what the police have to say about that."

Stepping to her side, Jennifer would have liked nothing better than to hand her the phone and let her have at it. But she had firsthand knowledge of how the press operated. Avoiding reporters' questions was one thing; embarrassing one in front of a restaurant full of customers, not to mention his camera crew, was quite another. If she had the annoying Mr. Lake thrown out, he could crucify her on the evening news.

"If we throw him out, another will only show up in his place," she told Molly quietly, stopping her before she could pick up the phone. "I can handle it."

Unlike last night, when he'd caught her off guard, she thought she was prepared for him this time. He immediately proved her wrong. "Some of the people of Sandy Bluff don't seem to have too much good to say about you, Ms. Hart." At her nearly soundless gasp, his eyes glittered with satisfaction. "That's right. I checked you out and got quite a surprise. You made quite a few enemies out there in West Texas. In fact, a lot of people think you're nothing but a troublemaker. What do you have to say about that?"

"Nothing," she said, lifting her chin. "I have no control over what other people think."

"That's true," he agreed. "Because if you did, I'm sure you would have controlled what the police thought of you when you came to them about Mrs. Elliot being attacked *before* she was beaten and robbed. At one time you were considered a suspect in that case, weren't you, Ms. Hart?"

"I really couldn't say," she replied. "You'll have to take that up with the police."

"But they did check out your background, didn't they?" he pressed. "And what they found wasn't very encouraging, isn't that correct? You have a history of going to the police with some pretty incredible stories. Do you thrive on sensationalism, Ms. Hart? Have you gone to the tabloids yet with your story?"

He was twisting everything, making it seem as if she was only out for self-aggrandizement, just as the reporters in Sandy Bluff had when she'd broken the story about the mayor. Now, as then, her first instinct was to shy away from confrontation. She hated having to defend herself when she hadn't done anything but come to the aid of two senior citizens who had desperately needed her help. But whoever was preying on the elderly of San Antonio was still out there, still free to stalk and rob and shoot any old person who had the misfortune to catch his attention. She owed it to them, the future victims, to do whatever she could to convince Jonathan Lake's viewers that the criminal was the story, the one people needed to be concerned about and on the lookout for.

"No, I haven't gone to the tabloids or the talk shows or anyone else who's looking for a way to exploit this story, Mr. Lake. If you knew anything about me at all, you'd know I'm not the least bit interested in that kind of publicity. I'm just concerned about the senior citizens of San Antonio. They're vulnerable and at risk, and in my head, I see when they're being attacked. If you don't want to believe that, that's your choice. But your lack of faith isn't my problem. I know what I see."

She stood tall and straight and made no apologies for the special talent that had been both a blessing and a curse all her life. Instead, she turned the focus of the conversation to the unprincipled man who, with just two robberies, had the city's elderly cowering in their homes. She couldn't say what he looked liked or even guess at his name, but deep in her gut, she knew what kind of monster he was. Her attention focused inward, she told of his cunning and charm and total lack of conscience, and, unconsciously, chilled the blood of everyone who heard her, including the usually unflappable Mr. Lake himself. With a sincerity that couldn't be doubted, she warned that the robber would continue to strike at will until he made a mistake, and although he hadn't killed anyone yet, he would if someone tried to get in his way. He was dangerous, and the citizens of San Antonio had good reason to be afraid.

It had been a hell of a night. After he'd torn himself away from Jennifer and made his way home, Sam had spent what was left of the night cursing himself and the lady and aching with frustration. He'd vowed he wasn't going anywhere near her or that café of hers again unless it was on official business, and so far he hadn't. Thanks to last night's shooting of Mr. Stubbings, the station had been flooded with calls from people who thought they knew who the perp was, and he and Tanner had gone in early to check out every lead. There'd been so many of them that they'd split up, and he'd been running all over the city ever since.

In a bear of a mood, he'd only had time to grab a doughnut for breakfast and he'd missed lunch completely. He was thinking about getting a hamburger somewhere when he unthinkingly turned onto West Commerce Street.

It wasn't until he saw the familiar blue-and-white sign over the entrance to Heavenly Scents that he realized what he'd done. Driving by her café had become such a habit that the second he let his guard down, his instincts led him right to Jennifer.

Swearing, he told himself he wasn't going to stop. There was no reason to—she'd given him a statement last night and told him all she could about the man who'd shot and robbed Mr. Stubbings. Unless she had another vision or remembered something new, they had nothing more to say to each other.

His jaw as hard as Texas limestone, he started to drive right past without even sparing the café a glance. Then he saw the truck from one of the local television stations parked at the curb. One look at the call letters and he knew Jonathan Lake was hassling her again. The bastard didn't know when to give up. "Dammit to hell!"

He didn't remember pulling over, but suddenly he was parked in a No Parking zone and reaching for the emergency flasher he kept under his seat. Turning it on, he slapped it on the roof. Seconds later he was striding into Heavenly Scents like an old-fashioned gunslinger looking for a fight.

But the woman who'd cringed from the cameras last night faced the veteran reporter with her chin up today. Her voice steady, she looked him right in the eye with a quiet dignity that demanded respect, and she got it. Jonathan Lake didn't hurl questions at her like darts as he had before. Instead, he waited until she finished speaking before asking her another question, this time in a civilized matter. Then, when *she* wrapped up the interview, he actually thanked her for her time.

Sam had had enough dealings with Lake himself to know that the guy didn't often lose control of an interview. He was impressed. But watching Jennifer from near the front door as Lake and his cameraman filed out, it was easy to see that the interview had cost her. The cool fire in her green eyes dimmed and her shoulders slumped. When she lifted a hand to push her hair back from her face, her fingers were visibly trembling.

Unable to take his eyes from her, Sam felt the same protectiveness he'd felt last night. She looked exhausted, as though she hadn't slept, and he had a feeling he was entirely to blame for that. Guilt curled in his gut. He needed to get the hell out of there, now, before she knew he was there; but when he ordered his feet to move, they moved toward her, instead of away. Then she saw him. Color flared in her cheeks, she looked wildly around as if she wanted to bolt, and any chance he had of walking away from her died on the spot.

"You handled that very well," he said quietly when he reached her. "What'd you do to Jonathan? Hit him over the head or something? I don't think I've ever seen him act so polite."

Caught between the front counter and the kitchen area and within full view of the dozen or so customers, she couldn't just turn her back on him when he was talking to her, which was what Sam had counted on. But neither could she look him in the eye. Moving to the counter to clear it of some dirty dishes, she kept her gaze firmly focused on the task at hand.

"I said what I wanted to say, and it was something he thought his viewers wanted to hear. There was no reason to go for the jugular when I was cooperating."

"That's never stopped him before, but I'm glad he didn't hassle you." His gaze roaming freely over her pale face, he frowned at the faint shadows under her eyes. "Are you okay? You look tired."

"I'm fine," she said. "It's been a busy morning." The counter cleared and wiped clean, she hurriedly set down a place setting complete with a menu. "I imagine you stopped by to eat. Have a seat and I'll be back in a minute for your order."

"If anyone needs to sit down and eat," Molly retorted from her position at the grill, "it's you. You haven't had anything but coffee all day, and if you don't eat something soon, you're going to fall flat on your face."

"I'm not hungry," she said.

Frowning, Sam looked her up and down. "You do look like you're wasting away to nothing. She's lost weight, hasn't she, Molly?"

"At least five pounds in the last week alone, and you haven't helped matters," she said with a disapproving sniff. "She's worrying herself sick over those old people getting robbed, and now that you believe her, the press doesn't. The phone's been ringing off the wall with people wanting interviews, and she can't even watch TV or read the papers without seeing pictures of herself. No wonder she's lost her appetite. I would, too, if I were her!"

"Then maybe she needs a change of scene," Sam said smoothly. And before Jennifer could guess his intentions, he turned her around and untied her apron. "We'll take two of your best sandwiches, Molly," he told the older woman. "Whatever you've got on the grill. *To go.*"

"Oh, but I can't go anywhere!" Jennifer said in alarm. "Rosa won't be in this afternoon—she gave her notice—and Molly can't possibly handle the place by herself."

"Says who?" the older woman demanded sassily. "The day I can't take care of a few customers all by myself is the day I need to be put out to pasture." Scooping two cheeseburgers off the grill, she quickly wrapped them in foil, stuffed them in a sack and handed them to Sam. For the first time there was a glimmer of approval in her eyes when her gaze met his. "You go on and take her, Detective. I'll be just fine."

Outgunned and outmaneuvered, Jennifer knew when she was beaten. She gave in graciously and let him escort her to the back door, but not before she glanced over her shoulder at Molly and called, "Traitor!"

Unperturbed, her friend only laughed and turned her attention to the café customers who'd been watching in fascination as the scene played out. "All right, how many hamburgers am I making?"

He only took her as far as her own back stairs. Surprised, she stopped at the bottom step. "You want to eat in my apartment?"

"No, just on the landing," he said, urging her up the stairs. "I'd take you to one of the Mexican places on the river, but neither one of us has the time. And it's too nice a day to spend inside, so this'll have to do. Have a seat."

It was a beautiful day, clear and cool, the kind that always drew tourists and locals alike to the River Walk. *That* would have been romantic; her back alley was not. Until Sam sat down next to her on the top step of the landing and his hip nudged hers as he stretched one of his long legs down the steps in front of them. Awareness shimmered through her, sending her heart tumbling into a fast breathless beat. She looked up—and fell into his eyes.

Why was he here? What did he want from her? She desperately wanted to believe he couldn't stay away, but that was a dangerous conclusion to draw after only a few kisses. Especially when he hadn't been able to get away from her fast enough last night. Considering all that, the only other reason she could think of he might have sought her out was that he was still worried she might be suffering some effects from the trauma of Mr. Stubbing's shooting.

He was just being nice.

She cringed at the word and the sour taste it left in her mouth. "You didn't have to do this," she said, breaking the silence that had fallen between them as he pulled their burgers from the bag and handed her one. "I really am fine, and I know you need to get back to work. You don't need to stay and baby-sit me."

"Are you throwing me out?"

A crooked smile curled one corner of his mouth, but it never quite reached his eyes. Dark and intense, they seemed to see all the way to her soul. "No, of course not," she said quickly, blushing. "But I heard on the radio you've been flooded with phone calls from people who think they know who the robber is. You must have things to do."

He didn't deny it. "I've been hunting down leads ever since I clocked in this morning. A man's got to eat, but I'd just as soon not do it in the car. I do enough of that as it is." Suiting his actions to his words, he took a satisfying bite of his burger.

Her appetite nonexistent, Jennifer only nibbled at hers. "So how's the case coming? Are any of the leads panning out?"

He shook his head. "Not yet, but we're not giving up. And we may have gotten a break last night. We found a scrap of paper with Mr. Stubbings's security code on it on the floor near the safe. It turns out he usually carries that in his wallet, but he lost the wallet a week ago."

"You think the thief found it?"

"Stole it more likely, but we found some prints on the

paper and we're checking to see if they belong to Stubbings."

Hardly tasting his own food, he watched her pick at hers and knew he was in trouble when he couldn't keep his mind on the case. Last night he'd come up with some good solid reasons to keep his distance, and not a damn thing had changed since then. He needed to get back to work, yet here he was, unable to stay away from her. She was too thin. Too pale. The shadows under her eyes too dark. And like it or not, he was worried about her. Until he was sure she'd eaten something and taken a few minutes to relax, he wasn't going anywhere.

Shifting to face her, he said casually, "Speaking of leads, you should have been with me this morning when I checked out a tip on the south side. There was this old lady who was sure her next-door neighbor's son was the one who shot Mr. Stubbings. Evidently he's been the neighborhood terror all his life, and just this week bought himself a brand-new sports car and paid cash for it."

"That had to set him back a pretty penny. He didn't use Mr. Stubbings's coin collection, did he?"

"Not hardly." He chuckled. "It seems he had a major crack operation going in the barrio."

"You're kidding."

"Nope. The DEA had been watching him, and when they heard we'd gotten a complaint on him, they decided to come in and shut the whole thing down. All the neighbors were standing outside cheering when they hauled him and his new Corvette away."

Laughing, Jennifer took another bite of her burger without even realizing it. "The old lady must have been thrilled. Will she get a reward for turning him in?"

He nodded. "'CrimeStoppers' had something out on the kid, but when I told her she was going to get some money for placing the call, she said she'd rather meet you."

"Me?" Jennifer was startled. "Good Lord, why?"

Grinning, he said, "There's this old geezer—her words, not mine—she met at church who's been hounding her to go out with him. She wanted you to look into your crystal ball and tell her if he's just after her body or really interested in her."

Jennifer wanted to laugh—he could see laughter in her dancing eyes—but she clamped down on her bottom lip until it was steady, then said primly, "I told you before I don't have a crystal ball. I don't need one."

"I know, but the old lady wanted all the bells and whistles and I didn't have the heart to set her straight. So will you talk to her or not?"

"Just how old a lady *is* she?"

Struggling to keep a straight face, he said, "I believe she's eighty-one."

"Eighty-one! And she's still interested in sex?"

He grinned. He couldn't help it. She sounded so shocked. "Her exact words were, 'I would never get married again and give up my husband's pension, but I think it would be nice to have a lover again, don't you?'"

Her eyes wide, hot color tinging her cheeks, Jennifer had no idea how appealing she looked. She leaned toward him as if they were sharing a secret. "What did you say?"

His voice as hushed as hers, he said, "I agreed with her. It would be nice to have a lover again."

The husky words caught on a whispering breeze and swirled around them, teasing and enticing and seducing. Her heart skipping a beat, Jennifer told herself he was still talking about the old lady. But his eyes held Jennifer's with a heat that stole all the moisture from her mouth, and there was something in his tone that made her breath lodge in her throat and her body go weak all over.

"Sam—"

"Her name is Margaret De La Garza," he continued easily as he pulled a business card from his wallet. "Here's her number. I wrote it on the back. She'd be thrilled if you could find the time to call her."

Dazed, Jennifer took the card he held out to her, her eyes searching his in confusion. His tone was normal, the warmth in his gaze nothing more than friendly. Blinking, she rubbed at her temples, sure she was losing it. Had she imagined his suggestive remark, or was she more tired than she'd thought?

Shaking her head at her imaginings, she forced a smile. "Sure, I'll give her a call. Though I can't promise I'll be able to advise her on whether she should take a lover or not."

"She'd probably be just as happy if you could give her some input on Saturday's lottery numbers. The jackpot's twenty-eight million."

She laughed, and the inexplicable tension that had sparked to life between them instantly drained away. Her appetite returning in a rush, Jennifer turned her attention back to her burger and never saw the satisfaction that gleamed in his eyes as she proceeded to finish it.

Jennifer couldn't remember ever laughing so much during a meal, and given the chance, she could have sat there for hours and just enjoyed his company. But they both had jobs to get back to, and all too soon, the burgers were history and there was no longer any reason to linger on the landing. An awkward silence fell between them. Without a word they descended the stairs to the delivery area behind the café.

Somber, her heart thumping painfully, Jennifer stared up at the set lines of his rugged face and wondered what had changed his mood, but she never got the chance to ask. Holding out his hand, he said stiffly, "Goodbye, Jennifer."

That was all he said, just goodbye, but the single word went through her like a lance, cutting straight to her heart. Stricken, she looked from his hand to his face and saw the end of anything else between them there in his eyes. And it hurt. She'd always known this day would come, but she hadn't expected it to be so soon, especially after the way he'd kissed her. For the life of her, she couldn't bring herself to place her hand in his.

"Goodbye?" she repeated faintly.

"We won't be seeing too much of each other unless you have another vision or remember something from the previous ones," he said flatly, dropping his hand back to his side. "All my time's going to be taken up with the case."

And when this case was solved, there'd be another. Then another. She knew that, accepted it, didn't have a problem with that. It was his job to catch bad guys, and they didn't always make themselves available for arrest from nine to five. But he had days off. He went home at night. He had time to eat, time for a social life. If he wanted to see her, there was time.

Obviously he didn't.

He'd kissed her and held her and made her want him in a way she'd never wanted a man before, and now he was going to turn his back and walk away as if he'd never been the least attracted to her. Why? Because she was psychic? Because he still couldn't accept who and what she was?

The thought struck a nerve right in her very vulnerable

self-esteem. All her life she'd had to fight for acceptance and understanding, usually without success. She couldn't do it anymore. Not with Sam. She didn't know how it had happened, but he'd come to mean too much to her. If he didn't know by now that he had nothing to fear from her, then he didn't know her at all. And that infuriated her. How could he be so dense? What did she have to do to get past that damn guard of his?

Angry, she stepped toward him, her green eyes blazing. "So this is a kiss-off? Is that what you're saying? Then at least do it properly."

And with no more warning than that, she grabbed him by the tie and pulled his mouth down to hers for a hot blistering kiss.

Chapter 7

In her fury she would have given anything to drive him to his knees and make him beg, but from past experience, she knew her bones were more likely to melt than his. So she had to be content with giving him just a taste of what he was walking away from. It lasted all of ten seconds. And when it was over, she found little satisfaction in the taking of something he had once given so freely. She hurt. And it was all his fault.

Resentment shoring up her chin and keeping her eyes dry of the tears clogging her throat, she abruptly released him. "That's the way you say goodbye," she said coldly, then turned and stormed through the café's delivery entrance, slamming the door behind her before he could even think about following her.

His head reeling, Sam stared after her like a man who'd just had his feet knocked out from under him by a two-year-old. What the hell had just happened here? He'd kissed the lady senseless more times than he cared to remember, and he'd known she was going to be hurt by his withdrawal. He'd hated the idea of hurting her, but in the long run, he'd known it was for the best. He'd braced himself for tears and, yes, even anger. But what had lashed out at him from her green eyes had been sharp with betrayal and a hell of a lot stronger than mere anger. And he had a right to know why.

Hurrying after her, he tried to pull the back door open, only to find it locked. That was when his own temper ignited. Pounding on the steel door with the side of his clenched fist, he roared, "Dammit, Jennifer, let me in!"

"Go away!" she yelled. "I have nothing else to say to you."

"The hell you don't! Are you going to tell me what that was all about or do I have to guess?"

"You're the detective," she retorted. "Figure it out."

The sound of the dead bolt hitting home scraped his nerve endings like a rusty knife, and for all of two seconds he considered going around to the front of the restaurant and demanding an explanation in front of all of her customers. But considering the mood she was in, he wouldn't put it past her to call the station and file a complaint against him.

Muttering curses, he strode angrily down the alley and around the corner, but to his car, instead of the café. Women! he thought furiously. Who the hell understood them?

The man sat in the gathering shadows of his darkened living room and watched the five-o'clock news with a snort of disbelief. Jonathan Lake was interviewing the psychic everyone was talking about. He didn't believe in that kind of garbage—it was just a hoax, a trick to increase ratings. He didn't know who the hell she thought she was, but there was no way the little blonde knew anything about him. He'd been too careful, too smart. He'd left no prints, no clues to his identity, and he'd taken steps to change his appearance for each job. Hell, he'd only hocked two pieces in San Antonio because he'd been desperate for cash, and the clerk at the pawnshop hadn't even looked him in the eye, let alone asked for ID. He'd given a fake name and gotten the hell out of there, and there was no way the police could trace the deal to him. They didn't have a damn thing on him, and he was laughing all the way to the bank.

But as he congratulated himself on his cleverness, the woman on the screen looked him right in the eye and described a man who was not only clever, but smooth and charming and diabolical. A man who had never had the things in life he thought he deserved and for some reason blamed the elderly. An angry resentful man who had finally decided to go after what he wanted and to hell with the consequences. A man who sounded an awful lot like him.

His blood turning to ice, he listened in mounting rage as she speculated about him. She couldn't give his name or even guess what part of the city he lived in, but she was close enough to the mark to scare him spitless. There were people who knew him, people who had no love for him and saw past the facade he presented to the world, who might, upon hearing her profile of the robber, put it all together and come up with his name. All they'd need was a few more details from the little psychic, and his butt would be fried.

He had to do something, had to find a way to shut her up or scare her into backing off. It was the only way. He'd come too far, made too many plans, to let some freaky little busybody mess everything up now. But how could he get rid of her, dammit? She was psychic! She'd told that nosy bastard Lake she had no control over the information she was given, but what if she knew things she wasn't telling? What if she knew even now what he was planning and she'd already gone to the police? The second he tried to get close to her, he could be walking right into a trap.

But his mama hadn't raised any dumb kids, and as he watched Jonathan Lake wind up his interview at the Heavenly Scents Café, a sinister smile of anticipation slowly curled his thin mouth. He knew where the lady lived and worked, thanks to Lake's exclusive, and there was only one way to find out what she knew. He'd have to pay her a little visit.

Not taking a chance that she might recognize him, he completely shaved his head and eyebrows, then glued on a black beard that made him look like one of those missionaries who was always trying to save lost souls. Colored contacts changed his eyes from pale blue to dark brown, and a long black coat covered him from his neck to below his knees. There was nothing he could do about his size, but with a low-slung hat on his head and a Bible in his hand, hopefully no one would notice.

His own mother wouldn't have recognized him in the getup, but when he approached the café on foot the next morning, he did so cautiously. Working both sides of the street, pretending he was looking for people to share his message with, he kept an eagle eye out for the cops. There were no uniforms in sight, however, or anyone else that seemed particularly interested in what was going on at the Heavenly Scents Café. Everyone seemed to be in a hurry to get to work, and those he was able to stop and talk to couldn't get away from him fast enough. If there was a trap anywhere within the vicinity, he couldn't smell it.

Pleased, his hard eyes bright with expectation, he crossed the street and walked into the café as if he'd been a valued customer for years. The little bell attached to the front door jingled, and almost immediately he found himself face-to-face with Jennifer Hart. It was almost as if she'd been waiting for him.

If he hadn't been a man who was quick on his feet, his shock would have registered right there in his eyes. But he instantly dragged on a stiff smile and ducked his head. "Mornin'," he mumbled. "Something sure smells good in here."

"Homemade cinnamon rolls and fresh coffee," she said promptly with a smile. "Would you like a seat at the counter or a table?"

He had no desire to sit out in full view of everyone while he watched her, so he took a table off to one side, against the wall, and ordered coffee and a cinnamon roll. He wasn't hungry, but he couldn't just sit there and stare at her without making her uneasy. And that wasn't what he wanted. Not yet.

He'd hardly settled into his chair when she was back with his order, but the bell tinkled over the door again, so she didn't have time to linger. She hurried off to greet the new arrivals and seat them, then refill coffee cups all around the room and chat. She dispensed smiles as easily as she did coffee, and when customers who obviously knew her well asked her about the interview with Jonathan Lake they'd seen on TV last night, she answered freely. When she finally got back to his table to refill his cup, he was ready for her.

"Hey, you were on TV last night, weren't you?" he

said with forced cheerfulness. "You're one of those psychics, huh?"

She nodded and gave him a faint smile. "I guess there's no point in trying to keep it a secret now. Apparently everyone in town watched Channel Seven last night."

"Yeah. It was pretty interesting. If I was that dude you were talking about," he dared, "I'd be fighting mad. Don't you know he could come after you, girl? 'Course, I guess you would know what he was going to do, wouldn't you? You could call the police and have a trap all set up for him."

"Well, no, actually I don't see things very clearly for myself. Not that I think I have anything to worry about," she added. "Why would I? I'm not a threat to the perpetrator. All I gave Mr. Lake were some generalities. Just a psychological profile. The police might use it to narrow their search, but by itself, it's not enough to identify anyone. Not when there are hundreds, maybe thousands, of men in San Antonio who fit the profile."

She sounded confident enough, but when she drifted away to another table, he didn't miss the troubled shadows in her eyes. Smiling to himself, he threw a couple of bucks on the table and pushed to his feet. *Now* he could make some plans.

Three nights later, lying in bed in the darkness, Jennifer accepted with a tired sigh that she wasn't going to be able to sleep. Just as she hadn't been able to the night before or the night before that. Her mind was too active, the images that flashed against the screen of her closed eyelids too vivid. Sam. He was like a burr under her skin, an itch that couldn't be scratched. He nagged and pressured and tormented, and he didn't say a word. He didn't have to. He was there in her head every time she closed her eyes.

If she could have gotten her hands on him, she would have strung him up by his thumbs and left him to twist in the wind.

But she hadn't seen him since he'd told her he wouldn't be seeing much of her anymore and she'd kissed *him* off. God, what had possessed her? She might as well have stamped it on her forehead that she cared. Not that that kiss or the way she felt had changed anything, she thought, pain squeezing her heart. Three days. It'd been three days since she'd seen that chiseled face of his, and she missed him. She hadn't expected that. At the oddest times she found herself looking out the front window of the café for his car and listening for the sound of his footsteps on the back stairs to her apartment. But he hadn't come and he wasn't going to. Even when her grandparents died within six months of each other, she hadn't felt this alone.

She wouldn't, however, cry. Because she was afraid that once she started, it might be a long time before she could stop. So when her eyes started to burn and tears clogged her throat, she turned over, punched her pillow and deliberately turned her thoughts to Saturday's baking. She'd make something sweet to go along with the bread she usually donated to the local shelters. Maybe some double-chocolate-chip cookies.

Lost in her thoughts, the sound of breaking glass in the living room was like an explosion. Startled, her heart jolting in her breast, she sprang up in bed, her eyes wide as she listened to a car tear off up the street. Had someone thrown a rock through the front window? It wouldn't be the first time she'd had a problem with some of the kids who lived in the projects on the south side of downtown, but they usually were content just to tag the Dumpster behind the café. They never actually broke anything.

Frowning, she started to grab her robe, and then she heard it. A strange *whoosh*, like the burners in the oven of her commercial stove in the café when she lit them. At the thought her heart stopped dead.

"*No!*"

Fear choking her, she jumped from the bed and ran into the living room, only to gasp in horror at the sight of the flames racing up the curtains that hung at the front window. Smoke was already billowing into the room, thickening at an alarming rate, and as she watched, the braided rag rug on the floor, one her grandmother had made herself, ignited. Sobbing, Jennifer grabbed an afghan off the couch and ran forward to beat out the flame, never noticing the broken glass from the windowpane that cut into her bare feet as she swung the afghan again and again.

Everything she owned, everything she had left of her family, was there in the apartment. Her grandmother's favorite rocker, the trophy her grandfather had won at the state fair for his sourdough bread, keepsakes that had been a part of her life for as long as she could remember. She couldn't, wouldn't, lose them!

Abandoning the afghan, she ran into the kitchen and filled the largest bowl she could get her hands on with water, then sprinted back into the living room to throw it on the rug. Smoke engulfed her, burning her eyes and choking her. Coughing, tears streaming down her face, she ran back to the kitchen, this time with the afghan, and soaked it in the sink. When she dragged it back into the living room, the couch was on fire and the smoke was as thick as tar. Even as she watched through blurry eyes, the picture of her mother hanging on the wall went up in flames.

"No, damn you! No!"

Furious, she snatched it from the wall, uncaring that it

burned her hands, and beat the flames out, while the fire snaked around her like a living thing. She had to get out. Now, while she still could, but first she had to save what she could. Grabbing the silver candlesticks that had been one of her grandparents' wedding presents, the crackling of the fire loud in her ears, she never heard the pounding at the door that led to the outside stairs. Then an ax cut through it and with three mighty swings the door was reduced to nothing but kindling. Pushing it aside, a fireman in full protective gear stormed into the apartment like some kind of invader from outer space. Before she could do anything but gasp, he grabbed her around the waist and hauled her outside.

It was the discordant blast of a firetruck's horn as the vehicle ran a light at the corner that first woke Sam. Groaning, he fumbled for his pillow in the dark and slapped it over his head, but it didn't help. The truck raced past the Lone Star Social Club at the speed of sound, its sirens screaming all the way down the block. Still lying in the same spot on the bed where he'd fallen an hour ago, Sam cursed in the darkness.

God, he was tired. He'd been working like a madman, pushing himself to the limit, trying to forget the look in Jennifer's eyes when he'd told her he wouldn't be seeing her anymore, but so far, nothing had worked. She'd looked at him like he'd stabbed her in the heart, and all he'd been trying to do was protect her, dammit! She was too young for him, too innocent, too...otherworldly. She could see and hear things, which he had a hard time accepting, and that wasn't ever going to change. For both their sakes it was better if they went their separate ways now, before somebody got hurt.

But remembering the shattered look in her eyes, he

knew he'd waited too long. Guilt ate at him, twisting in his gut like a snake. He'd checked out her background; he'd known there were no men in her life. She was a virgin—he knew it as surely as he knew she lit a fire in him the way no other woman ever had. She hadn't had a clue how to protect herself from him, and he'd kissed her, anyway. Held her, anyway. Wanted her and made her want him. And now she was hurting because of him, and it sickened him.

Another fire truck roared by outside, forcing its way into his thoughts. Frowning, he lifted his head abruptly, listening. A two-alarm. And it was close. For the first time he noticed that the truck had hardly turned the corner when it cut its siren. Rolling out of bed, he walked naked to the window in the dark and stared out across the river.

He couldn't see any flames, but the smoke was thick and gray and already climbing high into the night sky. And it appeared to be right over Jennifer's café and apartment.

For one frozen moment in time he just stood there staring blankly. Then it hit him, and with a hoarse cry he whirled and snatched up his clothes. Thirty seconds later, when he bolted out of his apartment and down the central stairs of the Lone Star, he had on his jeans and a pair of house shoes that kept slipping off his bare feet. Swearing, he kicked them off and sprinted barefoot through the back door and gardens. By the time he reached the wrought-iron gate that separated the grounds of the Lone Star from the rest of the River Walk, he was running flat out and daring anything to get in his way. Without bothering to check his speed, he vaulted the gate and kept on running.

"Oh, God! Oh, God!" The words fell from his lips like a chant, echoing the rhythm of his pounding heart as he raced over the first bridge he came to, then took the stairs that led to street level. Over the roar of the blood in his ears, he heard another siren and nearly stumbled. An ambulance. Someone had called for an ambulance.

No, dammit! She couldn't be hurt. He wouldn't allow it!

Dread like a fist in his throat, his lungs straining, he saw the ambulance whiz past, its lights spinning, just as he reached West Commerce. And for the first time he got a good look at the small two-story building that housed Heavenly Scents and Jennifer's small upstairs apartment. What he saw turned his blood to ice. Surrounded by emergency vehicles, smoke pouring from its upper windows, it looked as though it had been firebombed. And there was no sign of Jennifer anywhere.

His mind numb, his legs moving like he was running in mud, he searched frantically for her in the crowd. There were firefighters everywhere, their hoses crisscrossing the street as they hosed the building down, and cops already erecting barriers to keep the curious back. A TV-news crew had arrived, and he thought he caught a glimpse of Jonathan Lake, but he didn't spare the man a glance. His eyes searching the scene for one small golden-haired woman, he told himself she had to be there somewhere. The fire seemed to be upstairs at the front of the building she would have been able to get out the back door and run down the stairs at the first hint of smoke. She couldn't still be in there.

Then, without warning, the sea of humanity blocking his path parted and there she was, not fifty feet in front of him. Dressed in a gray flannel nightgown he suspected had been white earlier in the evening, her hair wet and dripping and her face streaked with black soot, she looked like a street urchin. A dirty, bedraggled, beautiful street urchin.

His knees weak, his eyes stinging suspiciously, he saw nothing but her. He stepped over hoses and around firemen, heading straight for her. "Jennifer?"

Locked in the hold of the burly fireman who'd pulled her from her apartment and was stubbornly trying to carry her out of the danger zone, she couldn't hear anything but the grunts of her captor as she struggled to free herself. "Let me go, damn you!" she cried. "I'm all right. I just have to get my things!"

"I'm sorry, ma'am. I can't let you do that. If you'd just calm down, you'd see—"

"I *am* calm!"

Her cry, high-pitched with hysteria, seemed to echo off the neigboring buildings, and then suddenly Sam was there, stepping out of the madness with a worried frown etching his rugged face. "Sam! Thank God you're here!" Relieved, she tore herself free of the fireman and launched herself at him. "Make him get out of my way!" she pleaded frantically. "I have to get back inside. All my grandparents' things are in there. Everything from my childhood. I can't lose it. It's all I have left of my family...."

"She was trying to save stuff when I broke down the back door," the fireman told Sam over her head. "There wasn't any time to waste."

"I knew what I was doing," she argued. "All I needed was five more minutes." Her hands clutching at him, she said hoarsely, "My grandparents' silver candlesticks are just inside the door. I dropped them when he grabbed me. Please, Sam, let me get them. That's all I want. Please. Just that."

She was begging, and she didn't care. She couldn't just stand there and watch everything she owned go up in flames. Panic pulling at her, she searched his face in growing desperation, sure he would help her. But then his arms tightened around her and the regret she saw in his eyes broke her heart. "I'm sorry, sweetheart," he said thickly. "It's just too risky. Your life's worth more than a pair of silver candlesticks."

The fireman, relieved that she was no longer his problem, turned to rejoin the fight against the fire, then glanced back over his shoulder. "The lady should be checked out by one of the paramedics. She doesn't appear to be suffering from smoke inhalation, but she was beating at the flames when I found her. In all the excitement, she could be burned and not even know it."

"I'm fine," Jennifer protested, but Sam had already grabbed her hands. When he turned them over and spit out a curse, she said, "What? What is it? I'm telling you, Sam, there's nothing wrong with me."

"The hell there isn't! Look!"

Feeling perfectly fine, she glanced down curiously at her palms—and sucked in a swift sharp breath. The skin was red and raw, blistered from her fingertips nearly to her wrists. "No," she murmured. "How could they be burned? They don't even hurt."

"You're in shock, honey," he told her gently, and swept her up into his arms. "Just hang on and the paramedics will have you feeling better in no time."

With long, sure strides, he carried her to the ambulance, then hovered protectively close while the paramedics worked over her. Numb, wrapped in a blanket as she lay back on a stretcher, she didn't so much as flicker an eyelash when the cuts on her bare feet were discovered and Sam swore like a sailor. She should be hurting big time just about now. Somewhere in the hidden recesses of her brain, she knew that, but as she dazedly watched the firefighters put out the last of the fire and shoot what seemed like millions of gallons of water into her apartment and café, she couldn't feel anything. Gone. It was all gone.

She was too pale, too still, too damn calm, Sam thought worriedly. She'd just watched everything she owned and loved go up like a bonfire, and she was entitled to scream and rage about it. But once she'd realized she wasn't going to save so much as a candlestick, all the fight just seemed to drain out of her. She just lay there on the stretcher, wrapped from her feet to her neck in a blanket, and stared at the water-logged smoking building, not an ounce of emotion in her green eyes.

Frustrated, feeling as if he could chew glass, Sam wanted to shake her until her eyes lost their glazed expression, then carry her off to a place where nothing and no one could ever hurt her again. But she couldn't leave. Not until they knew the fire was out completely and what had caused it. Standing around with his hands in his pockets had never been easy, however, especially when Jennifer seemed to draw more and more into herself. All he could do was take her to one of the patrol cars and let her sit there, out of the cold, while the firemen went over the building with a fine-tooth comb looking for the cause of the blaze. And all the while, she just sat in the back of the patrol car, hugging herself and staring off into space.

When the fire inspector approached them fifteen minutes later, Sam lifted a brow in surprise. He'd expected them to have to wait at least another hour or two. "That was fast," he told the inspector. "What was it? A loose wire or something? This old building looks like it hasn't been rewired in years. It's a wonder it didn't go up a long time ago."

His face grim, the older man shook his head. "No, sir, it wasn't the wiring. Someone threw a Molotov cocktail through the front window. If Ms. Hart hadn't taken steps to contain the fire until we got here, the whole place would have burned to the ground."

Chapter 8

Encased in numbness, Jennifer stared at Sam blankly, trying to understand why he was suddenly cursing furiously and the fire inspector looked so somber. But her brain was mush, and the traumatic events of the evening were starting to catch up with her. A hammer pounded in her head and she was so tired all she wanted to do was lie down and close her eyes. But both men were waiting for some kind of response from her, and she didn't for the life of her know what it was. Swallowing thickly, she said in a voice made raspy by too much smoke, "I don't understand. Was someone trying to hurt me?"

"We don't know, sweetheart," Sam said gently, his eyes hard, "but I'm going to find out. You stay here while I call for an evidence team, then I'll be back to take you home."

He strode off into the night, disappearing from view before she could remind him that her home was the charred mess on the corner. Staring at the blackened ruin, she knew on some level of her consciousness that she should be worried. She had nothing but the clothes on her back, not even a pair of shoes, and nowhere to go for the rest of the night. But she couldn't drag up the strength to be concerned.

Closing her eyes, she leaned her head back against the headrest, and just that easily time lost all meaning. When Sam finally returned and slipped into the back seat of the patrol car with her, she couldn't have said if two minutes had passed or sixty. Just opening her eyes was a struggle.

"The evidence team is on its way," he told her as a uniformed officer climbed behind the wheel and started the engine. "I'll come back later and see what they found out, but right now, Officer Stevens is going to drive us to my place. You're staying with me tonight."

He didn't ask, he *told* her what she was going to do, and she didn't offer a word of protest. That alone was enough to deepen the concern in his eyes as he slipped his arm around her shoulders and eased her against him, but she never noticed. Sighing, losing the fight to keep her eyes open, she melted against him trustingly and sank back into oblivion.

She would have been content to stay that way the rest of the night, but all too soon, Officer Stevens was braking to a stop. Jennifer stirred, then frowned bleary-eyed at the familiar lines of the Lone Star Social Club. She'd never been inside the old Victorian mansion, but she'd fallen in love with it the first time she'd laid eyes on it and made a point to walk past it whenever she visited the River Walk.

Still groggy, she glanced at Sam. "What are we doing here?"

"I live here," he said with a smile. "Second floor at the back on the right." Pushing open the car door on his side, he came around, opened hers for her and held out his hand. "C'mon. You need to get inside and change into something dry."

That sounded heavenly, but when she looked past him to the ten or more steps that led to the porch, she hesitated. Her feet had started to throb, and even though they were bandaged, she didn't see how she could even think about climbing stairs. "Uh...we've got a problem," she murmured.

"What? The stairs? You won't feel a thing," he promised, and in one smooth motion, he leaned down and plucked her from the patrol car as if she weighed no more than a feather.

Gasping, she clutched at him, but his arms were rock steady, his stride sure as he thanked the young rookie for the ride, then started up the steps, the blanket that still covered her trailing behind them on the walkway. In the time it took to blink, they'd reached the front door.

"Can you punch in the security code, honey?" he growled softly. "It's 6-5-8-1."

Her fingers were far from steady, but when he turned so she could reach the keypad, she managed to hit the right numbers. The lock clicked open, and he quietly shouldered the door open and stepped into the darkened front hall. Hushed silence surrounded them. Flipping on the light, he carefully started up the main staircase.

At any other time she would have memorized every detail of the old house and asked him a dozen questions about it, but her brain still felt as if it was encased in smoke, and she couldn't seem to think. Weary to the bone, she dropped her head to Sam's shoulder and closed her eyes. At that moment he could have taken her to the moon for all the attention she paid to her surroundings. She was just too tired to care.

His hands full of her, Sam felt the soft brush of a breast against his chest, the warmth of her breath against his neck as she sighed, and he clenched his teeth on a silent groan. She was hurt, he reminded himself grimly. And if not in shock, then damn close to it. She had to be or she'd have already remembered the last time they were together, when *she* had kissed him off. When tonight's trauma faded and she was herself again, she wouldn't be nearly so willing to accept his touch. He'd be lucky if she even spoke to him.

For now, though, she needed tender loving care and he needed to be the one to give it to her. She might hate him for it later and rail at him for taking advantage of the situation, but he'd just have to chance it. He had to get back to her apartment to learn what the evidence team had found, but he couldn't leave her. Not yet. Not when she seemed so lost and fragile in his arms.

Stepping into his apartment, he carried her into the bathroom and carefully eased her onto a stool next to the old-fashioned claw-foot tub. Grabbing towels and a washcloth from the linen cabinet, he frowned when he saw how she was trembling. "I know you're cold, honey, and you'd sleep much better if you could have a hot bath, but that's not going to be possible. Not with those bandages on your hands and feet. So I'm going to sponge you down, if that's okay with you. And find you something to sleep in besides that smoky nightgown. okay, Jen? Are you okay with that?"

She didn't so much as blink, but he knew she'd heard him. Something flickered in the depths of her eyes, and her poor bandaged fingers instinctively tightened on the blanket she clung to like a lifeline. Swallowing a curse, he hesitated, wondering what the hell he was going to do. She was visibly shaking now, her teeth chattering. She had to be miserable in that wet gown. But she'd already been through hell once tonight; he'd be damned if he'd drag her through it again by stripping her of her clothes against her will.

Hunkering down in front of her, emotions he couldn't put a name to tightening his chest, he reached out to trail a finger over her sooty cheek. Just the thought of someone trying to hurt her, to *burn* her, enraged him. His voice, however, was gentle when he said, "Would you like me to go downstairs and get my landlady to help you, instead? Considering the circumstances, I'm sure she wouldn't mind."

For a second he thought she was going to agree, but then her fingers loosened slightly on the blanket and she shook her head. "No. It's too late. I wouldn't want to wake her."

"Honey, she saw you on TV and thinks you're the greatest thing since sliced bread," he said ruefully. "Trust me, she wouldn't mind."

He spoke nothing less than the truth. Ever since Alice saw the interview with Jonathan Lake and learned Jennifer was not only psychic, but working with him, she'd been dying to meet her. If she had even a clue that she was here in his apartment and in trouble, she'd be pounding on the door.

He knew Alice—she truly wouldn't have minded—but he should have known Jennifer would never dream of getting anyone, least of all an old lady she didn't even know, out of bed just to help her. She was the caretaker type, not used to letting others help her.

"I trust you," she said softly, and let the blanket fall away from her as she tiredly closed her eyes.

Her words went through him like a streak of lightning, burning him from the inside out, and for the first time he doubted the wisdom of what he was about to do. With a will of their own, his eyes went over her hungrily, lingering on the shadow of her nipples and the tempting curves revealed by her damp clinging gown. She was pale and dirty and exhausted. And he wanted her. More than his next breath. That hadn't stopped just because he'd finally come to his senses and accepted the fact that she was all wrong for him. He couldn't remember the last time he'd crawled into bed without aching for her, and just the thought of touching her made him hard. But she trusted him, and he'd swallow ground glass before he'd give her reason not to.

Pushing to his feet, he wet a washcloth with warm water. If his fingers weren't quite steady when he lifted her face to him, she didn't seem to notice. At the first soothing stroke of the cloth over her brow and cheek, she murmured something unintelligible and went boneless. Before he could do anything but drag in a sharp breath, she was slumped against him, the side of her face resting against his belly.

Lust frying his brain, he never knew how he got through the next few minutes. He didn't strip her completely—he couldn't without going quietly out of his mind. Instead, he kept her covered as much as he could, pushing the sleeves of her gown out of the way when he wiped down her arms, then the hem high up on her thighs when he turned his attention to her legs. And when he found her a pair of sweatpants and a T-shirt to replace her gown, he did have the good sense to turn out the light. But it didn't help. Standing in the darkness right next to her as she clumsily struggled with the garments with her bandaged hands, every whispered movement sparked his imagination. By the time she was dressed again, he felt like howling at the moon. And he was sweating, for God's sake!

Mumbling curses, he lifted her in his arms and carried her to bed in the dark.

"I'm going to sleep on the couch," he said firmly, and wasn't sure who he was trying to convince—her or himself. He was worried that *she* might be worried about it, but evidently the thought hadn't crossed her mind. Already half-asleep, she turned into his pillow and snuggled under the covers the second he laid her down. It was all he could do not to crawl in there with her.

Grinding his teeth, he swallowed a groan and reminded himself that the evidence team would be winding things up at her apartment, if they hadn't already. He needed to get over there, but he didn't like to think of her waking up and finding herself alone in a strange bed in an even stranger apartment.

"Jennifer?"

He nudged her shoulder, but she was already dead to the world and didn't move so much as a muscle. After all she'd been through, he wasn't surprised she'd finally crashed. Sleep was the best thing for her. That didn't, however, make leaving her any easier. His hand lingered, lightly caressing the curve of her shoulder until he suddenly realized what he was doing. Swallowing an oath, he jerked back and got the hell out of there while he still could.

She awoke slowly, the unfamiliar quiet nagging at her subconscious until she groaned and was forced to face the coming day. Still, she couldn't bring herself to open her eyes. Luxuriating in the warmth that enveloped her, she buried her face in the pillow she clutched to her breast and sighed sleepily. Just a few more minutes, she told herself, then she'd get up. She had to get the coffee on and set the first batch of dough to rising. Maybe she'd make some beignets this morning…

Then she remembered.

The fire. The scorching heat and licking flames. The horror that cut her off at the knees as she watched everything she held dear ignite and burn.

No! she wanted to scream. It was all just a bad dream, a nightmare that couldn't possibly be real. All she had to do was wake up and she'd be back in her own bed, wrapped in the quilt she and her grandmother had made when she was thirteen. But even as she tried, she knew her imagination wasn't that good. Her apartment was on the street, the pulse of the city right outside her windows. Sam's was backed up to the river, away from traffic, and quiet except for the occasional laugh of tourists on the River Walk or the wail of a siren that was so penetrating it reached the back of the house. She was alone in his bed, wearing his clothes, because everything she owned in the world was now nothing but ashes.

The blessed numbness that had protected her last night cracked, and suddenly she was stripped bare of defenses. She felt the bandages wrapped around her hands and feet, the dull throbbing of her burns, the aching loss of things that could never be replaced. Hurt gripped her heart, clawing at her, tearing her apart, until she thought she would die from the pain. Curling into a ball, she buried her face in Sam's pillow and sobbed.

She cried until there were no tears left, until her eyes burned and her head pounded and shudders racked her. And it changed nothing. When she finally dragged herself into the bathroom and faced herself in the mirror, she looked into her red-rimmed puffy eyes and faced the harsh reality of her situation. She was homeless and didn't even own the clothes on her back. She would have been out on the street last night if Sam hadn't come to her rescue.

Shadowy images from the night flickered before her eyes, haunting her, confusing her. It was just days ago that he'd said he didn't plan to see her again. But he'd literally come running when she was in trouble. And not only had he helped her, he'd taken care of her when she hadn't been in any condition to take care of herself. Her memories of what happened after he brought her to his apartment were vague, but she could hear his husky voice in her ear, murmuring to her, assuring her everything was going to be all right. And his hands. She could still feel his hands on her, the warm wetness of the washcloth as he gently drew it over her arms and legs and face. She'd leaned against him and wanted it to go on forever.

But he'd carried her to his bed and made it clear he had no intention of sleeping with her. Last night, somewhere in her numb mind, she'd been grateful he wasn't the type of man to take advantage of a woman who'd practically draped herself all over him. But now, in the light of day, she had to face facts. He hadn't slept with her because he didn't want her.

The truth hurt, but she faced it squarely. She had to leave. Today. He'd never know how much she appreciated his hospitality, but she couldn't hang around any longer without looking like she wanted more from him than emergency shelter. That would only embarrass them both. She'd get dressed, write him a note...

She turned to hurry back into the bedroom, only to spy her nightgown hanging on a hook nailed to the back of the bathroom door. She stopped short, the enormity of her situation hitting her right in the face. God, what was she thinking? she wondered hysterically. She couldn't leave. Not unless she wanted to parade down the River Walk in

Sam's T-shirt and sweatpants. And even if she dared that, where would she go? The apartment? It was a charred ruin; she didn't even want to think about how long it would be before it would be habitable. A hotel? And pay for it how? With her good looks? Her credit cards and driver's license were in her purse, and that, too, had been destroyed by the fire.

Stunned, she stumbled into the living room where she sank onto the couch and stared blindly into space. What was she going to do now?

Ten minutes later she was still sitting there, racking her brain for answers, when the doorbell rang. Startled, she jumped, wondering how she could answer the door dressed the way she was, when a woman called out, "Jennifer? Are you all right, dear? Sam had to run an errand and asked me to look in on you. I'm his landlady, Alice Truelove. I've got coffee and doughnuts, but I can come back later if you'd rather."

Glancing down at herself, Jennifer groaned. She was hardly in any condition to deal with strangers, but the landlady sounded so friendly and concerned she didn't have the heart to send her away. Hurrying to the door, she pulled it open to find a small elderly woman standing in the hall. Dressed in a colorful running suit, her white hair curling about her head, two bags of doughnuts in her hand, she had a smile as big as Texas.

Her own smile wobbly, Jennifer automatically lifted a hand to her hair, which she knew still bore the unmistakable odor of smoke. "I'm sorry. I know I must look a fright...."

Her faded blue eyes alight with sympathy, Alice clicked her tongue and scolded good-naturedly, "Don't be ridiculous, dear. Considering what you went through last night, you look darn good. From what I heard, you're lucky you're not toast.''

Put that way, Jennifer couldn't help but laugh. Liking the woman immediately, she pulled the door open wider and stepped back. ''I suppose you're right. Please, come in.''

The landlady headed straight for Sam's galley-style kitchen and began to rummage in the cabinets for plates and coffee cups, chattering all the while. ''I know you must think you've lost everything this morning, but things really aren't as bad as they seem. I know—I've been there.''

Surprised, Jennifer hesitated in the kitchen doorway. ''You were in a fire?''

Alice nodded. ''When I was just about your age, as a matter of fact. My husband and I were newly married and living in a ratty apartment, which was the only thing we could afford. One day when we were both at work, it burned to the ground. We lost everything we owned and didn't have two nickels to rub together.''

Instantly sympathetic, Jennifer moved to the small round kitchen table and sat in a chair. ''What did you do?''

''There was nothing we could do but start over and thank God that neither one of us was hurt.'' Pulling plastic-foam cups of coffee from one of the bags she'd set on the table, Alice poured the steaming contents into thick mugs and pushed one across the table to Jennifer. Then with a plate of assorted doughnuts on the table between them, she took the chair opposite Jennifer. ''Things can get broken or stolen or even burned,'' she said with all the wisdom of her seventy or so years, ''but nobody can take your memories. They're always there, right there in your heart.''

"But I have nowhere to live. And the café... God, I haven't even thought about that! How am I going to earn a living?"

"The same way you did before—with your café. The building didn't burn to the ground. Sam said the fire inspector said most of the damage was contained to the living room of your apartment, thanks to you." Suddenly realizing what Jennifer had said, she frowned. "What's this nonsense about having nowhere to live? You'll stay right here."

Startled, Jennifer nearly choked on a jelly doughnut. "What do you mean, *here?* I couldn't impose on Sam—"

Her blue eyes twinkling, Alice laughed gaily. "There are other ways of imposing on a man without living with him, but that wasn't what I meant. You can stay with me, of course. I have plenty of room and you'd be close to the café, which will be convenient once you start making repairs."

"Oh, but I couldn't!"

"I don't see why not," Alice replied. "I realize we don't know each other, but you're a friend of Sam's, and that's all the reference I need. And you wouldn't be imposing on me. You'd be helping me as much as I'd be helping you."

Jennifer didn't see how she could possibly help anyone when she didn't even own the clothes on her back. "How?"

Eyes sparkling, Alice could barely contain her excitement. "I've always said that if these old walls could talk, I could write the next *New York Times* bestseller. Can you imagine the stories they'd be able to tell? And, well, I was hoping, since you're a psychic and everything, that you could...you know..."

"...see what I can pick up on the people who once lived

here?'' Jennifer finished for her, amused. ''Is that what you're trying to say?''

''Oh, would you, dear? When I saw you on TV, I could tell you were extremely sensitive and just the person I needed to talk to. I know more about this old place than just about anyone, but stories get lost down through the years, and there's no way a person can know everything.''

''Especially when a house is as old as this one is,'' Jennifer agreed, grinning. ''I wasn't in much shape to appreciate it last night, but it's just full of spirits, you know.''

''You picked that up, too? Oh, how wonderful! I thought it was just me.'' Pleased with the turn of events, she said eagerly, ''So you'll stay? Please say yes. I'd love to have you.''

Touched, Jennifer knew it was the logical solution to her problem, and she didn't doubt for a minute that she and Alice would get along just fine. But Sam would be right upstairs; he would have to pass Alice's apartment every time he came in or out the front or back door. She wouldn't be able to walk in the garden or step into the entrance hall without possibly running into him.

Her heart jolting painfully at the thought, she regretfully shook her head. ''I can't, Alice. I'm sorry. It's really sweet of you to offer, and if circumstances were different, I would take you up on it in a heartbeat. But I don't think it would be a good idea.''

''Because of Sam,'' Alice guessed shrewdly.

Jennifer nodded miserably. ''He brought me here last night because I had nowhere else to go, and I appreciate it. But it would be best for both of us if I found somewhere else to stay besides the Lone Star Social Club. That doesn't mean, however, I can't go through the house with you. Why don't I come back on Sunday afternoon and we'll do it then?''

Thrilled, Alice jumped at the offer. ''I'll make lunch. But I still want you to think about my offer. If you change your mind, I've got plenty of room.'' Deliberately changing the subject, she reached for another doughnut. ''Now that we've got that cleared up, let's talk about Jonathan Lake. Is he really as arrogant as he appears on TV?''

Alice took her mind off the fire and the future and made her laugh, but she couldn't keep her company all morning. Once she left, silence pressed in on Jennifer, and too late she remembered Molly. She'd probably shown up for work that morning without knowing a thing about the fire! Quickly hunting through the apartment, she found the phone next to Sam's bed and called her at home.

''Thank God you're okay!'' the older woman cried the second she recognized her voice. ''When I got to work this morning, I almost had a heart attack! I probably would have if Detective Kelly hadn't been there. He told me you were at his place.''

''Sam was at the café at six this morning?''

''He sure was. He didn't know my number and knew I'd be worried about you when I heard about the fire. You know, Jen, I think I misjudged that man. The more I get to know him, the more I like him. Is he taking good care of you?''

It was a simple question with an equally simple answer, but as she remembered those moments in the bathroom, when he'd so tenderly seen to her needs, she could feel his hands on her, the gentle rub of the washcloth against her skin, the husky tone of his voice as he murmured to her. There were, she realized as an ache lodged in her heart, different ways for a man to take care of a woman.

If Molly was talking about taking care of all her burns and bruises, that was one thing. Her growing physical need for him was something else entirely.

Heat staining her cheeks, she said, "I don't know what I would have done without him last night. Did he say where he was going after he left you this morning? He was gone when I woke up. Maybe he had to work—"

The words were hardly out of her mouth when she heard a key in the lock. "That must be him now," she said quickly. "I've got to go. I just wanted to let you know I was all right so you wouldn't worry."

Hanging up with a promise to call her after she checked out the damage at the café, Jennifer stepped out of his bedroom, her stomach a jumble of nerves, just as he walked through the apartment door. She had what she'd say all worked out in her mind—she'd thank him for his hospitality, then find a way to get out of there. God only knew where she'd go, but she'd worry about that later.

However, the second she saw him, the words she'd carefully rehearsed flew right out of her head. He'd obviously been shopping—his arms were laden with packages—but it was the tiredness that etched his face that drew her eye.

When he'd carried her to bed sometime between three and four in the morning, he'd claimed he was going to bed down on the couch, but now, she had to wonder if he had. She'd fallen asleep almost immediately and hadn't a clue what he'd done after he'd walked out of the bedroom and shut the door behind him. If he had stretched out on the couch, he'd put the covers up before he'd left. Had he slept at all?

Walking into the living room, he stopped short at the sight of her, something hot and intimate flaring in his eyes before he quickly blinked it away. "You look better," he said by way of greeting. "You must have slept well."

Her pulse skittering wildly, she nodded. "I did, thanks to your taking such good care of me. But you shouldn't have let me have your bed. You didn't sleep at all, did you?"

"I stretched out on the couch for a couple of hours," he said with a shrug. "That was all I had time for. After you went to sleep, I went back to your apartment to confer with the evidence team."

"My God, you must be dead on your feet! Here, give me those things." She took the packages from him. "What are you doing going shopping, anyway? I just talked to Molly..." Suddenly suspicious, she added up the numbers in her head and scowled. "You didn't sleep, did you? How could you? You left here around three to go back to the apartment and Molly said you were still there when she got there at six. Darn it, Sam, you should have let me take the couch so you could have your bed! What are you grinning at?"

"You." He chuckled. "You really are a caretaker, but I guess you know that. You might want to try those things on," he added, nodding at the packages she was still clutching.

"What things?" she asked, eyeing him warily. "What have you done?"

"Bought you a few clothes until you can pick some things out for yourself. I thought you'd be more comfortable in something besides my old sweats and T-shirt."

"You went shopping for *me?*"

He nodded. "I guess I could have dragged some of those blackened jeans and shirts from the closet in your apartment, but I figured you'd rather not walk around smelling like a barbecue pit. But if you want me to take them back…''

She knew he was teasing, but she wasn't taking any chances. Clutching the bags to her chest, she took a quick step back. When his grin only deepened, she couldn't help but laugh at herself. ''I'm a little bit paranoid about clothes right now, so I guess I should warn you that if you even think about trying to take these from me, I'll have to break both your arms.''

''Hey, never let it be said that I got between a lady and her clothes.'' He threw his hands up in mock surrender. ''They're all yours, sweetheart.''

Warmed by the amusement glittering in his eyes, she felt her heart turn over at his thoughtfulness, and suddenly, to her horror, she found herself battling tears. ''I'm sorry.'' She sniffed and waved him off when he cursed and stepped toward her worriedly. ''Don't mind me. My emotions have been going up and down like an elevator all morning. I just didn't expect you to buy me clothes.''

''It's nothing fancy, honey. Just the basics. Jeans and shirts. Underwear. Some new nightclothes. Oh, and a pair of loafers. You can't walk around barefoot all day.''

It could have been biker shorts and polyester and she still would have treasured it. Sinking onto the couch, she opened the bags to see what he considered the basics and then glanced back up at him in surprise, her mouth trembling with a smile. ''Everything's the right size. Even the shoes. How did you know?''

He never moved, but something shifted in his eyes, something hot and knowing and masculine that stroked her from the top of her head all the way to her toes. ''I've got a good eye,'' he said roughly. ''Go try them on and see if you like them.''

Caught in the heat of his gaze, she nodded dazedly, her

heart thundering wildly. He hadn't laid a finger on her, but he hadn't needed to in order to make her want him. How she made it to the bathroom without running into a wall, she couldn't have said.

Everything fit, including the shoes, once she removed the bandages on her feet and replaced them with Band-Aids. Staring at herself in the mirror, she flushed and had to admit that he did, indeed, have a good eye. The jeans he'd picked out for her were a flattering cut, and the forest green turtleneck brought out the green in her eyes. But it was the new bra and panties that stole her breath. Hardly more than lace and promises, they were the sexiest underwear she'd ever worn. Just thinking about them in his hands made her burn.

If he noticed how pink her cheeks were when she rejoined him in the living room, he didn't let on, but simply assessed her with knowing eyes and nodded in approval. "Good, they fit." Once again a detective investigating a case, he was all business as he motioned for her to take a seat on the couch. "I know you'd rather not talk about the fire now, but you need to while your memories are still fresh. What do you remember?"

"The sound of breaking glass." The answer came automatically, the images sharp before her eyes. Too restless to sit, she prowled over to the window that overlooked the Lone Star's famous back garden. Surrounded by an antique wrought-iron fence and bordered on one side by the River Walk, it was beautiful with fall flowers.

But her gaze was focused on last night, and Jennifer saw nothing but her own apartment. Flames licking up the walls and the scent of smoke pungent and burning in her nose. "I was in bed when I heard glass breaking in the living room. By the time I got up and ran in there, the curtains and rug were on fire."

"Did you see anyone on the street? Hear anything?"

"No. It all happened so fast." A faint memory pulled at her. "Wait, there might have been a car. It seems like I heard one racing up the street, but I was so busy trying to put out the fire I didn't pay any attention."

"All right, that's a start at least," he said, relieved. "We know the bastard wasn't on foot. Do you know anyone who would do something like this to you?"

Astonished, she whirled. "Of course not!"

"Don't be so quick to answer," he cautioned. "Think about it. I'm not talking about a friend or even an acquaintance. It could be a stranger. Can you think of someone you might have accidentally ticked off without even knowing it? Maybe a customer who didn't like the way his eggs were scrambled? Someone you cut in front of in the bank line or wouldn't let in on the expressway? Anyone."

"No. I'm sorry."

"What about Rosa's boyfriend?"

"Carlos? Oh, I don't think so."

"He never made a secret of the fact that he didn't like you, did he? He even talked her into quitting to get her away from you. What if that wasn't enough? What if he felt like you were always going to be an influence in her life—unless he got rid of you? You know him better than I do. Would he try to burn you out if he got mad enough?"

Would he? She didn't want to think she was such a poor judge of character that she hadn't even guessed the guy had been capable of that kind of vindictiveness, but she couldn't be sure. And that was what really worried her. The world was full of nutcases who really got off on terrorizing women. How many of them had she had dealings with without even knowing it?

Her knees suddenly turning to jelly, she plopped down in the nearest chair. "I don't know," she said hoarsely.

"Maybe. How can anyone know what someone else will do if they crack?"

"Then we'll check him out and see if he has an alibi for last night." Making a note in the small notebook he drew from his pocket, he shot her a penetrating look. "All right, who else? Maybe a supplier you don't order from anymore? Or a neighbor who's sick of you getting up before the crack of dawn to bake?"

"No, no one. I don't have any neighbors—just other businesses, so it's not like I'm disturbing anyone or anything. And I've been using the same suppliers ever since I opened the place." Rubbing at the ache that had lodged between her brows, she frowned. "God, I can't think! Business has been good—great, in fact! Ever since that interview with Jonathan Lake—"

Suddenly realizing what she'd said, she froze, her eyes wide as they lifted to his. "Oh, God, that's it, isn't it?" she whispered, horrified, and saw the answer in his eyes. "You knew, didn't you? You knew this could be linked to whoever shot Mr. Stubbings."

"I knew it was a possibility when I heard how the fire started," he said grimly. "That's why I called in the evidence team and went back to your apartment after you went to bed last night. I got to thinking about that interview with Lake. Even though you couldn't give a physical description, the psychological one was pretty damning. If our boy was watching when it aired—and according to the overnight ratings, most of the city was—he had to be sweating bullets by the time the interview concluded. If you nailed him like I think you did, he was one desperate son of a bitch."

"So you think he was trying to kill me?"

A muscle ticked in his jaw. "Either that or scare you into shutting the hell up."

"Oh, God." Shivering, she wrapped her arms around

herself, but it didn't help. She was cold all the way to the bone. "That guy who came into the café the day after the interview aired," she muttered half to herself, "he warned me this could happen, but I just laughed. I never dreamed—"

"What guy?" he asked sharply.

"He was just some customer," she said absently. "The place was packed and everybody was talking about the interview. He was curious like everyone else and wanted to know what I could see."

"And he told you you could get hurt?"

"Well, yes, but—"

"And you didn't tell me?" he roared. "Dammit, woman, what were you thinking? He was threatening you!"

"No, he wasn't," she said, taken aback. "He was a customer. He was just making conversation."

"No," he snapped. "He was a *stranger*. Wasn't he? You didn't know him, did you?"

"Well, no."

"He was never in the café before?"

"No, but—"

"Then how do you know he wasn't the same bastard who shot Stubbings and tried to choke the stuffing out of Agatha Elliot?"

It was a logical question, one that drained the blood right out of her cheeks. Stricken, she took a step back. "No. I would have known."

"Would you?" he asked quietly. "You said you usually can't see things for yourself. Isn't it possible you could have waited on this jerk, talked to him and never suspected he was going to come back in the middle of the night and torch your place?"

God, was it? She didn't know, couldn't think. *Could* she have been so blind as to not sense a monster when he was standing right in front of her? What kind of psychic was she?

"I don't know," she said, blinking back the sudden sting of tears. "If you'd asked me this last week, I would have said no way, but now—" she shrugged "—maybe. I don't know. I guess anything's possible." Suddenly remembering the rest of the conversation, she groaned. "God, I even told him I couldn't see things for myself! Damn! How could I have been so stupid?"

"You weren't stupid," he replied. "Just trusting. How were you supposed to know he was insane enough to walk right into the café and talk to you? *If* that was even him. Sit down and tell me what you remember about him. I don't suppose there's any chance he told you his name."

Shaking her head, she sat, but only on the edge of the couch. Not surprised that she popped right back up again, he said, "Okay, we've got no name. What did he look like? Was he short? Tall? Ugly? Fat? What?"

Most people, when they were put on the spot to give a description, started with the basics—height, weight, eye color. Not Jennifer. Staring into space as if the guy stood right in front of her, she said, "He was odd."

"Odd? What do you mean by that? Odd how?"

"I don't know. Like he didn't add up or something. It's hard to describe."

"Try."

Closing her eyes, she frowned and pinched the bridge of the nose, as if bringing the picture in her head into focus. "It's like the parts didn't add up to the sum of the whole. At first glance, he looked like he was Amish or something. He was dressed in a long black coat and had a shaggy beard that looked as if it hadn't been trimmed in years. He even carried a Bible. But when I looked into his eyes, there was this coldness there that made my skin crawl."

Understanding, Sam nodded. "Go on," he said gruffly.

"And his coloring was all wrong. His skin was really white, but his eyes were nearly black."

"He could have been wearing contacts. What else was odd about him?"

"He had this strange face. I only caught a glimpse of it because he kept his head down and he was wearing a slouch hat, but his features were kind of flat, almost expressionless. I—" Blinking suddenly, she glanced up at him in amazement. "I've been racking my brain trying to figure out why he looked so weird, and it just hit me. He didn't have any eyebrows!"

"None?"

"Not a one," she said firmly. "Come to think of it, I don't even know if he had any hair at all except for his beard."

Now they were getting somewhere, Sam thought, pleased. A bald guy walking around with no eyebrows was bound to draw some attention from someone. "He probably shaved his head so he wouldn't be recognized when his hair grew out," he told her. "What about his eyelashes? What color were they?"

"Blond," she said decisively. "Which would explain his light complexion." Somber, her gaze locked with Sam's. "He does sound suspicious, doesn't he? You think he's the one? The one who burned me out and shot poor Mr. Stubbings?"

It was a logical conclusion, one Sam couldn't dismiss, not when his gut was telling him they were on the right track. "It could be a coincidence, but I don't think so," he said truthfully. "It fits. Why would anyone go to that much trouble to change their looks unless they were up to no good?"

Chapter 9

"All right, that should about do it," Emma Kitchen said in satisfaction. "What do you think?"

Seated across the table from the police artist in one of the small interview rooms at the police station, Jennifer looked at the drawing the woman held out to her and felt her blood turn to ice. When Sam had asked her if she'd mind going to the station to work with Emma, she'd reluctantly agreed, but she really hadn't thought it would do much good. Not when she only had fleeting impressions of the man she'd talked to at the café. Emma, however, had pulled things out of her she hadn't even realized she'd seen. Now, staring at the finished sketch, she wondered how she'd ever thought she hadn't gotten a clear look at the man. The image that gazed coldly back at her was, without question, the man who'd warned her she was in danger.

"That's him," she said flatly.

Standing behind her, where he'd hovered protectively

ever since they'd walked into the room, Sam squeezed her shoulder reassuringly. "Good girl. You did great. You okay?"

She nodded. "If he's the one who threw that firebomb through my window, I'll be a lot better when he's behind bars. What happens next?"

"We show the picture around, feed his description and MO into the computer to see if he's got any priors, look for witnesses."

"Witnesses? D'you think there were any?"

"It's too early to say," he said with a shrug. "Just because no one's come forward yet doesn't mean no one saw anything. Sometimes people don't realize what they've seen until days later."

"But it was so late," she argued. "Who would have been downtown at that time of night?"

"You'd be surprised," he replied. "Tourists coming in late to hotels on the river, shift workers, truck drivers. The city's never completely deserted, and a speeding car draws a lot of attention on an empty street. Someone blocks away might have seen it racing for the nearest freeway and not given it a thought. Then when they see the story on the news or read about it in the paper, they start to think about it and give us a call. If we're lucky, they not only can tell us the make and model of the car, but the license number."

And if they weren't lucky, there would be no license number, no description of the car, no witnesses. And the man who had tried to shut her up, who may have hoped to kill her, would remain free to try again.

Sam didn't say the words, but he didn't have to. She wasn't an idiot. Last night's fire was the act of a desperate man, a man who'd felt his back was to the wall, or he never would have taken such a risk. The fact that he'd failed to eliminate her as a threat would only make him more determined to succeed. It went without saying that he would be watching her. And waiting.

For one quick unguarded moment, fear clutched at her heart, and every instinct she had screamed at her to run, to hide, to find a place to lie low until the nightmare was over. But she cringed at the thought of living her life in fear. She wasn't a coward, nor as trusting as she'd been yesterday. She'd made a mistake when she'd overlooked a stranger. It wouldn't happen again.

Pushing to her feet, she said simply, "Then I guess there's nothing I can do now but wait."

She thanked Emma for making the procedure less of an ordeal than she'd anticipated, then let Sam escort her back to his car. "I want to go home," she said as soon as they were buckled up. "I've put it off long enough."

He didn't try to talk her out of it, but drove her right to the café and parked in the alley at the back. When he came around to open her car door for her, however, his face was grave. "No one would think any less of you if you put this off until tomorrow, you know. You don't have to torture yourself this way."

"I have to see how bad the damage is," she said stubbornly and stepped from the car.

But when she started toward the back entrance of the café, it wasn't damage she saw streaming out the back door, but a crowd of familiar faces coming toward her, led by Molly. Howard and Amos and Tina and a dozen others—customers from the café, people from the homeless shelters she baked bread for on Saturdays, neighbors from the businesses up and down the street. Dressed in their grungiest clothes, their hands and faces filthy with soot, they looked like a bunch of kids who'd been playing in a mud puddle.

Molly, reaching her first, hugged her fiercely, then drew back to frown down at her bandaged hands. "What's this? I thought you said you weren't hurt."

Used to her friend's scolding, she said, "I'm okay, Mother." She held up her hands and wiggled her fingers. "See? Just a few superficial burns, nothing to worry about. I didn't even have to go to the hospital, so don't scold."

"You were lucky," Molly sniffed, then hugged her again.

When she released her, Jennifer was wearing nearly as much soot as Molly was. Glancing down at herself, she looked back up and grinned quizzically at Molly and the motley group assembled behind her. "Would somebody like to tell me what's going on here? What are you doing?"

"Cleaning up," Amos Armstrong said, his lined face creased with good cheer. A security guard at the bank down the street, he ate bacon and eggs every weekday morning at the café. "I had some time coming, so I took the day off and came over to see if you could use a strong back."

"The kids are in school and I'm working the evening shift at the shelter tonight," Tina Chandler chimed in. A volunteer at one of the city's homeless shelters and the wife of one of the city's most successful trial lawyers, she had a blatant weakness for Molly's banana-cream pie and had been known to drop by several times a week for a slice. "I didn't have anything to do till school's out, so here I am. Larry said to tell you he'd try to stop by, too, after court."

The others, people she'd talked to over coffee and doughnuts and fresh bread without ever knowing too much about their personal lives, had similar stories and didn't seem to think it was the least unusual that they'd taken time from their busy schedules to help her. Emotion clogged her throat and stung her eyes. "I don't know what to say," she whispered, her smile tremulous as she blinked back tears. "You didn't have to do this."

"Yes, we did," Molly said affectionately. "What kind of friends would we be if we let you go through this all by yourself? You've been here for all of us and we're here for you. Now, enough of this maudlin stuff. You'll be happy to know that the fire never reached downstairs to the café, but we've got some serious cleaning up to do before you can even think about getting a crew in here to repair all the smoke and water damage. Why don't you find a seat inside, put your feet up and supervise?"

She couldn't of course. Not when there was so much to do. Not when friends she hadn't known she had were there to help her. "Later," she promised, and followed Molly inside.

Smoke had blackened most of the dining area, and so much water had leaked through from upstairs that it was two inches deep on the floor. She grabbed a mop and bucket and was trying to mop it up when she remembered Sam.

"Oh, God!" She hadn't even thanked him for bringing her home!

She whirled, her eyes wide, only to stop short at the sight of him standing on a chair removing soggy ceiling tiles that were in danger of falling. "What are you doing?"

"Taking these down before they hit someone on the head," he said matter-of-factly.

"But you don't have to do that. Don't you have to report back to the station?"

"Not until later. My shift doesn't start until four." He

glanced down, his eyes steady as they met hers. "You care if I stick around for a while?"

She shouldn't have let him. For a man who wanted nothing to do with her, he'd already done too much. But when she looked up into his face and felt the almost physical touch of his gaze, she couldn't for the life of her recall that moment when he'd told her goodbye. Instead, she heard the groan that rumbled through him when he kissed her and the soft reassuring words he'd murmured to her last night when he'd taken care of her better than she could have taken care of herself. He wanted to stay and she couldn't deny him.

"No," she said quietly. "But you've already done so much. I don't like imposing."

Amused, he arched a brow at her. "Are you kidding? Sweetheart, imposing is when you stop to help someone with car trouble and they not only want you to take them to get the damn car fixed, but they want you to pay for it and pick their kids up at school, too."

"You're making that up!"

"I'm not." He chuckled. "I swear. You wouldn't believe the number of people who think that because cops are public servants, we're just here for their convenience. This is nothing. Anyway," he added huskily, "I want to help."

Something passed between them then, something hot and sweet and breath-stealing that neither of them could look away from. All around, her friends were cleaning up the mess, but all she saw, all she heard, was the drumming of her own heart. Then someone dropped a pan in the kitchen and the moment was gone, shattered like the front window in her living room upstairs.

She jumped and suddenly realized that she was staring up at him with her heart in her eyes. Revealing color seeping into her cheeks, she quickly glanced away. "Just don't feel like you have to stay all afternoon. I'm sure you must have other things to do."

He did, but none of them could have dragged him away from there, from *her,* at that moment, and he didn't question why. She hadn't batted an eye at the damage the fire had wreaked in the café, but she hadn't been upstairs to her apartment yet. There was no way in hell he was letting her go through that alone. When she headed that way, he planned to be right there at her side.

"A few," he admitted, "but nothing that can't be put off until later. I'll let you know when I have to leave."

Someone called her away then, and for the next twenty minutes she was busy bailing water and hauling ruined supplies out of the pantry. Staying where he was, Sam continued to pull down the soggy ceiling tiles and never let Jennifer out of his sight. Caught up in the messy work, laughing and talking with her friends, who were determined to keep her spirits up, she seemed, at first glance, to be totally focused on the work that had to be done. But he knew the lady now, knew how she put on a smile for others so they wouldn't worry about her when in reality she was miserable. From the corner of his eye, he watched her like a hawk and wasn't surprised when her eyes darted to the café's back entrance and the outside stairway beyond. She looked away almost immediately and laughed at something Molly said, but Sam wasn't fooled. Any second now she was going to slip out when no one was looking and go upstairs to her apartment.

It took her another ten minutes before she made her move, but when she did, Sam made his, too. Everything seemed to get in his way, however. By the time he wound his way through her friends and stepped through the back entrance, Jennifer was already at the top of the stairs. He glanced up and saw her push aside the lumber the fire department had put up to block the entrance to the apartment after they destroyed her front door with an ax. He swore and hurried after her, but he'd only taken two steps when she disappeared inside.

He half expected to find her in tears, but when he quietly followed her into her apartment, she was standing just inside the entrance, tenderly wiping soot from a silver candlestick. She never looked up, but somehow she knew it was him. "This was one of my grandparents' wedding presents," she told him. "They got married in 1942, and right after the ceremony my grandfather left to join the army and fight in the war. Gran didn't see him again for more than two years."

"Must have been a tough way to start a marriage," Sam said quietly. "How long were they married?"

"Fifty-four years. Pop went first, then Gran six months later. She went to bed one night and didn't wake up. I don't think she could live without him."

She described a relationship, a marriage, that most people only dreamed of. "They must have loved each other very much."

"They finished each other's sentences and never seemed to notice." She looked up and smiled ruefully. "I guess that says it all, doesn't it?"

Shaking off her reflective mood, she changed the subject just by looking around. There was no question that the apartment was a daunting sight. The walls were black, the furniture barely recognizable charred masses. The smell of smoke was still strong, and it would be at least a week before the place dried out. Burned floors, woodwork and walls would have to be replaced, but the structure still appeared to be sound and the ceiling and roof were intact. All in all, things could have been considerably worse.

That, Sam knew by the look on her face, was little consolation. True, she'd managed to save her grandmother's candlesticks, but few of her other treasures. She had insurance for the café and apartment—the money, minus whatever deductible she carried, would be there for any and all repairs necessary to make the place livable again. But even if she'd had the foresight to insure her personal belongings, a generous check from her insurance company couldn't replace pictures of her parents and grandparents or items that had been in her family long before she'd been born. Those things were priceless—and gone forever.

He wanted to reach for her then, despite the sure knowledge that he shouldn't, but he buried his hands in his pockets and deliberately drew her attention from her loss to the positive. "This old building's tougher than it looks—the fire inspector said the beams in the floor are two feet thick, which is one of the reasons it didn't go up like a pile of matchsticks." Hitting a solid door frame, he grinned. "See? Built like a stone fort. Once the actual repairs themselves are started, you ought to be able to move back in in a week."

"A week?" she gasped. "You think all this can be fixed in a *week?*"

"Once you get estimates from your insurance company and get bids from a couple of reputable contractors? Sure," he said easily. "I know it doesn't look like it right now, sweetheart, but it's going to take longer to get all the bids and paperwork done that it is to do the repairs. You replace the floor and plasterboard, check the wiring and put in new trim and paint, and you're in business."

He made it sound so simple. Frowning, she turned to

examine the far end of the living room with new eyes and felt his hands settle on her shoulders from behind. "Look," he urged softly, his warm breath stirring her hair and caressing her ear. "Not at what's burned, but at what's not."

She tried, she really did, but any chance she had of concentrating on what was right there in front of her eyes died the second he touched her. He was behind her—she couldn't even see his hands—but when she stood still as a doe and stared straight ahead, she saw nothing but Sam. Sam, holding her, his strong hands gentle on her shoulders. Sam, leaning whisper close, his tall hard body brushing hers, setting every nerve ending tingling. Sam, all but surrounding her, warming her, melting her bones one by one. All she had to do was shift the slightest bit and she would be in his arms.

"Jennifer? You still with me, sweetheart?"

No, she almost groaned, jerking back to attention. She was way ahead of him.

Thankful he couldn't see the hot color that rushed from her toes to the roots of her hair, she nodded. "Don't mind me," she told him in a raspy voice that made her wince. "I've been drifting off all day."

Instantly sympathetic, he kneaded her shoulders and had no idea how close she came to dissolving into a puddle at his feet. "You did have a rough night," he murmured. "Maybe you should go back to my place and take a nap. Molly can keep the crowd downstairs in line."

She wanted to. God, how she wanted to! But she couldn't forget why he was back in her life. If it hadn't been for the fire, he wouldn't even be speaking to her right now, let alone offering her his bed.

Galvanized by the thought, she never remembered making a conscious decision to move, but suddenly she was all the way across the room and words were tumbling unchecked from her tongue. "No! I can't. You're used to having your space, and the apartment's too small. The bed…"

Unable to finish that thought, she shied away from it and blurted, "Alice has invited me to stay with her until I can move back in here. I'm going to do it, so you can have your bed back. I'll move in tonight."

His eyes as dark as midnight, he didn't so much as blink at her announcement. "I don't remember saying I wanted my bed back."

He hadn't, and they both knew he wouldn't. He would let her have his bed for as long as she needed it while he made do with a couch that was four inches too short for his frame. And they'd both lie alone in the dark, aching, until one of them did something about it.

Looking anywhere but at him, she said, "You didn't, but this is for the best. Please don't give me a hard time about it."

There were a dozen things she wasn't saying, and he heard every one of them. The attraction between them wasn't going to go away—that was a given. With every day it grew stronger, and to even think about living together, even for a short time, was asking for trouble. He'd kept his distance last night, but only because she'd been injured and he'd had to work. But he had to come home eventually, and she needed to be gone before he did.

He knew he should thank his lucky stars that she was being so sensible. But just the idea of letting her walk away from him made him want to throw something. God, he was pathetic! He'd already told her goodbye once. Why did he have such a hard time remembering that?

His jaw rigid, he said in a reasonable tone, which didn't come nearly as easily as he would have liked, "Just because I took you to my place last night doesn't mean you're under any obligation to continue to stay there. It was late, I didn't think you should be alone, and frankly, I didn't know where else to take you. But it was only intended as a temporary measure. You don't have to apologize because you found somewhere else to stay.''

"I'm not apologizing,'' she said, then grimaced. "Well, not exactly. It's just that what you did went above and beyond the call of duty, and I don't want you to be offended.''

"Do I look offended?'' He held his arms wide and gave her a crooked smile. ''You'll enjoy Alice, and she's going to love having you. She doesn't get much company. I'm glad you decided to take her up on her invitation. It'll be good for both of you.''

Her eyes searching his, Jennifer had to admit that he hardly looked like a man who was nursing injured feelings. But later it struck her that he hadn't hung around long after their conversation. They'd gone back downstairs to the café to join the others, and he'd left with the excuse that he needed to get some sleep before he reported to work.

Missing him already, needing some time to herself, she escaped to her office, but she'd barely settled into the chair behind her desk when there was a tap at the door. Expecting Molly, she glanced up with a smile only to gasp at the sight of Rosa standing hesitantly in the open doorway. "Can I come in?'' she asked diffidently.

"Of course!'' A pleased smile stretching across her face, Jennifer jumped up to give her a fierce hug. "What are you doing here?''

"I heard about the fire.'' Returning her hug, Rosa drew back and frowned worriedly. "Are you okay? On the news they said you were hurt.''

With a wave of her hand, Jennifer dismissed the injuries that rarely now even gave her a twinge. "It was just a few minor burns and some cuts, nothing serious. So how have you been? I thought about calling you a dozen times, but I figured you were busy, and you'd call when you could. Is everything okay at home? Sit down and tell me."

"Everything's fine. I'm still in school. And passing." She sank onto a chrome chair that was relatively free of soot. "Graduation's June second. We order our caps and gowns in January."

"That's great! Are you excited?"

"Yeah," she said softly. "It's going to be pretty neat." But her smile didn't quite reach her eyes and she couldn't seem to sit still. At last she jumped up like a jack-in-the-box and began to prowl around the office.

Jennifer leaned back in her chair and watched her. Rosa wasn't one of those teenagers who was always flitting around and couldn't sit still. Extremely self-possessed for a girl her age, she was seldom, if ever, restless.

Jennifer arched a brow at her. "You want to tell me what's wrong, or do I have to guess?"

"I..." Apparently unable to find the words she was looking for, Rosa hesitated, and suddenly her eyes flooded with tears. "God, I'm sorry."

"For crying? Don't be ridiculous, silly," Jennifer scolded. She got up and placed an arm around the girl's shoulders, then steered her back to her chair. Snatching a tissue from the box on her desk, she pressed it into her hand. "There's plenty more where that came from, so if you need to cry, you cry. But it might help to talk about it."

"I—I know. I j-just feel s-so stupid." Wiping her eyes, Rosa drew in a deep breath and let it out slowly. "It's Carlos," she said finally, shakily.

Not surprised, Jennifer didn't say a word, but she didn't have to, for Rosa went on, "I know you never liked him and you thought he was bad for me, but I really thought he cared for me. He was always so protective."

"He wasn't protective, sweetie—he was possessive. There's a difference."

Rosa nodded miserably. "I know. *Now.* I should have known it when he talked me into quitting my job with you, but I was so confused. I was working a lot and I didn't get to see him as much as I wanted to, and he made me feel guilty. I didn't know what to do, so I quit. I thought it would make things easier."

"And did it?"

"No." She sniffed. "Every time I tried to get another job, he found reasons for me not to. He didn't like the idea of me driving so far, or the hours weren't right, or he'd heard the boss couldn't keep his hands to himself. Before I realized it, I'd gone through most of my savings."

"Everything you'd been saving for college? Oh, no!"

Rosa nodded. "It was a stupid thing to do, but at the time I couldn't see anything else to do. I didn't realize how much he was controlling me—I just knew we were arguing all the time. Then this morning, when I saw the fire on the news and wanted to come right over, he *ordered* me to stay away from you and Molly and all the friends I'd made here."

The amazement in her voice changed to outrage. "Can you believe that? He was acting like my father or something and actually thought I'd say, 'Yes, sir, whatever you say, sir,' and do as I was told like a good little girl."

Her black eyes snapping fire, steam practically pouring from her ears, Rosa obviously hadn't fallen meekly into line as expected. Fighting a grin, Jennifer said dryly, "I gather you didn't."

"When you were in trouble?" Rosa said indignantly. "Of course not! We had this huge fight, a real knock-down-drag-out—"

Jennifer sobered. "Did he hit you?"

"No. He's not that stupid. But he did grab me and leave a few bruises. I don't know who was more surprised— him or me."

Outraged, Jennifer immediately reached for the phone. "I'm calling Sam."

"Detective Kelly? Oh, God, Jennifer, don't bring the police into this!" she pleaded, grabbing Jennifer's hand before she could punch in the number. "It's just a few bruises, and it's not like I'm going to see him again or anything. He took off and he won't be back—not after I told him I'd call 911 if he ever dared show his face on my doorstep again." She added with a slight grin, "I think I wounded his pride. He said I didn't have to worry. He wouldn't cross the street to see me dance naked. It's over, Jennifer. Let it go."

Any man who deliberately hurt a woman didn't deserve clemency, Jennifer thought, but if he was really out of Rosa's life, she could, for her sake, let the matter go. "All right." She sighed and replaced the receiver. "But if he ever shows up here again, I will call the police."

"Then I can have my old job back?" Rosa asked eagerly. "Three days a week after school and all day Saturdays? Pleeease? You said yourself I needed a trade to support myself when I got out of school. How'm I gonna do that if you don't keep teaching me the baking business?"

Jennifer would have liked nothing better than to hire her on the spot, but there was a slight problem. "You

know the job's yours, sweetie, *when* I reopen the café.
Trouble is, I don't know when that's going to be, and you
need a job now."

"So hire me to help you with all the work that'll have
to be done before you can open up again," Rosa suggested. "I can do anything you need done—clean up, run
errands, swing a hammer, paint. Anything! You're going
to be so busy coordinating everything, you're bound to
need some help."

"Molly will be here—"

"That's true," Rosa said quickly, "but you don't have
to wait until the rest of the place is ready to have the
kitchen up and running. We can open a to-go window.
That way, you'll be bringing in an income and we won't
lose all our customers to the competition. I can run it and
that'll leave you free to supervise the construction workers. You know how they are—if you don't keep an eye
on them, they're bound to do something you won't like,
and then it'll take more time and money to change it."

Laughing, Jennifer surrendered. "Okay, okay, I give up.
You've got a job, same hours as before. Can you start
tomorrow?"

"Tomorrow?" Rosa scoffed, dark eyes dancing. "What
are you talking about? I'll start today!"

When Sam walked into the squad room to report for
work, his co-workers took one look at his stony face and
cut a wide path around him. All, that is, except Tanner.
Sprawled comfortably behind his desk, he took one look
at his partner and immediately sat up straighter, amusement sparking in his eyes. "Uh-oh. Somebody's got
woman problems and it's not me. What's the little psychic
done now?"

"Stuff it, Tanner," Sam growled, dropping into his chair. "I don't want to talk about it."

Far from discouraged, his friend only grinned. "It's your own fault, you know. You play white knight for a lady, and the next thing you know, you're the one who's falling like a ton of bricks. Happens every time. Just like that." He snapped his fingers. "So when's the wedding? You're inviting old lady Truelove, aren't you? Now there's a gal who's probably dancing a jig. Has she said 'I told you so' yet?"

Torn between a grin and the need to bust him one, Sam jerked out of his chair and said through gritted teeth, "No, and she's not going to. There isn't going to be a wedding—at least not between me and Jennifer Hart. You got that? She's just a kid, and kids fall in and out of love a dozen times before they settle down. I've been that route once. Never again."

His voice took on that hard edge it always did whenever he spoke of his ex-wife, and that was usually all it took to warn anyone who got in his way that they were treading on thin ice. But Tanner was like a brother to him, knew things about him that no one else knew, and it took a hell of a lot more than a growl to make him back off.

"She's not Patricia, Sam," he said softly. "Not even on her worst day. She's a nice lady, and you could do a hell of a lot worse. Just because she's not an old stroke like you is no reason to write her off."

"I'm not an old stroke."

"Then the age difference shouldn't be a problem," he said simply, flashing him a triumphant grin. "Admit it, pal. You're hooked."

"And you're worse than Alice," Sam retorted. Ignoring his partner, he picked up the phone and made arrangements for a black-and-white to park across the street from

Heavenly Scents while Jennifer was there. When he hung up, Tanner was grinning from ear to ear. "You gotta say something, then say it, Bennigan! Don't just sit there grinning like a jackass."

"Oh, how the mighty have fallen." Tanner chuckled, wiping at the tears of laughter that streamed from the corners of his eyes. "I never thought I'd live to see the day."

Tanner was in one of those moods, the kind that made Sam want to laugh and shake him at the same time. There was no dealing with the guy. Grinding a string of exasperated oaths from between his teeth, Sam pushed to his feet. "Go ahead, have yourself a good laugh. I'm going to check out some things about last night's fire. If you're coming with me, you'd better get it in gear."

He didn't wait for an answer, but headed for the door. He'd only taken two steps when Tanner started in behind him, still grinning like an idiot. "I'm right behind you, partner," he said. "Lead the way."

Sam took him at his word and drove to one of the worst public housing projects in the city. Located on the west side of downtown, it was a complex of two-and three-bedroom apartments divided by paper-thin walls. Drug dealers regularly conducted business there, and in spite of frequent raids by the police, it was a hotbed of illegal gang activity.

The car was unmarked and Sam and Tanner wore no uniforms, but Mario Sandoval and the rest of the thugs who made up the Terrors made them the second they turned into the complex. Nearly six feet tall and skinny as a fence post, Mario, like his buddies, thought he was the toughest thing that had ever walked on two legs, and anybody who came onto his territory uninvited had to deal with him. By the time Sam and Tanner stepped from the car, Mario and the other gang members had them surrounded.

Sam didn't have to even glance at Tanner to know that he didn't show any more fear than he did. Lowlifes like Mario thrived on intimidation and got off on fear. If he and his fellow thugs were looking for their daily jollies, they could damn well look somewhere else.

"Look, Tanner, we got us a welcoming party. Ain't that nice?" Sam drawled. "Now we've only got to ask our questions once. Now, who wants to tell us about the hot little cocktail that was thrown through the window of an apartment on Commerce last night at about one-thirty? It had the Terrors handwriting all over it."

"Oh, no, you don't!" Mario said harshly. "You're not pinning that one on us! We wasn't anywhere near Commerce last night."

"Yeah, and we're Santa's little helpers," Tanner retorted. "If you weren't lighting fires downtown, then where were you?"

"You wanna know, you take me to the station and ask me in front of my lawyer," Mario said coldly. "Otherwise, I ain't talking."

"You'd rather have us haul you in than cooperate?" Sam taunted. "Whatever makes you happy. We'll haul all your asses in. Tanner, get on the radio and call for backup—"

"No!"

His eyes stone cold, Sam growled, "Then talk. The Terrors have a reputation for hurling cocktails at anyone who rats on them, and whoever threw that one last night headed straight this way. Give me one good reason why we should believe you aren't in this up to your neck."

"Because we were at the gym playing midnight basketball," he said triumphantly. "If you don't believe me, ask the security guard there. He'll tell you we didn't leave until two-thirty."

Chapter 10

By the time she thanked everybody for their help and made her way back to the Lone Star Social Club, Jennifer was so tired she could hardly put one foot in front of the other. Every bone in her body ached, and all she wanted was a hot bath and a bed, in that order.

She'd called Alice earlier in the day to let her know she was taking her up on her offer to stay there until she could move back into her apartment. When she stepped through the older woman's front door now, dinner was cooked and waiting for her on the back porch, where Alice was lighting candles on an old wonderfully ornate wicker table. She'd already brought out the food and filled their tea glasses, and in the flickering light of the candle, the scene looked like something out of *The Great Gatsby*.

Delighted, Jennifer must have made a sound because Alice looked up from lighting a second candle, her blue eyes sparkling. "I hope you don't mind eating out on the veranda, dear. I know it's almost November, but it feels like spring, doesn't it? If I didn't know better, I'd swear I could smell the mountain laurel in the air.''

Closing her eyes, Jennifer sniffed, a smile tracing her lips, only to feel her heart lurch in surprise as the sweet scent of mountain laurel drifted teasingly under her nose. Her eyes flew open. "My God, you're right! But how can that be? Mountain laurels don't bloom until March or April."

Not the least disturbed, Alice smiled serenely. "It's the house, dear. There's a magic in the air here that you won't find anywhere else. Time, seasons, *years* just seem to ebb and flow from one to the other and back again. Sometimes, if you sit very still and just listen to your heart, it's impossible to tell if you're in this century or the last."

Jennifer could just imagine what Sam would say to that, but she, more than most, knew just how possible the impossible was. Intrigued by the idea of looking back in time, she closed her eyes and let her mind drift. And just for a second, against the backdrop of her closed eyelids, the restaurants and shops along the River Walk faded, then disappeared altogether, and from the back veranda of the social club, she caught a glimpse of a San Antonio that hadn't existed for a hundred years.

Fascinated, she wanted to see more, but then someone at a riverside table at the restaurant across the river laughed, and the image vanished. When she glanced up, Alice was watching her with a knowing twinkle in her eyes. "You saw something, didn't you?" she said.

Jennifer nodded. "The river before the River Walk was built. But I don't understand how. I've always been able to look into the future, never the past."

Understanding perfectly, she reached for Jennifer's plate and served her a healthy portion of the chicken casserole she'd made for supper. "There are some people who come into this house and never see anything but the here and now. Then there are others, like you, who are more sensitive, who catch scents and sounds and images no one else can. It always amazes me who sees what. Can you pick up anything else besides the flowers?"

Jennifer would have sworn she was too tired to see anything, but when she closed her eyes, she couldn't help but chuckle. "Is there a place on the stairs that always makes you feel like laughing?"

Alice gasped. "Why yes, there is! But I never told anyone about it because I thought it was just my imagination."

Her eyes still closed, Jennifer grinned. "There was a cowboy sometime after the Civil War—he must have been a real rounder. But the women loved him. One summer night he rode his horse right up the stairs to the ballroom."

"Oh, my!" Alice laughed. "I had no idea."

Enthralled, Jennifer told her stories of lovesick cowboys, an outlaw judge and a railroad baron's daughter from the East who tamed the most dangerous man in town. They were outrageous tales, and if only half of what she saw really happened, she could see why stories about the Lone Star Social Club still circulated through the city almost a hundred years after it closed its doors.

Caught up in the stories, they both ate with hearty appetites and never noticed the passage of time. Then, just when Jennifer was sure she couldn't eat another bite, Alice produced a chocolate cake that had to have ten thousand calories. "Stop!" she groaned. "Sam just bought these jeans for me. You keep feeding me like this, and I'm going to need a bigger size by the end of the week."

Grinning, Alice cut her a piece that would have done a pro football player proud and set it in front of her. "You could use a little weight on you—you're too thin. A man likes a woman with some meat on her bones. If your jeans get a little tight, I'm sure you won't hear Sam complaining. He's nuts about you.''

"Alice!"

"Well, it's true, dear. Just because I'm old doesn't mean I don't still have eyes in my head. He'd walk across a burning bridge for you—he just doesn't realize it yet. But he will. It's only a matter of time. I've seen harder men than him try to fight the power of love, but they can't win. Not in this house.''

Confused, Jennifer frowned. "What does the house have to do with anything?''

"What does it have to do..." Surprised she even had to ask, Alice laughed. "Why, everything! Haven't you heard about the legend?'' At Jennifer's blank look, she exclaimed, "My God, you haven't! Oh, dear. That might change things, but I don't see how. It never has before. I keep forgetting that you've only lived here a short while. I guess that's why I just assumed you knew...''

Amused at her rambling, Jennifer arched a brow. "Assumed I knew what? Alice, I haven't got a clue what you're talking about.''

The old woman grimaced. "I know. I'm sorry. In case you hadn't noticed, I do have a tendency to go on at times, especially about this house.'' Gathering her thoughts, she drew a calming breath and let it out with a smile. "You already know the house has a special magic to it...''

"Yes, the spirits—''

"No, it's more than that. People didn't stop falling in love here just because social clubs went out of fashion. I guess you could say bringing people together, helping them find their mates, is ingrained in the very walls. And whenever a single person moves in here, the magic just seems to rub off on them.''

"What do you mean? How?"

"They meet someone and fall in love within the year. *Every single time.*"

She was so serious, Jennifer couldn't help but laugh. "Oh, c'mon, Alice! You don't really believe that, do you? What about Sam? He's lived here a lot longer than a year, hasn't he?"

"True, but he was married when he moved in, and his divorce wasn't final until six months ago. I've never seen a more bitter man," she confided solemnly. "He told me that if he ever even looked at another woman under thirty again, I had his permission to shoot him with own his service revolver. And he was serious! That was just this past summer. Now he's involved with you."

"But not romantically," Jennifer said, blushing. "Oh, he's kissed me a couple of times, I admit, but that doesn't mean anything. To be perfectly honest, I don't even know if he likes me!"

Grinning at her miffed expression, Alice cut herself a generous portion of cake and said dryly, "I've seen the way he looks at you when he thinks no one's watching, and he much more than likes you. Just be patient. He'll come around. And while you're waiting, you might start looking at wedding dresses. You're going to need one."

"Alice!"

"Well, it's true," she said, grinning. "I've lived here a long time—I've seen the spell this house weaves around people. Trust me, it packs a powerful punch when just one of the parties lives here. Now that you and Sam are both under the same roof, you haven't got a chance."

Her stomach flip-flopping at the thought, Jennifer told herself that Alice was just kidding. No one believed in the mystical powers of the universe more than she did, and there was no denying that the house had an aura distinctly its own. But there was no way four walls and a roof could bring together two people and make them fall in love. It was nice in a fairy tale, but such things didn't happen in the real world.

Alice, however, believed the legend with all her heart. One glimpse at the confident glint in her eyes and Jennifer knew she could talk until she was blue in the face and it wouldn't change the woman's mind. "I guess time will tell, then, won't it?" she said easily, and let it go.

Later, however, when the lights were out and she was comfortably stretched out in the bed in Alice's guest room, so weary she should have dropped right off to sleep the second she was horizontal, the conversation replayed itself again and again in her head. Disgusted, Jennifer told herself that only a desperate old maid would make the mistake of buying into such a tale.

But what if it was true?

The thought tempted and tantalized and enticed, and then, as if on cue, she heard the music. Soft and low, it was hardly more than a whisper on the night air. She caught her breath for a second and cocked her head to listen. One of the nightspots farther up the river must have turned up their speakers, she decided. But as she tried to figure out what the haunting melody was, she realized it was a waltz. A lilting, old-fashioned, romantic waltz.

And it was coming from the ballroom in the attic.

She went perfectly still, the thumping of her heart loud in her ears as she recalled the stories Alice had told her about the ballroom and the music that could sometimes be heard coming from there. Could anyone else hear it now? How could they not? It seemed to grow louder by the second.

Rolling onto her back, she stared up at the darkened ceiling and could have sworn a live orchestra was playing two stories above her. What was going on up there? If she listened harder, could she hear the slide of feet on the wooden floor as couples twirled in time to the music? If she went up there, could she see them? Before the thought had fully registered, she was throwing back the covers and padding in her bare feet to the guest-room door.

The apartment was dark and from the other side of Alice's closed bedroom door came the steady drone of snoring loud enough to wake the dead. Grinning, Jennifer silently stole through the shadowy apartment and let herself out into the hall. There, the music was clearer, sweeter. Humming, her eyes already adjusted to the lack of light, she started up the stairs in the dark.

With every step she climbed, the music got louder. By the time she neared the third-floor landing, she didn't know how anyone in the house slept. Surely they had to hear it! But no lights flickered on downstairs and the rest of the house's occupants continued to sleep. Amazed, Jennifer took the final step into the ballroom and stopped dead in her tracks.

Candles. They were everywhere. Long white tapers dripping wax from wall sconces and chandeliers, they cast a golden glow over a ballroom that looked like something out of an old Currier and Ives lithograph. In a corner on the opposite side of the room, a small but complete orchestra played a waltz, while in the center of the ballroom, women in hooped dresses dipped and swirled and turned to the lilting strains of the music. It all looked so real that Jennifer could have reached out and touched them if she'd just lifted her hand, but she was afraid to move, afraid to chance shattering the magic of the moment.

All his senses on alert, his service revolver loaded and in his hand, Sam silently followed the shadowy figure up the stairs and wondered how the hell the sneaky bastard had gotten in. The front door had been locked when he'd come in at the end of his shift, just as it always was, the security system armed and ready to scream at the first sign of a break-in. The house was silent, however, which was why he'd been so shocked when he'd spied someone clinging to the shadows and creeping up the stairs like a thief in the night. Who the hell was it? And why the devil was he going all the way up to the attic? Nothing was up there but a few old pieces of furniture. He knew—he'd helped Alice cart them up there for storage.

His eyes trained on the shadowy figure above him in the darkness, he closed the distance between them, instinctively avoiding all the squeaky spots on the stairs. A little closer and he'd have the jerk, he thought grimly as the intruder reached the top step and just seemed to hover at the entrance to the attic. What the hell was he looking at?

His fingers tightening on the butt of his revolver, he was two steps from the top when the faint light from the attic windows illuminated the woman standing on the landing. Swearing, he quickly reholstered his weapon.

"Dammit, Jennifer, what the devil are you doing up here in the dark?" he asked. "I thought someone had broken into the house!"

She whirled to face him and didn't seem to have the least idea how close he'd come to taking her down like a common crook. "Sam! Thank God you're here!" Her eyes shining, she grabbed him by the arm and tugged him up beside her. "I want someone else to see this besides me. Look!"

Turning back to the attic, she motioned to the huge shadowy expanse that opened before them like a cavern. Cloaked in murky darkness, there was nothing to see but a few hulking wardrobes that were crowded together in one corner and shrouded in dust covers.

From the glow on her face he could see even in the poor light, Sam knew he was missing something, but for the life of him he didn't know what. "Okay," he said in a gruff whisper that wouldn't float down the stairwell and wake the rest of the house, "I give up. What am I supposed to see? It's just an attic. Most old houses have them."

"Just an attic?" She stared up at him amazement. "My God, you really don't see it, do you?"

Puzzled, Sam glanced back at the obscure shadows that stretched before them. "If you're talking about something besides a dark attic, then no, I guess I don't. What am I missing?"

She gazed at the festive scene unfolding before her, a smile curling her mouth. "A ball," she said huskily. "You know—like something out of *Cinderella*. There are all theses candles and flowers, and the orchestra in the corner is playing a waltz. Can't you hear it? It's wonderful. The women are wearing these incredible hooped dresses that sway when they dance, and the men are all stiff and formal as they hold their partners at just the proper degree of closeness. It's wonderful."

She closed her eyes and hummed the melody that only she could hear, her body unconsciously swaying in time. Watching her, hearing nothing but the melody she hummed, seeing nothing but her, Sam only just then realized she was barefoot and wearing nothing but the flannel gown he'd bought her that morning.

He felt heat curl into his gut and knew he had no business being alone with her up there in the attic in the dark. She was decently covered—he could barely see her—but a smart man would have escorted her back to Alice's apartment before he was tempted to do something stupid. But even as the thought nagged at him, he gave in to an insane desire to pull her into his arms for a waltz only she could hear.

He should have felt like a fool. There were no candles, no lights, no other couples swirling around them. It was just the two of them whirling around the dusty floor in the unlit attic, dipping and swaying to the music of an orchestra that hadn't played there for a hundred years. If any of the other occupants of the social club's apartments had chanced upon them, they'd have thought they'd both lost their minds. But if this was insanity, he wanted to drown himself in it. Nothing had ever felt so right in his life.

He was in trouble, but he didn't care. Not when it seemed like forever since he'd held her. With a murmur of pleasure she melted against him as if there was nowhere else in the world she'd rather be, and just that quickly, any chance he had of keeping his head flew right out the window. She felt like heaven in his arms. Her cheek found the hollow of his shoulder, her breasts nestled against the hard wall of his chest, and her hips sweetly brushed his. Need settled hot and hard in his loins.

And for one heart-stopping moment he could have sworn he heard the haunting strains of a waltz.

He told himself it was nothing more than his imagination.

Something that drifted downriver from one of the restaurants that specialized in romance. Something his mind had conjured up at her suggestion. A fantasy. That was all it could be.

But the woman in his arms was no fantasy. She was soft and sexy and probably naked under her gown. And he wanted her so badly that he could hardly remember a time when just the thought of her hadn't made him hard.

When he whirled with her in his arms and she looked up, laughing, it seemed the most natural thing in the world to lean down and kiss her.

A kiss. Just one. He swore that was all he'd intended. But the second his mouth settled on hers and he tasted the heat of her response, he was intoxicated. The floor could have fallen away beneath his feet and he never would have noticed. Murmuring her name, he tightened his arms around her and lost himself in the sweetness of her.

Her senses swimming, her heart pounding, Jennifer clung to him and tried to remember why she shouldn't. But his hands were slow and sure, caressing her, claiming her as if he had every right, and she couldn't think. *This* was what she wanted, what she'd ached for in the middle of the night when there was a fever under her skin and she couldn't sleep. Sam kissing her, holding her, sweeping them both into passion without a care to tomorrow. Nothing mattered but this...Sam...the two of them together... finally.

If he'd found a dozen reasons to walk away from her in the past, tonight he couldn't seem to let her go. Drawing her up on her toes, he wrapped his arms around her as if he would draw her into his very heart, and she gloried in it. Then he kissed her again. Then a third time. Long hot searing kisses that aroused and seduced and mesmerized. And all the while the music, the magic, throbbed in her blood.

Somewhere in the back of her mind she knew she'd lost all reason, but she couldn't find the strength to care. Unfamiliar yearnings twisted and coiled in her, driving her on. Blindly moving against him, seeking something she couldn't name, she rubbed her breasts, swollen and sensitive, against the hard wall of his chest, but it only intensified the ache that had lodged low in her belly. Whimpering, she crowded closer.

She couldn't have said what she needed, but he knew. Fighting the folds of her gown, he dragged up the soft material until it bunched around her waist, then filled his hands with her bare bottom and pulled her tight against his arousal. Her knees buckled, and in the hushed darkness of the attic, her muffled cry echoed to the rooftop.

"Easy, sweetheart," he soothed thickly, even as his fingers stroked and teased and drove her crazy. "God, your skin's like silk. I've got to touch you, just for a minute...."

Her mind blurring, no longer aware of anything but the liquid fire in her center that burned hotter with every stroke of his fingers, she tugged at his clothes, desperate to touch him as he touched her. "Make love to me," she moaned. "Please, Sam. I want you to make love to me."

He groaned and almost lost it right there. But as much as he wanted her, he hadn't completely taken leave of his senses. She was a virgin, ignorant of men, and didn't even know what she was asking for. For no other reason than that, he should have found the strength to put her from him. But right from the beginning he hadn't been able to keep his distance from her, and instead of easing her away and taking a couple of deep breaths to clear his head, he tightened his arms around her.

Every instinct he had urged him to sweep her up and carry her off to his bed. Now. While the world was asleep and they had the night all to themselves. Before she remembered how hard he'd tried to walk away from her. But he had to be able to look himself in the mirror in the morning, and he couldn't do that if he rushed her into something in the heat of the moment that she wasn't really ready for.

Drawing back slightly, his eyes met hers in the darkness. "Be sure this is what you want, honey," he said fiercely. "Because I want you so much now my teeth ache. If I get you in my bed, get you under me, I don't know how I'd find the strength to let you go if you changed your mind."

Heat fired her cheeks at his bluntness, but her gaze never flinched from his. "I won't," she promised huskily. "It's what I want."

"How can you be sure of that when you've never made love before?"

If she was surprised that he'd guessed she was a virgin, she didn't show it. Instead, she took his hand and dared to lift it to her heart. "I know it here," she said softly, making him suck in a sharp breath. "That's all I need to know."

Up until then he'd liked to think he was in control of the passion she stirred in him so effortlessly. But when she cupped his fingers on her breast and looked up at him with such trust in her fathomless green eyes, he knew he'd never been in control, not even in the beginning. She smiled and made him burn. She touched him, sweetly offered herself to him, and she destroyed him. Helpless to resist her, he scooped her up in his arms. "Not here," he said hoarsely. "I want you in my bed."

He carried her down the stairs and through the door of his apartment, going straight back to his bedroom without bothering to turn on a single light. Later, he promised himself, he would turn on the bedside lamp and treat himself to the sight of her, but this first time, he couldn't seem to let go of her long enough to do anything but jerk back the covers and set her down in the moonlight that streamed in through the window to pool in the center of his bed. A split second later he was lowering himself beside her, his arms closing around her as his mouth found hers.

She turned to him and gave him back kiss for kiss, but he felt the tension in her, the nerves that wouldn't let her completely relax, and suddenly the control he'd thought had deserted him was back. Clamping a lid on the need that clawed at him, he reminded himself that she was an innocent. If he came on to her like a sex-starved maniac, he was going to scare the hell out of her.

Gentling his mouth on hers, he kissed her softly, sweetly, his tongue teasing, stroking, tenderly seducing. When she sighed in pleasure, the sound hardly more than a whisper in the night, all his fine resolves nearly came undone. He wanted her now, naked beneath him, opening to him, taking his aching flesh into her hot, wet, silken depths. But somehow he kept his touch light, his kiss slow and easy, as if he had all the time in the world. And slowly she responded, like a flower in the sun. The tension drained out of her, the stiffness in her muscles melted away, and her hands reached for him, drawing him closer.

"That's right, sweetheart," he murmured. "Just relax and let me take care of you. You know I won't hurt you."

Deep in her soul, she knew he'd cut off his right arm before he'd let anyone, including himself, harm her. She could trust him, or she never would have let him come anywhere near her. But although she knew the rudimentary facts about making love, it was the little things she didn't know that made her nervous. Like when did you take your clothes off and what was she supposed to do with her hands? What if she was frigid? How did a woman know something like that about herself if she'd never made love before?

Horrified that she was and he would be terribly disappointed in her, she stiffened. "Oh, God, Sam, what if I'm frigid?"

His mouth twitched, unexpected amusement gleaming in his eyes before he quickly blinked it away. "Trust me, honey, you're not frigid. You could never respond to me the way you do if you were. So quit worrying, Okay? Everything's going to be fine."

Her eyes still troubled, she stared up at him in the darkness. "You'll tell me if there's a problem?"

"You'll be the first to know," he assured her solemnly, then stopped any further protests with a fierce kiss. He didn't give her time to worry about disappointing him, but simply set about the business of slowly driving her out of her mind. Tearing his mouth from hers, he kissed his way down her throat while his fingers worked unsuccessfully at the buttons of her gown. Swearing, he gave up in defeat, palmed her breast through the material of her gown, then took her straining nipple into his mouth.

"Sam!"

"I know, sweetheart," he growled, curling his tongue around her nipple, undeterred by the thin dampened fabric. "It feels good, doesn't it? It'd feel even better if you unbuttoned those itty-bitty buttons for me. They weren't made for my fumbling hands."

Caught in the heat of his gaze, her breast throbbing from the wet warmth of his mouth, she lifted trembling fingers to the series of small pearl buttons that marched down the center of her chest. With little effort the buttons slid free one by one. Heat climbing in her cheeks, she slowly parted her gown, baring her breasts, and then his mouth was on her, sucking, and she could hardly bear the pleasure. She moaned and clutched him to her, wanting the moment to never end.

But there was more. Much more. Her head was still

spinning when he stripped the gown from her, then tore off his own clothes. As his weight carefully pressed her into the mattress, they were both gloriously naked, and nothing had ever felt so good.

On fire for her, Sam groaned at the feel of her under him. God, he wanted her! Hot and fast, slow and easy, any way he could get her. He wanted to make her cry out at his touch and come apart in his arms. Capturing her hands, he dragged them above her head and anchored them to the mattress with one of his own. In the darkness he saw her eyes widen, felt the shudder of awareness that rippled through her. Then his free hand was sliding down her body, caressing her breasts, measuring the narrowness of her waist, dipping lower to tease and flirt with the soft heated heart of her femininity.

She cried out, startled, her eyes glazed. Swooping down, he took her mouth in a savage kiss, letting her taste the need that licked at him like fire. And all the while, his fingers circled and dipped and gently played with her sensitive flesh, making her gasp and whimper and plead.

Torture. It was the sweetest kind of torture. His own needs raking at him, he groaned as her hips instinctively lifted to his stroking fingers. "That's it, baby," he murmured. "Go with it. God, you're sweet!"

Through the cloud of passion that fogged her brain, she heard him whispering to her, coaxing her to give herself to him. And she was helpless to resist. Sobbing, needing to touch him, to wrap herself around him and find release in his arms, she strained against his hold. "Sam, please! I can't stand this! Let me go!"

But he wouldn't listen. Not until he had her writhing under him, her body tight with need. Before she'd even realized he'd released her hands, he parted her thighs and settled himself between them. In the warm darkness, her eyes met his and she never thought to be afraid. Not of him. Never of him. If she knew nothing else in life, she knew that.

Because she loved him.

The thought slipped out of the darkness to steal her breath, and she could do nothing but stare at him. Where? How? When? The questions flew at her from all directions and she couldn't answer any of them. Not when he was this close, and she ached for him with every fiber of her being.

She wanted, needed to tell him. But then his fingers linked with hers, and he began to slowly ease into her, filling her, inexorably pushing until he came up against the wall of her virginity. She instinctively stiffened against the pain, but there was no escaping it—not then, and not when the delicate tissue suddenly tore free and he surged into her with a low rumbling groan of satisfaction.

Gasping, a flood of emotions swamping her in waves, Jennifer felt tears well in her eyes and could do nothing to stop them from spilling over her lashes. She'd read enough books and seen enough movies to know what to expect, but no one had warned her that simply by taking her, he would stake a claim on her very soul. It was beautiful, frightening, overwhelming. And terribly, so terribly intimate.

His expression as fierce as a hawk's, he leaned down to kiss away the tears that silently trailed down her cheeks. "Are you okay?" he rasped.

She nodded, her smile tremulous. "I didn't expect..."

She couldn't find the words, but he understood. "I know. I didn't, either." Then he moved, and she gasped at the sensations that rippled through her like heat lightning. Urgency filled her and fueled her blood, and with a sob, she lifted her hips to his again and again in a rhythm that pounded like thunder in her veins. She heard him murmur encouragement to her, felt his hands close around her hips and lift her into his thrusts, and thought she was surely going to die of the hot unbearable tension that consumed her.

Insanity. There was no other way to describe it. He'd taken control of her head and her heart and her body, and was driving her unrelentingly toward an end she couldn't see. Then, before she was ready, they were upon it, and she could no more have pulled back than she could have stopped the rising and setting of the sun.

With a cry that rose to the rafters, she hurtled over the edge into the unknown.

Dazed, pleasure rippling through her like wildfire, she dimly heard Sam's own shout, and then he was convulsing in her arms. At last he collapsed against her, his body heavy, his breath warm and enticing as he buried his face in her neck. Feeling boneless, she curled her arms around him and held him close, a sleepy smile tugging at the corners of her mouth. So this was what all the fuss was about. Now she could see why people did stupid things for love. She'd never felt more complete in her life.

Chapter 11

Sam reached for her twice more during the night. He couldn't help himself. She was in his blood, a thirst he couldn't seem to quench, and in the all-concealing darkness, there was no tomorrow, no yesterday to make him stop and think about what he might be getting himself into. There was just Jennifer, in his bed, in his arms.

But with the coming of dawn, there was no darkness to hide behind, no shadows to conceal the love lighting her face when he awoke to find her lying close, smiling at him dreamily. His eyes tracing the enticing curve of her mouth, he felt his heart shift and knew that if he wasn't already in love with her, he was damn close. If things had been different...

But they weren't. And no one regretted that more than he did. She might be twenty-four years old, but if last night had done nothing else, it had proved to him once and for all just how innocent she was. No doubt she thought she was in love! But she'd never even had a boyfriend before, let alone a lover. For the first time in her life, she was dealing with good old-fashioned lust, and just like every young girl with stars in her eyes, she thought it was love. When she was more experienced, she'd know better.

His gut clenching at the thought of another man touching her, something of his feelings must have shown in his face. The soft glow in her eyes dimmed. "Obviously I don't have any experience with mornings after," she said quietly. "Is this where you tell me last night was a mistake?"

He winced, unable to deny it. "I don't want to hurt you."

"No, I don't think you do," she agreed, surprising him. "But that's not going to change anything, is it? You're still dumping me and turning last night into nothing but a one-night stand." With a dignity he couldn't help but admire, she clutched the covers to her bare breasts and sat up against the headboard to face him. "I think I've got a right to know why."

Any other woman would have cried and raged and accused him of leading her on just so he could get her into bed. But not Jennifer. Oh, no. Unconcerned that the only thing hiding her nakedness from him was a sheet, she looked him right in the eye, her hurt as obvious as an open wound, and insisted that he explain himself. He'd never felt more like a heel. God, she was something!

"I'm not dumping you," he said irritably.

She laughed, but there was little humor in the sound. "That's easy for you to say. Trying sitting where I am and you might change your mind."

"You don't understand..."

"No, I don't. So make me."

Swearing, he threw back the covers, reached for his

jeans and rose naked from the bed. He heard her gasp, but he was too agitated to worry about her sensibilities. Stepping into his jeans, he hauled up the zipper and just barely missed injuring himself.

Then he whirled to confront her. "Do you think I like doing this? I care about you, dammit! And after last night, you sure as hell can't deny I want you. But that isn't always enough. Believe me, I know, honey. I've got the scars to prove it."

Pacing, he didn't see her go pale. "You're talking about your ex-wife."

"She was a kid when I met her, barely twenty-two. Not much younger than you," he said. "And an innocent. She wanted a husband and babies and a life right out of 'Father Knows Best,' and she thought I could give it to her. The only problem was I wasn't Robert Young, and the real world's nothing like a TV show. I couldn't be home every night at five for the dinner she'd slaved over all afternoon. Hell, there were times I had to work double shifts and was lucky if I got to see her two or three nights a week."

"You're a cop," Jennifer said stiffly. "She must have realized when she married you that you were never going to work banker's hours."

He shrugged. "Maybe. To be perfectly honest I didn't know what was going on in her head. We never had that much in common, but I figured as long as I loved her and we got along in bed, nothing else mattered. Six months after we were married, she was bored and lonely and went looking for someone to keep her company. It was three months before I even had a clue she was fooling around. I came home unexpectedly one night when I was supposed to be working and found her in our bed with another man."

"So are you saying that because one woman cheated on you, another one will? That *I* will?"

"You're young," he said flatly. "And inexperienced. And like most young girls, I'm sure you want the fairy tale—the husband, the castle and happily-ever-after."

"Did I say I wanted those things? I don't remember even hinting at anything of the kind."

She didn't have to. He could see the pain of disenchantment in her eyes. And he hated it. Hated himself for putting it there. The last thing he wanted to do was hurt her, but this was a discussion he'd put off for too long.

"No, you didn't say anything," he retorted, "but just for the record, don't get caught up in Alice's stories about this house. That's all they are—stories. Happily-ever-after doesn't exist in real life, and magic doesn't last."

His words cut her to the bone, but it was the disillusionment in his eyes that really hurt her. He was wrong. True love *did* last—she'd seen it every day of her life in her grandparents' eyes when she was growing up. She just hadn't thought she'd ever find it for herself. Now that she had, she wanted what her grandparents had had. She wanted fifty or more years of waking up in his bed, finishing his sentences, loving him to distraction. She would, in fact, settle for nothing less; and the sooner he knew that, the better.

"If that's the way you feel, I can't do anything about that. But just for the record, I'm the best thing that ever happened to you. I love you," she said boldly, knowing he would rather not hear the words but saying them, anyway. "And it's got nothing to do with the magic that really is in this house. If we'd met on a mountaintop in Tibet, I'd still feel the same, and that's not ever going to change. If that makes you uncomfortable," she said when his brows snapped together in a scowl, "I'm sorry, but I thought you should know."

"I'm not uncomfortable, dammit! I'm just concerned about you."

"Don't be," she said with a rueful smile. "Because although I can't see anything for myself, I know you've got something wonderful waiting for you down the road, and I've got to believe that it's me."

Unfazed by his fierce scowl, she said lightly, "Now that we've got that settled, I'd appreciate it if you'd hand me my gown so I can get out of here. I want to hit the ground running at the café today, and the sooner I get over there, the better."

He wanted to argue—she could see it in his eyes—but her smile was steady, her attitude all business, and what, after all, could he say? He'd wanted her out of his bed and she was leaving without a fuss. Grinding an obscenity between his teeth, he grabbed her gown up from the spot he'd tossed it last night and handed it to her without a word. Striding to the window, he turned his back to her, giving her privacy to dress.

She'd meant every word she'd said about his future and her place in it, but that didn't make leaving him any easier. How she got out of there without falling apart, she never knew. Once she was decently covered by her gown, she felt more in control, but when he walked her to the front door of his apartment, she was horribly afraid he was going to insist on escorting her all the way downstairs to Alice's door, and that she couldn't have borne.

Stepping over his threshold into the upstairs hallway, she stopped and turned to face him. It was still early, the house quiet, her voice low as she said, "There's no need for you to walk me downstairs. It's not that far and I know the way. Goodbye, Sam."

She would have held her hand out to him and ended it all with a businesslike handshake, but one look at his stony expression and she changed her mind. This was what he wanted, she reminded herself as she turned toward the stairs and started down them. After the hell of his ex-wife's betrayal, she could understand how leery he would be of letting her or any other woman get close to him. But *she* wasn't the one who'd hurt him. Giving him the time he needed to realize that was going to be the hardest thing she'd ever done.

In spite of all her firm resolve, though, she couldn't believe he would just stand there and let her walk out of his life. But every step she took brought her farther away from him, and he never said a word. She reached the ground floor, and the only sound from above was that of his apartment door quietly, but firmly, shutting. He couldn't have hurt her more if he'd stabbed her in the heart. Still, she didn't cry. She couldn't and not still hold on to the hope that she was his destiny.

She'd already decided she wasn't going to tell Alice anything about their breakup and put the woman in the uncomfortable position of choosing sides. But the minute Alice opened her apartment door to her quiet knock, she took one look at her face and said, "What's wrong?"

Jennifer had to smile. Alice hadn't batted an eye at the sight of her standing in the hall in her bare feet and night-gown, but one look at her sad face, and she puffed up like a mother hen.

Suddenly the words came tumbling out. "I'm in love with Sam and he dumped me because he thinks I'm just like his ex-wife. He even warned me not to believe the stories about this house because there's no such thing as happily-ever-after and magic doesn't last."

Wiping at her eyes, she half expected Alice to bristle

at the dig about the house, but amazingly she only laughed. "Oh, he did, did he? Well, I'm glad to hear it. Because the more someone fights the magic of this old house, the harder he falls. You hang in there, dear. He'll come around. You just wait."

Considering the circumstances, there was nothing Jennifer *could* do but wait. Time, she convinced herself, was her best friend. And living at the Lone Star Social Club could only help her cause. She would be close, but just out of reach. And that just might be what Sam Kelly needed to shake him up.

Or at least that was what she thought until she walked through the Lone Star's front door later that afternoon and came face-to-face with Sam. He was on his way out, his thoughts elsewhere. He looked up, saw her right in front of him and stopped dead in his tracks. He nodded a greeting, but his expression was grim, as was the silence that neither of them seemed able to break. When he finally stepped around her and continued on outside, it was all she could do not to cry.

If she'd had anywhere else to go, she would have moved out that night. As much as she hated to cut and run like a coward, she knew now she couldn't stay there for long, not if Sam was going to freeze up every time he saw her. She couldn't bear it. She'd just have to get her apartment fixed up as soon as possible. It was the only solution.

The first thing she did the next morning when she arrived at the café was haul out the telephone book and start calling contractors who specialized in remodeling. She pleaded and begged and bullied and finally convinced four of them to stop by as soon as they could that day to assess the damage and give her a bid. When the first one arrived before noon and walked through both her apartment and the café, she could have cried with relief when he told her he could get started on the job by the end of the week if she accepted his bid. The three others told her the same thing when they arrived that afternoon. By the time she was ready to lock up at the end of the day, she was feeling better than she'd dared to hope. Once she got the verbal bids in writing and checked references, all she needed was the go-ahead from her insurance company to get started later in the week.

Half-afraid she would run into Sam in the hall again, she spent long hours at the café and her apartment cleaning and hauling out debris. And whenever she was there, there was always a patrol car parked across the street. She knew Sam was responsible for that and liked to think he'd ordered the extra security because he loved her and wanted to make sure she was safe until the thug who tried to burn her out was caught. In the back of her mind, however, a caustic little voice reminded her that she was the only one who'd seen the perpetrator without a mask. In all likelihood, Sam was just protecting a valuable witness.

The truth hurt, but she had a lot of work to do, and that helped. On Friday morning workers arrived at dawn to begin the repairs to her apartment. Charred walls and burnt flooring were torn out, and soon the whine of electric saws, followed by the pounding of hammers, was so loud you could hardly hear yourself think. Jennifer loved it.

By the time she got back to the Lone Star that evening, she couldn't stop rattling on to Alice about how much work the construction crew had accomplished in only a day. At the rate they were going, she could move back home just as soon as the broken front window was replaced and the apartment had been rewired.

"Oh, surely not so soon!" Alice cried, surprised. "You just moved in. And you haven't seen Sam at all."

"Because that's the way he wants it," Jennifer told her. "And what do you mean I just moved in? I've been here a week already. And it's not like I'm moving out today or tomorrow. I just wanted you to know that if the rest of the repairs go as well as they did today, it won't be too much longer until I'm out of your hair."

Alice sniffed at that. "It's not my hair you should be in. It's Sam's."

She seemed so put out that Jennifer couldn't help but smile. "I agree, but he's avoiding me, Alice. Pretending otherwise won't make that hurt any less. I appreciate all you've done for me, but I need to go home. If Sam wants me, he knows where to find me."

"I know. But if you could just stay a little longer..."

Pain squeezing her heart, Jennifer shook her head. "I can't. I've already stayed too long as it is."

Nothing if not persistent, Alice tried to change her mind. For nearly a week she took advantage of every opportunity to bring the subject up and had no idea how close she came to success. The nights were cold and lonely, and Jennifer would lie in her borrowed bed and ache for the feel of Sam's arms around her. The holidays were coming up—Thanksgiving was only two weeks away—and there was only one person she wanted to spend them with. But she flatly refused to hang around like a lovesick teenager waiting for a chance to run into him in the hall.

Anything was better than that, so two weeks to the day after she moved in with Alice, she moved back to her apartment. The paint fumes were still strong, the place bare of furniture except for the few old pieces Alice had lent her, but it was home. If she was lonely and miserable, no one had to know that but her.

Work had always been a panacea for her in times of

trouble, and now was no different. The damage to the café had turned out to be minimal, and after scouring the entire place from top to bottom and installing new ceiling tiles, the place looked as good as ever. The same day she moved home, the city health inspector gave her permission to reopen for business. She couldn't have been more thrilled if he'd told her she'd just won the lottery.

Molly was thrilled, too, when she heard the news, but reopening wasn't quite as simple as turning the Closed sign on the front door to Open. There were supplies to be ordered, deliveries to talk suppliers into making that afternoon, the dining area to get ready. Tables and chairs that had been stored in the back while the whole place was painted had to be carted to the front of the café, and customers from nearby businesses had to be notified that Heavenly Scents would be open regular hours tomorrow.

Molly was so happy about the opening she would have been willing to stay up all night if necessary, but with her help and Rosa's—and the cooperation of the suppliers, thank God—they had just about everything in place by eight o'clock that evening.

"Well, that's just about it," Jennifer told the others as the last table was set in place. "I want to get everything organized in the pantry, but you guys don't need to hang around for that."

"Are you sure?" Molly asked, frowning. "I don't mind staying."

"I know you don't, but there's no need. I can handle the rest. Once the word gets out that we're open, we're going to have our hands full, so go home and get some rest. Tomorrow's going to be a long day."

No one could argue with that, and because Jennifer had only a little left to do, Molly and Rosa left her to it, locking the door behind them as they let themselves out. Humming to herself, Jennifer turned back to the pantry. Ten minutes, tops, she decided, and she could close up and go upstairs to her apartment. As exhausted as she was, she'd be lucky if she even heard the alarm when it went off at four-thirty.

So tired she could hardly think, she never noticed when the scene before her eyes began to change. One second she was arranging spices, and the next she found herself looking at the interior of a convenience store. It was one that belonged to a national chain, and the clerk behind the counter was pale as a ghost as she raked the contents of the cash register into a paper bag. A masked man was holding a gun on her. Just as the trembling clerk started to hand him the bulging bag, Sam walked through the front door.

As quickly as the vision appeared, it vanished, and she was once again staring at the contents of the café pantry. Blinking, she gasped. "Oh, God. No!"

Horror chilling her blood, she stumbled out of the pantry into the kitchen and grabbed the phone. Before she thought, she punched in 911, only to slam the phone down again. No! What was she thinking? She needed the police department itself, not the emergency operator, and she didn't have a clue what the number was. Snatching up the phone again, her fingers shaking so badly she could hardly hold the receiver, she dialed information.

"Please, please, let him be there," she prayed when she finally got the number and punched it in.

But it seemed to take forever for anyone to answer in the squad room. It rang and rang, and with every ring, her panic grew. When someone finally answered, she was almost in tears.

"I need to talk to Detective Kelly," she said quickly. "Please, it's an emergency. Is he there?"

"He was a few minutes ago, but I think he was on his way out on a call. Hang on, and let me see if he's still here."

A clunk echoed in her ear as the phone was thrown down on a desk. Terrified she'd missed him, she was wondering how she was going to reach him when he came on the line twenty seconds later. "This is Kelly."

"Sam! Thank God! I was afraid I'd missed you and I didn't know what to do—"

"Jennifer?" he asked sharply. "What is it? What's wrong? Are you okay?"

"I'm fine," she assured him, ignoring the headache already pounding at her temples. "It's you I'm worried about. I had a vision." After quickly telling him about the robbery she'd seen, she said, "I know you have a hard time accepting this kind of thing, but please be careful! The convenience store has a poster for an upcoming charity dinner for the Hispanic College Fund in the window—it's right by the front door. Don't go in there, Sam. *Please!* If you do, the robber won't even think twice about shooting you."

"Nobody's going to shoot me, honey. I never go into convenience stores. You're worrying about nothing."

His tone was calm and soothing and logical, and it grated on her nerves like sandpaper. He didn't believe her! Agitated, she said, "Dammit, Sam, you have to listen to me! I know what I saw, and it's going to happen if you're not very very careful!"

She was so desperate to make him believe her that if she'd been there at the station, she would have shaken him until every tooth in his head rattled. And something of her desperation must have finally reached him.

"I'm always careful," he said soberly. "I have to be or I wouldn't have survived my rookie year, but I'll keep my eyes and ears open and watch what I'm walking into for the next couple of days. Okay?''

It was the best she could hope for, but the sick feeling in the pit of her stomach wouldn't go away. "Just be ready for anything," she said huskily. "If you don't, you could be in trouble before you even realize anything's wrong."

"Believe me," he said dryly, "I don't make a habit of letting people with guns surprise me. Nothing's going to happen."

Not sure if he'd completely reassured her when he hung up a few minutes later, he almost called her back just to hear the sound of her voice. God, he'd missed her! And it was killing him, dammit! She was all he thought of, dreamed of. If he could just see her... But he wouldn't be able to do that without touching her, and if he ever got his hands on her again, he didn't know if he'd be able to let her go.

"Sam? Was that Jennifer?"

Glancing up to find Tanner frowning at him, Sam nodded. "She had another vision. She saw me walk into the middle of a holdup at a convenience store and get shot."

Arching an eyebrow at that, Tanner said seriously, "I hope you listened to her. So far she's been batting a thousand when it comes to those visions of hers. I don't know how she does it, but it's pretty damn impressive."

Long since past the point where he needed to be convinced of Jennifer's psychic abilities, Sam had to agree with him. "You heard me tell her I'd keep an eye open, but this time I think she missed the mark. I can't remember the last time I stopped at one of those places."

Tanner knew his habits as well as his own and had to agree with him. "Just the same, watch yourself," he said stubbornly. "The lady saw something, and after the way she saved old man Stubbings's life, only a fool would ignore one of her warnings."

"I'm not ignoring anything," Sam growled. "I just don't think anything's going to happen. But I'll keep my eyes open," he said quickly before Tanner could nag him again. Changing the subject, he said, "So what's this tip someone called in about a coin collection? Any chance it's Stubbings's?"

"Probably not. Some lady on the west side was visiting her boyfriend and caught a glimpse of some coins in a desk drawer before he put them away. Apparently he's a shady character and she wouldn't put much past him. She saw the reward Mr. Stubbings is offering and decided to give us a call."

Sam groaned. The reward the old man had posted had been both a godsend and a curse. People were scouring the city, looking for those damn coins, and they'd gotten a ton of calls about them. But most of them were false alarms. He and Tanner had checked out everything from a pile of loose change on a bedside table to buried treasure in some kid's backyard. And so far they'd turned up nothing.

And this time was no different. The coins the girl saw at her boyfriend's house turned out to be quarters, not the silver dollars and gold pieces Mr. Stubbings collected, and the only reason the guy hid them from her was that he was afraid she'd get her hands on them and spend them.

He and Tanner laughed about it as they left the house, but it was getting to be damn frustrating. Where the hell was the rest of Agatha Elliot's jewelry and that damn coin collection? The items should have surfaced by now, but they hadn't, and there'd been no more robberies. Even the slip of paper that was found with Mr. Stubbings's security code turned out to have nothing but his fingerprints on it.

And things weren't going any better in the investigation of the fire at Jennifer's apartment. No witnesses had come forward and no one had recognized the composite sketch of the suspect he and Tanner had shown around the area. They'd talked to every informant they had, and no one knew anything.

Disgusted, wondering when they were ever going to get a break, Sam took the wheel as they headed back to the station, taking one of the main thoroughfares into downtown, instead of the interstate. He never had a clue anything was wrong with the car until steam started pouring out from underneath the hood.

"What the hell!" Caught in the inside lane of a four-lane avenue, he swore, checked his mirror to make sure no one was coming up on his right and swung into the first driveway he came to. It wasn't until he braked to a stop and cut the engine that he realized he'd pulled into the parking lot of a small convenience store.

Tanner, however, noticed right away. "Speak of the devil." He whistled softly. "Ain't this interesting."

"It's just a damn coincidence," Sam snapped. "I wouldn't even have pulled in here if I hadn't been forced to."

"So? Jennifer didn't say *why* you stopped at a convenience store, did she? What exactly did she say, anyway? You never said, except that she saw you getting shot when you interrupted a holdup."

"That was about it," Sam replied, glaring at the small store in front of them. "And if I wasn't careful, I'd be in trouble before I realized it. There was a poster for some kind of dinner for the Hispanic College Fund in the window...."

Even as the words left his mouth, he spied the poster wedged in a corner of the store's wide plate-glass window.

Beside him, Tanner swore. "I don't know about you, buddy, but this is close enough for me. You want to take the back door or the front?"

Not convinced yet there was a problem, Sam studied the store's only two occupants through the window. The clerk, a small skinny woman who couldn't have weighed more than a hundred pounds, stood behind the counter talking to a customer. The man had his back to the window and his hands in his jacket pockets. He looked harmless enough, but there was something about the way he was hiding his hands that raised the fine hairs on the back of Sam's neck. That was all he needed to warn him that something was wrong.

"The front," he said, drawing his gun. "When you kick in the back door, I'll make my move."

Tanner, his own gun already in his hand, nodded. "Since he's got his back to us, I should be able to slip around the side of the building without him seeing me. Give me till the count of ten."

They'd worked together too many years for Sam to make his move too soon. Adrenaline pumping through him, he quietly slipped out of the car as Tanner disappeared around the corner of the building. The count slow and measured in his head, he approached the front door and just had time to wonder what he and Tanner were going to say if they'd misjudged the situation when he ran out of time.

Tanner kicked in the back door, startling both occupants of the store. The clerk screamed and dropped behind the counter just as the lone customer pulled a .38 from his pocket and whirled to face the opening that led to the back storage area. He didn't see Sam slip through the front door.

"Freeze!" Sam yelled, pointing his service revolver

right at the middle of the robber's back just as Tanner burst in from the back yelling, "Police."

"You even look like you're going to squeeze that trigger, and you're dead meat, pal," Sam snarled. "Drop it."

Still on the floor behind the counter, the clerk began to sob. "Oh, thank God! Thank God!"

His gun still trained on the robber, Sam never spared her a glance. He couldn't. Not when the bastard had Tanner in his sights and was just itching to shoot him. Sam could see the temptation in the way he hesitated, and he knew what the guy was thinking as clearly as if he'd spoken aloud: he could drop them both if he moved fast enough.

"You're not that fast, cowboy," he said silkily. "We were first and second in marksmanship at the academy. You might get one of us, but not both, not without taking a bullet in the heart. You don't believe me, you just try it."

For a second he thought he was actually going to have to shoot the idiot. The man hesitated, his fingers tightening on the .38. Then with a muttered curse, he dropped it. Before he could lift his hands into the air, Sam was on him, kicking the gun out of reach, then forcing him up against the wall to search him. The entire procedure had taken no more than sixty seconds.

It took well over an hour for them to tie up loose ends and get back to the station. They had to wait for backup, then call for a tow truck when they discovered they'd blown a radiator hose in their unmarked car. And all the while Tanner badgered Sam to call Jennifer.

"It's the least you can do," he told him for what seemed like the tenth time when they strode into the detectives' squad room. "Dammit, she saved your life. Mine, too! If she hadn't warned you, we'd have walked into that store to get something to eat while we waited for a tow truck and gotten our heads blown off. You owe her a thank-you, if nothing else.''

"I know that," Sam said curtly. "And one of these days I'll find a way to do that. But right now, I think it's better if we keep our distance."

"You're making a mistake, man. Can't you see you're miserable? And you're making me miserable, too, walking around with a long face all the time. Quit being so damn stubborn and call her!"

His jaw set in granite, Sam said tightly, "Stay out of this, Tanner. I know what I'm doing."

"The hell you do. You wouldn't know a good thing if you tripped over it. Jennifer Hart is a damn fine woman and you know it. You're just running scared because of what Patricia did to you, and there's no reason for it."

His mouth compressed in a flat line, Sam refused to even discuss it. Wanting to bust him one, Tanner made a snap decision and grabbed the phone. "Then if you won't call her, I will. What's Alice's number?"

"I'm not talking to her."

"Nobody asked you to. Give me the damn number!"

Swearing, Sam gave it to him, then sat at his desk, stone-faced, as his partner made the call. He'd rather not have listened, but he didn't have much choice when Tanner sat right there and glared at him as he spoke into the phone. "Hey, Alice," he said when the old lady came on the line. "Tanner Bennigan, here. Can I speak to Jennifer for a minute?"

Knowing Alice, Sam expected her to chat awhile with Tanner before handing the phone over to Jennifer, but seconds later Tanner hung up. Surprised, he said, "That was fast. What's the matter? She already in bed?"

"Nope. She's not there," he retorted. "Alice said she moved back to her apartment this morning."

Chapter 12

It was the pounding at her front door that woke her. Groggy, her head thick, she fumbled for her alarm clock, squinting at it in the dark. One o'clock! God, who would bang on her door at o'clock in the morning? But even as she asked herself the question, she knew. Sam. Somehow he'd discovered she'd left Alice's, and judging from the force of his blows against her new steel door, he was more than a little miffed that she hadn't consulted him first.

Go away! she wanted to shout at him. She wasn't in any shape to deal with him tonight— she was tired, and moving back into the apartment, seeing again everything she'd lost, had been an emotional roller coaster for her. But she knew Sam. He wasn't going to go away until he spoke to her.

Grabbing her robe, she struggled into it on the way to the door. "Hold your horses," she grumbled. "I'm coming, dammit!"

Checking the peephole to make sure it was him, she

released the dead bolt and slid the safety chain free, then jerked the door open to find him glaring down at her in the dark. She barely had time to step back before he was surging inside. "What the hell do you think you're doing?"

She didn't so much as blink at his angry greeting. All innocence, she looked up at him with drowsy eyes. "The same thing most people are doing at this time of the night," she answered sassily in a voice that was still husky from sleep. "And if you don't mind, I'd like to get back to it. I've got to be up at four-thirty to fire up the ovens and start the morning baking."

As far as hints went, she couldn't have gotten much blunter. But he didn't budge. His eyes as dark as midnight, he looked her up and down, then growled, "Go pack your clothes. You're going back to Alice's."

"Oh, no, I'm not! In case you hadn't noticed, this place is back to normal, so there's no reason for me to impose on Alice."

"Think again, sweetheart," he retorted. "Whoever threw that firebomb through your front window is still walking around free, and we're no closer to catching him now than we were the night he burned you out. He could have killed you. There's nothing to say he won't come back and try to finish the job if he finds out you're here alone."

"And chance getting caught? I don't think so. Only an idiot would try something when there's a cop sitting across the street twenty-four hours a day, and this guy's no idiot."

"No, he's been pretty damn smart up to now," Sam agreed. "But you're a threat to him, and he knows you didn't die in the fire. He's got to be getting desperate, wondering when those little voices in your head are going to tell you something about him we can use to identify him. And that makes him twice as dangerous. A desperate man doesn't always use his brain. So get your keys. You're staying at Alice's until he's caught.''

"I am not. I won't be driven from my home by a piece of trash who hasn't got the guts to come out of the darkness and do his dirty work in the light of day. He's a coward, and if you really think he's going to come after me, then put another watchdog in the alley. But I'm not leaving and you can't make me!''

It was the wrong thing to say to a man who'd spent the last four hours of his shift worrying himself sick about her. Dammit, what did he have to say to get it through that pretty head of hers that she was in danger? Yeah, he could put another uniform outside her door—hell, he could put ten men out there! But that wouldn't necessarily keep her safe. They weren't dealing with a man who played by the rules. The bastard had shot Stubbings, and the old guy hadn't even been much of a threat to him. If he had any connections on the street at all, he had to know there was a sketch of him making the rounds of every pawnshop in the city, and only one person could be responsible for that. Jennifer. If he wanted to get rid of her, all he had to do was get a long-range rifle and take her out from any one of the surrounding rooftops.

It was that thought that had sent him rushing over to her place just as soon as his shift was over. He'd pictured her hurt and bleeding, and all the time he'd been battling with the need to race to her rescue like a damn knight on a white charger, she'd been sound asleep.

Staring down at her flushed cheeks and mass of sleep-tousled curls, the bare toes that peeked out from beneath the soft crushable flannel of her gown and robe, something in him seemed to snap at the thought of anyone hurting her. Muttering a curse, he reached for her.

The second his fingers closed around her flannel-covered arms he knew he never should have touched her. Not when she was warm and rumpled from sleep and he remembered all too clearly what it felt like to carry her off to bed and lose himself in her. God, he wanted her! She was a craving in his blood, a fire that should have begun to burn itself out by now. So why the hell hadn't it? She'd obviously accepted the fact that they didn't have a future; for the past two weeks he'd barely caught a glimpse of her.

And there'd been no mention of the L-word since that one time she told him she loved him; he only had to remember how she'd drawn into herself when she'd left his apartment that morning to know she'd never bring it up again. He should have been thrilled. Wasn't that what he wanted? Instead, he couldn't walk into his damn apartment without remembering what it was like to make love to her. It—*she*—was driving him crazy!

"You *are* leaving, and I *can* make you," he said between his teeth. And before she could do anything but sputter, he bent down and slung her over his shoulder.

"Sam! Dammit, what are you doing?"

"Taking charge," he said. "If you won't listen to reason, then I'll just have to do what I think is best. Quit squirming."

"Oh! You...you Neanderthal! Put me down!"

He should have carried her over to Alice's right then and there, but he knew he wasn't going to do that. The second he'd snatched her up, all he could think of was finding a place to lay her down and make love to her. Striding over to the front door, he turned the dead bolt and set the chain. Ten seconds later he was striding into her bedroom.

"What are you doing? I thought you were taking me out of here."

"So did I," he said roughly. "Looks like we were both wrong." Leaning down, he dropped her on her back on the bed and immediately followed her down. She was still gasping when his mouth covered hers.

She should have punched him one. She at least should have demanded to know why he was sweeping her off to bed now when just two weeks ago he'd gone to such painful lengths to make it clear he wanted nothing more to do with anything that even hinted at a relationship with her. But every night of those two weeks had been too long, too lonely, and already her arms were lifting to encircle his neck as her body softened to accommodate his much larger, harder one. And the sweetness of it nearly overwhelmed her. Tears stung her eyes, then trailed silently down her cheek. Dear God, how she loved him!

He felt her pain, tasted her tears—she'd known he would, but there was nothing she could do to hide her emotions from him. She was an open book where he was concerned, and when he pulled back suddenly and tenderly cupped her cheek in his rough palm, his eyes searching hers in the darkness, she couldn't look away.

"Did I hurt you?" he asked.

"No," she whispered, pressing a lingering kiss to his palm. "Ever since the fire, I cry about the craziest things. Molly says it's just the stress of losing everything and starting over."

"You shouldn't have left Alice's, sweetheart. You were safer there."

"I know, but I needed to come home," she said simply. "Even if it's not the same as it was before, this is where

I belong." Afraid he would press her to go back to the Lone Star again, she distracted him by pushing his jacket from his broad shoulders.

In the darkness his eyes glinted down into hers. "What do you think you're doing?"

He spoke in that husky growl she loved, stroking her with just his voice alone. Flashing him a mischievous smile, she lifted her fingers to his tie and began to loosen it. "Trying to distract you. How'm I doing?"

With gratifying swiftness, he settled himself between her thighs and moved against her. "I don't know," he murmured wickedly. "You tell me."

Caught off guard, she gasped. He was hot and hard and flush against her, tugging her gown up out of the way before she even knew what he was about. Against the tender skin of her inner thighs, the fabric of his slacks was a breath-stealing caress. A shudder rippled through her, dragging a soft moan from her. Abandoning his tie, she pulled him back down to her for a long hungry kiss.

Fire licking at her veins, she was almost past reason when he gently tugged her arms from around his neck and returned her hands to his tie. When she groaned in protest, he chuckled and dropped another kiss to her mouth. "Finish it, honey," he rasped. "Get me out of these clothes."

He didn't have to tell her twice. Before he could blink, his tie went flying. A heartbeat later, her fingers were rushing down the center of his chest, making short work of the buttons. In ten seconds flat she had his shirt off and her hands were at his belt. And no one was more surprised by her own daring than Jennifer. He watched her eyes widen and her cheeks bloom with color, and his heart turned over. Lord, she was something!

When she hesitated, he covered her hands with his and felt her fingers tremble. Too late, he remembered how new she was to lovemaking. Tenderness welled in him as his eyes met hers. "You want me to do the rest?" he asked hoarsely.

He expected her to nod and look away, but he hadn't counted on the depth of her need. Her eyes turned fierce and sensuous, her hands sure as his zipper growled in the darkness under the play of her fingers. He sucked in a breath, but then she had him naked, and he didn't for the life of him know how she'd managed it. She not only touched him, she stroked and caressed and took infinite pleasure from the differences in their bodies. His jaw clenched, sweat beading on his brow, he let her explore him to her heart's content and somehow just managed to hang on to his sanity.

Then she pushed him onto his back and kissed him, her tongue darting into his mouth to torment and tease, and what was left of his self-control shattered. His blood roaring in his ears, he never heard the groan that ripped from his throat, never remembered hauling her up over him until her hips were straddling his. With one stroke, he was buried deep, her cry echoing in his ears. With the second, she came undone around him. With the third, he forgot his own name.

When the alarm went off at four-thirty, Jennifer groaned and hit the cut-off button. Beside her, Sam only mumbled something in his sleep and buried his face in *her* pillow. Memories of the loving they'd shared warming her, she smiled sleepily. When he hadn't been reaching for her during the night, he'd been stealing her pillow, until they'd finally ended up sharing it.

An experienced woman would have had a spare, but she hadn't allowed herself to dare hope for his company when she'd bought a bed, complete with new mattress and bedclothes, to replace her smoke-and-water-damaged one. That, she suspected with a grin, might have been a mistake. He could shout it to the rooftops that there was nothing more between them than desire, but every time he'd touched her, kissed her, during the night, she'd felt a love that had brought tears to her eyes. He loved her, and she had to believe that one day soon he would realize it.

She had no intention of making the same mistake she'd made the first time they'd made love, however. She'd keep her heart out of her eyes and give him the space he needed, she promised herself as she quietly eased from the bed and padded into the bathroom. And if she was lucky, it wouldn't be too much longer before it hit him that space was the last thing he wanted from her.

She was taking the first batch of cinnamon rolls from the oven when she heard Sam's footsteps on the outside stairs. Her heart lurching, she threw him an easy smile as he stepped through the back door and tried not to notice how good-looking the man was in the morning. But she was fighting a losing battle. He wore the same thing he'd worn last night of course, but he'd left off the tie and his shirt was open at the throat. She wouldn't have minded if he'd used her razor, but he hadn't, and his granite jaw was shadowed with stubble.

He looked rough, sexy, wonderful, and she wanted to go to him so badly she ached. But that was something she'd sworn not to do. Turning her attention back to her baking, she said with a cheerfulness that didn't come quite as easily as she would have liked, "Good morning. C'mon in. These are ready and the coffee's on. Grab yourself a cup while I put another batch of rolls in the oven."

All business, she shoved another pan of cinnamon rolls into the oven, then looked behind her to find him still standing right inside the door, as if not quite sure how to take her. Biting back a smile, she could almost see the wheels turning in his head. He knew she loved him—she hadn't been able to hide it during the night—and he obviously expected another emotional confrontation with her. He didn't know what to make of her casualness, she thought, pleased. Good. The more she could shake him up, the better.

"Molly will be here in a few minutes if you'd rather wait for bacon and eggs," she said when he made no move to help himself to a sweet roll. "Normally I'd be happy to cook it for you, but we're going to have a real crowd this morning and I've got to get this baking done."

"I'll have something later," he said in a voice still gravelly from sleep.

He didn't, in fact, give a damn about food, but she was another matter. Was this the same woman who'd told him she loved him the first time they'd made love? he wondered, scowling. The same one who'd surprised herself and almost set the sheets on fire loving him last night? He'd expected blushes from her this morning and that loving light in her eyes that always made him want to haul her close and kiss her. Instead, her smile was friendly—*friendly*, dammit! Like they were best buddies or something! And nothing out of the ordinary had happened between them last night. And he didn't like it one little bit.

"Are you okay?" he asked.

"Of course," she said airily. "Why wouldn't I be? We reopen this morning, and I'm back home where I belong. Things couldn't be better."

His eyes narrowed at that. "You're not staying here alone. You might not think you're taking a chance, but I know you are. So if you won't go back to Alice's tonight, then I'm moving in here. And don't give me a hard time about it. I've made up my mind and I'm not changing it."

If he'd wanted to knock that irritating smile off her face, he couldn't have found a better way. "Oh, really," she purred, her eyes snapping. "And just who died and left you in charge? This is my place. *Mine,* dammit! And you're not moving in or doing anything else I don't want you to do just because we had sex a couple of times."

"Sex?" he repeated, stung. "You think what we shared was just *sex?*"

"Of course. What else could it be?"

"What else..." Realizing he sounded like a damn parrot, he ground his teeth together and reached for her before he could stop himself. "So you think we just had sex, do you?" he said grimly. "Then maybe I need to show you the difference between that and making love."

"Sam!"

"Don't you dare *Sam* me," he growled. "You asked for this and you know it."

He never would have hurt her, but he was so infuriated he would have taken her right there on her work table. But before he could do anything but start to draw her into his arms, Molly arrived.

A blind woman couldn't have missed the tension in the room, and Molly was sharper than most. Making no effort to hide her surprise at finding him there at that hour of the morning, she drawled, "Looks like I interrupted something. I'd offer to make myself scarce, but we open in fifteen minutes, and I need to fire up the grill and get things ready."

Groaning silently, Sam forced a tight smile. "Don't let me get in your way. I've got to be going, anyway. I was just keeping Jennifer company until you got here."

Far from fooled, Molly grinned. "Keeping company, huh? I haven't heard it called that in a while."

His mouth twitched at her teasing, but his eyes were

dead serious when he turned back to Jennifer. "Don't think for a second that this discussion is over. I'll be back later when you've got more time to talk." Stepping close, he caught her off guard with a hot hard kiss that drew a chuckle from Molly and a gasp of indignation from her. She was still sputtering when he walked out.

The man hiding in the recessed doorway of the building across the street froze as the detective strode out the front door of the café and folded his long body into the un-marked police car that had sat parked in front of the build-ing for most of the night. So the son of a bitch was finally leaving! It had taken him long enough.

He'd been watching the place as best he could the past two weeks, dodging the cops and construction workers who seemed to be constantly underfoot, cursing himself for not eliminating her when he'd had the chance. All she'd had to do was shut her yap after the fire like he'd wanted her to and he'd have left her alone. But, no! She'd gone to the cops, instead, and told them all about him. Now they knew what he looked like, and for that, she was going to pay.

Last night he'd finally thought his time had come. She'd moved back to her apartment, and the black-and-white that had sat across the street like a watchdog drove off the second Kelly arrived. He figured she was his as soon as the bastard left. But he'd stayed all night.

And with every passing hour his rage had grown. Kelly was finally leaving and the damn café was opening in fifteen minutes. If he didn't get his hands on the little bitch now, when he only had that old cook of hers to deal with, there was no telling when he might get another chance. Customers would stream in and out all day, and Kelly was bound to be back that night. It was now or never.

The decision made, he moved soundlessly in the pre-dawn darkness, blending in with the shadows as he peeked out from his hiding place. A quick glance in either direction assured him that the street was still dark and empty, the first customer nowhere in sight. His face twisted and ugly with purpose, he darted around the corner and sprinted down the street to where he'd parked his van. Seconds later he turned into the alley behind the café.

Still steaming long after Sam had disappeared from view, Jennifer wished, just once, she was the type of person who threw things when she was mad. She'd have already thrown every pot she owned out the front door after Sam. The nerve of the man! Who did he think he was, anyway? He'd made it clear he wanted no part of anything that even hinted at commitment, and just when she obliged him and cut herself out of his life, he came swaggering in like John Wayne, ordering her around just because he'd slept with her. He had no right, damn him. None! Even if she did love John Wayne.

Amusement sparkling in Molly's eyes as she gathered the eggs and bacon and sausage she would need to feed the crowd that would soon descend on them, she said, "You want to tell me what that was all about, or do I have to guess?"

"The man's insufferable!"

"All men are," Molly retorted without missing a beat. "But we can't seem to live without them. What'd he do?"

Still bristling, Jennifer raged, "He thinks he can boss me around! But God forbid I should think I'm in love with him. Oh, no, that's not allowed. He doesn't want to get involved with me. I'm too young, too inexperienced. I can't be trusted to know my own mind."

Amused, Molly couldn't help but grin. "Seems like you know it pretty good to me."

"You're darn right I do," Jennifer snapped, then just as quickly laughed when she thought about what Sam's unreasonableness meant. "Oh, Molly, I love him!" She laughed, suddenly feeling as if she was walking on air. "He's fighting me every step of the way, but this morning I think I finally made a little progress."

"If you're talking about that clinch I saw when I walked in," she drawled with dancing eyes, "then I'd say you were making a heck of a lot more than a little progress. The man definitely looked hot and bothered."

Pleased, Jennifer grinned. "Oh, he was. I turned the tables on him, and he didn't know if he wanted to strangle me or kiss me. And he's got no one to blame but himself. I played by his rules and now he doesn't like the game."

Jennifer knew she was going on like a lovesick schoolgirl, but she couldn't stop talking about Sam. Chatting happily as she helped Molly whip up batter for pancakes and French toast, she never saw the man who slipped through the back door as soundlessly as a cat. One second it was just her and Molly busily preparing for the morning rush, and the next they found themselves face-to-face with a stranger with a gun.

Horrified, Jennifer froze. She felt Molly stiffen at her side, but she couldn't take her eyes away from the intruder who stood just inside the back door. Her heart slamming against her ribs, she wanted to believe this was just a simple holdup, but she knew with sickening dread that it wasn't.

He looked different from the last time she'd seen him—the black beard that had looked so incongruous with his coloring was gone, and without a hat, it was obvious he'd shaved his head fairly recently. Pale reddish blond hair, cropped short and standing in spikes, poked through his scalp. In spite of the changes, she knew he was the same man who'd sat right here in her café and questioned her about her psychic abilities, then warned her she was in danger. The same man she was sure who'd choked Mrs. Elliot and shot Mr. Stubbings. The same man who'd tried to burn her place to the ground.

He wanted her dead. She could feel his hatred. Like a physical thing, it slapped her right in the face and seemed to suck the very air from her lungs.

Don't let him see your fear, a voice whispered in her head. *It's your only hope. He's the kind of monster who thrives on taking advantage of anyone weaker than he is.*

Stiffening, she said contemptuously, "If you're here to rob the place, you're too early. We haven't been open for two weeks, and the only money we've got is fifty dollars in change in the cash register. Take it and get out."

"Oh, no, lady," he said softly. "I've been waiting a long time to get my hands on you. I'm not going anywhere without you."

Outraged, Molly gasped. "The hell you're not! If you know what's good for you, you'll get out of here before her boyfriend comes back. He's a cop and he won't mess around with trash like you."

"Her *boyfriend,*" he sneered, unimpressed, "is long gone. I saw him leave, and he looked madder than hell. I don't think he'll be coming back." Pulling a black scarf from his pocket, he tossed it at Jennifer. "Tie the old battle-ax up and be quick about it. We're running out of time."

Fear chilling her blood, Jennifer searched his soulless eyes and knew she didn't have any choice but to do as he said. If she gave him the slightest bit of trouble, he'd shoot them both and be done with it. Reluctantly she turned to Molly. "I'm sorry, Moll."

"Don't be," she said gruffly. "You just be careful."

"Quit your yammering!" he growled, "and get on with it!"

His eyes shifting to the clock, then to the front door, he was too busy watching for the first customer to notice that Jennifer not only bound Molly's hands in front of her, she twined the scarf around her wrists and tied it in a slip knot that any four-year-old could have gotten out of.

"All right, she's tied," she told him, then immediately distracted him before he could check her handiwork too closely. "If you're planning on getting out of here before anyone sees you, you'd better hustle. Mr. Libberman is always here at six-thirty sharp, and it's already six-twenty-two."

His eyes widened in panic, and then he was hustling them both toward the rear of the kitchen. "What's in here?" he demanded, and pulled open the door of the pantry to see. It was a small windowless room, and without even looking at Molly's bindings, he shoved her inside. "In you go, Grandma."

Ignoring her sputterings, he slammed the door in her face, then saw, too late, that there was no lock. He spit an oath, then grabbed a chair and shoved it under the doorknob. Her heart pounding, Jennifer turned to run, but she'd only taken two steps when he reached out and snared her hair.

"No!" she screamed.

"Oh, yes," he snarled, and hauled her back to him by her hair until he could lock an iron arm around her and shove the gun into her side. "I've got you, lady. You can make this as hard or as easy on yourself as you want—it makes no difference to me. But you even think about getting away from me again, and you're dead on the spot. You hear me?''

''Y-yes. I hear you.''

''Good. Then get your ass outside.''

His fingers biting into her arm, he dragged her after him out the back door and over to a battered orange van. The sliding door on the passenger side was already open, waiting. His mouth twisting into a cruel mockery of a smile, he chuckled when she balked and planted her feet.

''You want to end it all right here?'' he taunted.

''You wouldn't!''

''Do you really want to take that chance?''

He had her there and he knew it. She had to buy whatever time she could until Alice could get free and call Sam. It was the only chance she had.

Without a word she stepped into the van and never saw him lift the gun. A split second later, he slammed it down on the back of her head. A blinding flash of white light exploded behind her eyes. Without a sound she crumpled to the floor.

Chapter 13

"Sam? Thank God you're home! You have to come. He's got her. I tried to stop him, but..."

His conversation with Jennifer still spinning annoyingly in his head, it took Sam a second to recognize Molly's voice. And even then, her words were so jumbled, so frantic, he could hardly understand her. Alarmed, he said, "Slow down, Molly. What's wrong? Who's got whom? *Where's Jennifer?*"

"That's what I'm trying to tell you!" she sobbed. "She's been kidnapped!"

"What? When? Dammit, she couldn't have been! I just left her!"

"Right after you'd gone, he came in here, big as life, and took off with her. He made her tie me up, but she didn't. Not really. I got out of the pantry just as they drove away."

A muscle twitching in his jaw, Sam snatched a pen and

paper from the counter in his kitchen. "Did you see the vehicle? Get a license number?"

"You're damn right I did!" Quickly rattling off the information, she said furiously, "They headed west on Commerce. You catch him, Sam. And when you do, I want a piece of him. He's going to kill her."

"The hell he is," he growled in a voice that would have chilled the devil himself. "He so much as harms a single hair on her head, and I'll make him wish he'd never been born."

Without another word, he slammed down the phone and immediately picked it up again to call the police dispatcher to issue an all-points bulletin. Seconds later he grabbed his gun and ran out the door.

The streets were still relatively deserted that early in the morning, and by the time he hit Commerce, he was flying low. Grim-faced, his siren blaring, he dared anyone to get in his way. No one did. There was, however, no sign of the orange van.

Where the hell was the bastard? What if he didn't catch up to him in time?

Fear knotted his gut. No, dammit! he thought angrily. He couldn't afford to think that way or he'd go out of his mind. Jennifer had to know he was coming for her. She was counting on him, and by God, he'd find her. Even if he had to tear the city apart. And when he did, he was never letting her out of his sight again!

"Calling all units in the vicinity of North Flores and I-35," the emotionless voice on his police radio droned. "An orange Ford van, license plate number 213 KJY, has been spotted in the two hundred block of North Flores heading north..."

Sam didn't wait to hear more. Snatching up the mike

to his radio, he called in to report that he was on his way.
"Have you got an ID to go with that plate number?"

"Affirmative. The vehicle is registered to a Paul Masterson at 635 North Flores."

He was going home. The idiot was winding his way
through downtown and leading them straight to his house!
Ordering all available units to Masterson's house, Sam
turned right at the next corner and hit the gas. If he got
on the freeway, he might just be able to beat him there.

He hit the entrance ramp going sixty. After that he
didn't even look at the speedometer. The world passed in
a blur, but it seemed like he was hardly moving. Then the
North Flores exit was rushing at him, and he was forced
to slow down to keep all four wheels on the ground as he
shot off the freeway.

Backup was on the way, but when he saw a rusty orange van pull into a driveway two blocks ahead, Sam
knew there was no way in hell he was waiting for anyone
before going in after Jennifer. His jaw granite hard, he
floored the accelerator. Thirty seconds later, tires screaming, he slammed to a stop behind the van just as the driver
jumped out.

In the time it took to kick open his door, Sam was out
of his car and taking cover behind the front fender. His
gun steady as a rock in his hand, he yelled, "Freeze!"

Three black-and-white units came roaring down the
street with sirens blaring, but Sam never spared them a
glance. One second he had Paul Masterson in his sights,
and the next the son of a bitch had jerked Jennifer out of
the van, pulled her in front of him and pressed a gun
against her chest. Sam stiffened, his heart stopping in mid-
beat at the sight of her. She was as pale as a ghost, her
eyes dazed as she visibly swayed on her feet. What had
the bastard done to her?

"Jennifer? Are you all right?"

"He hit me—"

"Shut up!" Masterson barked, "or I'll do more than that to you. And you back off," he told Sam shrilly. "I mean it! This little revolver here has a hair trigger, and my fingers get real clumsy when I'm upset. You back off or you can start planning the bitch's funeral. It's your choice."

In all his years on the force, Sam had never once lost control on the job. He'd never even come close. But at that moment, seeing Jennifer's terrified eyes as Masterson ground the barrel of the gun into her breast, he could have easily killed the lowlife scumbag with his bare hands. "Let her go, Masterson," he said coldly. "Look around you, man. We've got you surrounded. Let her go and nobody gets hurt."

"Yeah, right," he jeered. "Like I'm gonna walk out of here alive. Who do you think you're dealing with, Kelly? A moron? Get back!" he screamed when one of the uniformed officers edged closer. "All of you back off, or I swear I'll kill her right here!"

He was just jittery enough to do it, Sam thought grimly. If his gun had the hair trigger he claimed it had, all he had to do was jerk when he thought someone was getting too close, and he'd shoot Jennifer right in the heart. She'd be dead before she hit the ground.

But he couldn't back off, dammit! He couldn't just stand there and let the son of a bitch haul her into his house. Here, surrounded by cops, she had a chance. If Masterson got her alone with him inside, in a hostage situation, the odds on her surviving were slim to none.

"You're not that stupid," Sam said with a calm he was far from feeling. "So far, all you have against you is a kidnapping charge. You don't want to add murder to that.

Think, man! We can end this thing peacefully. Let's just talk about it.''

She was going to die.

Pressed tightly back against the monster who held her, her head throbbing viciously from the blow she'd taken, Jennifer felt the tension in his big body, the rage he directed solely at her, and knew she was doomed. He didn't care that he was surrounded, that one bullet from a police sharpshooter would blow the top of his head off. In his twisted mind she was the cause of all his problems, and if he could just eliminate her, he wouldn't have a care in the world.

She had to do something. Think! she told herself fiercely, trying to clear her pain-clouded brain. A small army of cops encircled them. Sam even had her kidnapper in his sights, but he couldn't chance doing anything without endangering her. So it was up to her. She could literally feel the waning seconds of her life ticking away. If she didn't come up with some course of action soon, it was going to be too late.

She never made a conscious decision, but one second she stood stiffly in the grip of the man who wanted her dead, and the next she went boneless.

"What the hell! Stand up, you stupid bitch!" Caught off guard, her captor instinctively shifted his hold to grab her and shore her limp body up in front of him. In the process he tightened his grip on his gun.

The bullet slammed into her with the force of a speeding freight train and knocked her off her feet. On the edge of her awareness, she heard Sam's bellow of rage, then the sound of another shot being fired. A split second later, her kidnapper grunted in pain and his gun when flying. Before he hit the ground, the cops were swarming them.

Stunned, her shoulder on fire, Jennifer lifted a trembling hand to the wound and felt blood spurt between her fingers. Only then did she realize she'd been shot. "Oh, God!"

"Jennifer? Sweetheart?" Suddenly Sam was there, down on his knees beside her, his rugged face gray with worry as he bent over her. "Somebody call an ambulance. And get a first-aid kit over here stat!" he yelled as he tugged a handkerchief from his pocket and hastily pressed it to her shoulder. "You're going to be okay, baby," he told her huskily when he brought his eyes back to hers and found her watching him dazedly. "Just lie still."

"I had to do something," she said thickly. "He was going to kill me."

"I know, honey. I saw it in his eyes. You did fine." A uniformed officer came running up with the first-aid kit, and in record time, Sam had a thick pad of gauze pressed to her shoulder. But in spite of his best efforts, the wound still oozed blood, soaking the pad in a matter of moments.

Alarmed, he reached for her with his free hand and crushed her fingers in his. "I can hear the ambulance now, sweetheart," he said. "You hang on, you hear me? The hospital is less than fifteen minutes away. Don't you dare check out on me!"

Her smile feeble, she couldn't seem to keep her eyes open. "There you go bossing me again," she said weakly. "Are you sure you weren't a general in another life?"

"Oh, God," he groaned. "Don't tell me you believe in reincarnation, too!"

"Of course. Doesn't everyone?"

She was so blasé about it he almost laughed. Then he felt her fingers go slack in his and his heart stopped cold.

"Jennifer? Honey? Dammit!" he cried. "Where the hell's that ambulance?"

* * *

She was in surgery for two hours. It was the longest two hours of Sam's life. He made regular calls to Molly, who would have been there in a heartbeat if there'd been anyone else at the café to cook for the crowd of customers who'd shown up as soon as Jennifer was kidnapped, but there wasn't much he could tell her. He didn't know anything about her condition except that it was serious and was driving him crazy. He paced and swore and paced some more. And always, he watched the clock. He could have sworn it never moved.

What the hell was taking so long? he fumed. The shot was a clean one. It might have been a little low, but dammit, it wasn't anywhere near her heart! It couldn't have been. She would have been bleeding a lot more...

Images of her blood soaking the bandage he'd pressed to her shoulder flashed before his eyes, haunting him. He could still feel that same blood seeping through his fingers.

God, he loved her! How could he have been so blind? He'd known he was in trouble the night he'd found her in the ballroom of the Lone Star, and then again the next morning when she'd bravely admitted she loved him. She'd been so sure she'd scared him spitless, and he'd been running from the truth ever since. He'd clung to Patricia's betrayal like a shield that could protect him, but by then, it had already been too late. It was too late the first time he touched her.

But like a jackass, he'd tried to convince himself she was another Patricia just because she was young and romantic and seemed to have her head in the clouds. He couldn't have been more wrong. It wasn't lack of age or experience that made a woman betray her husband—it was lack of character. And Jennifer had plenty of character. She was loyal to her friends and people she cared about, and she stood up for what she believed in even when it wasn't always the smart thing to do. And she loved him as much as he loved her. If he knew nothing else about her, he knew that. And nothing else mattered. The rest was just details.

"Detective Kelly?"

Caught up in his thoughts, he didn't see the surgeon, still dressed in his scrubs, until he called his name. Whirling, he strode quickly toward him. "Dr. Rhodes! Thank God! How is she? She's going to be all right, isn't she? She lost so much blood...."

"Because the bullet nicked an artery," the doctor explained. "We were able to repair the damage, and she came through the surgery just fine. She's in recovery now and should be taken up to her room in an hour or so."

Until that moment, when relief took all the starch from his knees, Sam didn't realize just how scared he'd been of losing her. "Can I see her?" he asked hoarsely.

The doctor hesitated, but one look at the determined set of Sam's jaw, and he gave in to the inevitable. "Just for a couple of minutes. She's still under the anesthetic," he warned. "She won't even know you're there."

If they'd been talking about any other woman, Sam would have agreed. But not Jennifer. Smiling, he said, "Oh, yes, she will. Jennifer's got a sixth sense about this kind of thing. Where's recovery?"

"To the left at the end of the hall. You can't miss it. And remember," he called after him when Sam moved off. "Only two minutes."

He didn't, Sam thought, need that long to tell her he loved her. But when a nurse showed him to her bedside and he saw how still she was, how pale, he knew he was going to take every second of that two minutes and more if he could manage it. Then, when she was back on her feet and out of here, he was taking a lifetime.

Ignoring the nurses and the machines that beeped and gurgled all around them, he took her right hand and enclosed it in his, only to feel his heart twist when her fingers remained unmoving. "You're going to be all right, sweetheart," he whispered gruffly. "The doctor said I can't stay long, but I wanted you to know I'm here. I'll always be here, honey. You hear me? I've never loved anyone as much as I love you, and I'll always be here for you."

A nurse came up on soft-soled shoes to check the machines Jennifer was hooked up to, but Sam hardly noticed her. His voice pitched low and deep, he told Jennifer how stupid he'd been, how she should have given him a good swift kick where it would do the most good, how sometimes a man had to get hit with a sledgehammer before he could see what was right there in front of his eyes. He poured out his heart to her, and when he looked at the clock again, ten minutes had passed.

Her fingers still limp in his, Jennifer hadn't so much as twitched an eyelash the entire time. Logic told him she couldn't possibly have heard him. But as he went upstairs to wait for her in the room she would be brought to, he smiled for what seemed the first time in hours. She'd heard every word—he'd bet money on it.

Feeling as if she was swimming up through a black fog, Jennifer struggled toward consciousness, so tired she could hardly open her eyes. When she did, she frowned at the monitor next to her bed and realized abruptly that she was in the hospital. Her mind a blank, she couldn't for the life of her say why. Was she sick? Had she been in an accident?

Her groggy mind supplied no answers, however. She should have panicked, but then her gaze found Sam.

Slumped in a chair on the opposite side of the bed, his feet propped on the mattress, he was sound asleep.

I've never loved anyone as much as I love you.

He didn't stir, didn't move a muscle, but the husky admission came to her through the darkness of the night and the sweetness of a dream only just remembered, wrapping around her heart like a caress. He loved her. Somehow while she'd slept, he'd come to her in her dreams and told her he loved her.

She must have made a sound—she swore she only smiled—but he was so finely attuned to her that somehow he knew the second she was awake. His eyes snapped open and in the next instant he was on his feet and right beside the bed, his fingers closing around hers in way that felt endearingly familiar.

"Hi, sleepyhead," he growled softly. "How are you feeling?"

"Tired," she said, and was shocked by the weakness of her voice. "What happened? I can't remember—"

The words were hardly out of her mouth when the blackness shrouding her memory lifted and the events of that morning swept over her like a tidal wave. "Oh, God!"

"It's all right, sweetheart," he assured her quickly, squeezing her hand. "I talked to your doctor, and he said you're going to be just fine. There's no permanent damage and you'll be back to your old self in no time."

Her fingers still caught in his, he fought the need to snatch her up in his arms. He needed her close, heart to heart. But more than that, he needed to tell her he loved her and wanted to spend the rest of his life with her. But she was so damn weak. And so fragile-looking that he was afraid he would hurt her just holding her hand. When he proposed, he wanted her strong and healthy and in his arms, holding him as tight as he planned to hold her.

Resigned to waiting at least another week, he said quietly, "It's over, honey. The bastard who put you in here is in custody at the jail infirmary, and he's not coming anywhere near you again. We got him, sweetheart. His name's Masterson, and after Tanner found enough evidence at his home this afternoon to put him away for the next twenty years, he spilled his guts. He's been hocking stuff in Austin, but the idiot still had some of Mrs. Elliot's jewelry and Stubbings's coin collection."

"He confessed?"

Sam nodded grimly. "According to Tanner, he hung out in places where he could strike up conversations with senior citizens who lived alone. He'd make friends with them, feel them out about their hobbies and valuables, then find out where they lived and rob them. He even watched the obits."

"That's sick!"

Sam had to agree. "He met Mrs. Elliot when she had a flat tire—he'd stopped to change it for her. He did some moonlighting with Stubbings's yard service and took advantage of the opportunity to make friends with the old man and learn the layout of his house. Somehow, he got his hands on his wallet and got the code for the security system. He was making plans to go after a widow in Alamo Heights and would probably have hit her place by now if it hadn't been for you and that profile of him you came up with in your interview with Jonathan Lake.

"You nailed him, honey," he said proudly, stroking her brow. "He had a couple of rich old aunts who didn't leave him a dime after he took care of them, and he felt cheated. When he saw your interview with Lake, he didn't sleep all night. He just knew some of his relatives saw it and recognized the profile of him. That's why he went after you. He figured if he didn't shut you up, you were eventually going to lead either us or his relatives right to him.''

There were other things Masterson had admitted to Tanner, such as how he'd watched Jennifer from across the street from her café and how he'd planned to kill her nice and slow as a payback for all the trouble she'd caused him, but that was something Sam didn't ever plan to tell her. With the kidnapping and attempted-murder charges added to all the others against him, the bastard would never see the light of day again except through prison bars.

Her eyes drooping heavily as sleep threatened to overtake her again, Jennifer murmured, ''But I couldn't see his face clearly. It was on the news and everything. I wasn't a threat to him.''

''He thought you knew what he was doing every time he stepped out of his house, and he couldn't take the pressure. So he cracked.'' He saw her frown, trying to gather her thoughts, and he leaned over and kissed her softly on the mouth. ''That's enough for now, baby. Go back to sleep. You're tired.''

He didn't have to tell her twice. Before he straightened away from her, she was asleep.

The next time she woke up it was morning and Sam was gone. The wound in her shoulder a tight dull pain, she shifted carefully into a more comfortable position and told herself he'd probably gone home to shower and change. There was no reason to get all teary-eyed and emotional—he'd be back later, after he checked in at the station and caught up on his sleep.

But noon came and went, Rosa paid her a visit and so did Molly, and still no sign of Sam. All she could think about was that he'd told her he loved her in a dream, but not face-to-face. What if her imagination had just been playing tricks on her? What if, now that the case was solved and Masterson was behind bars, the love she was so sure she'd felt in his every touch was just lust that had burned itself out? Was his absence another way of telling her goodbye?

No! she cried silently. She hadn't imagined anything, least of all how much he loved her. He'd be back; she just had to be patient. He had a job, responsibilities, that couldn't be put on hold just because she was in the hospital.

But as the afternoon dragged by, fears she wanted no part of crept silently into her room to torment her. Her shoulder throbbed, but it was her heart that ached, and all she wanted to do was go home, lock herself in and not come out until her bruised heart had mended. Considering the way she was feeling, that might take another twenty or thirty years.

When Dr. Rhodes dropped by to see how she was doing, he refused even to think about releasing her early. "Sorry, Jennifer, but it's out of the question. That bullet hit an artery and you lost quite a bit of blood. You've been through an ordeal, young lady, whether you know it or not, and I'm not letting you out of here until I'm sure there aren't going to be any complications."

"But I'm not going to do anything but lie in bed. I can do that at home just as well as I can here."

"True, but you're still very weak and you live alone. Infection is always a risk after surgery, too. I want you here so I can keep an eye on you." Looking up suddenly, he smiled at the sight of Sam striding through the doorway. "Come in, Detective. I seem to have a restless patient on my hands. She wants to go home."

His brows snapping together in a frown, Sam said, "Isn't it a little early for that? She just had surgery yesterday."

"My point exactly," the doctor replied. "She doesn't realize how weak she is, and even when she does go home, she's probably going to need help."

"That won't be a problem," Sam told him. "I'm taking her to my place when she's released."

"I—I can't let you do that," she sputtered. Why would he say such a thing when she was no longer his concern? "Molly will be right downstairs during the day, and Rosa has already volunteered to stay whenever I need her. And you have to work."

"I've got some time coming. I'll take a few days off." Moving to her bedside, he took her hand and said, "Anyway, I want to take care of you myself."

Her heart lurching in her breast, she stared up at him in confusion and never saw Dr. Rhodes's knowing smile. "Then I can leave her in your hands," he told Sam. "I've got rounds to finish. I'll be back later tonight, Jennifer."

Her eyes searching Sam's, Jennifer nodded, then suddenly they were alone. Tension hummed in the air between them. In the silence that seemed to spin out indefinitely, he had to hear the thundering of her heart. "Why are you doing this?" she asked softly. "Is it because of the shooting? Because you feel responsible somehow? You're not—"

He hushed her simply by tightening his fingers around hers and drawing her hand to his mouth for a lingering kiss. "Don't you know how I feel about you, honey?" he murmured. "I could have sworn you did. I know I acted like a jackass, but I've never loved anyone as much as I love you...."

His words, drifting straight out of her dreams, were as

familiar to her as the beating of her own heart. In a voice rough with emotion, he told her how stupid he'd been, how a man sometimes had to get hit with a sledgehammer before he could see what was right in front of his eyes, and she realized that the dream she'd thought she'd had after surgery hadn't been a dream at all. He loved her.

Tears spilled over her lashes and she could do nothing to stop them. "Oh, Sam," she choked. "I love you, too! I know you think I'm too young to know my own mind, but I never have been one of those women who falls in love with someone new every other month. I never even looked at a man until I saw you."

"I know, honey. I was the one with the hang-ups. If it wasn't your age, then it was the visions and the way you seemed to know everything about me without even asking."

"Not everything," she said quietly. "I didn't know if you would ever be able to accept me for what I am."

Cursing himself for ever hurting her, he sank onto the side of the bed and carefully eased her into his arms. He hadn't meant to do this now—he didn't even have a ring for her yet!—but a man needed to hold the woman he loved when he bared his soul to her.

"I can't deny you threw me for a loop, love," he admitted huskily. "I couldn't figure out how the hell you knew the things you did—I still can't. But I don't know how birds know when to migrate, either. Or why every unattached person who moves into the Lone Star Social Club falls in love within a year, but it happens. Every damn time!"

Her lips twitching at his wry tone, she teased, "I thought you didn't believe in that kind of thing."

"How can I not believe it when it happened to me?"

He shook his head. "Honey, love was the last thing I was looking for when I met you. Now look at me."

He kissed her then because he couldn't help himself, because he couldn't stand the thought of her doubting his love for her even for a second. Softly, fiercely, with an aching tenderness, his mouth devoured hers. "You made me believe in forever when I didn't think such a thing was possible," he said roughly when he finally dragged his mouth from hers. "And when I'm ninety-five and you're eighty-five, I'm going to love having a young wife."

She started to laugh, and only just then realized what he'd said. Her eyes wide, she gasped. "You want to marry me?"

Delighted with her shock, he grinned. "You mean now or when you're eighty-five?"

"Sam! I'm serious!"

Sobering, he took her hand and carried it to his heart. "So am I," he said quietly. "I'm not psychic. I don't know what's going to happen down the road. I don't know anything except that I'll always love you and I want to spend the rest of my life with you. Will you marry me?"

Another woman might have needed some time to think, but she never had and never would be like other women, thank God. She looked up at him with a love in her eyes he somehow knew went soul-deep and trustingly gave him her heart. "Yes."

Just yes, nothing more. With a simplicity that stole the very air from his lungs, she made him the happiest man on earth.

Epilogue

Everyone had said she was crazy to plan a garden wedding for Valentine's Day. Everyone, that is, except Sam. His blue eyes glinting with amusement, he'd merely lifted a brow at her. "All this fortune-telling stuff is your thing, not mine. How do you think the weather'll be?"

"Sunny and eighty-one, with a light wind out of the southeast," she'd said promptly, grinning.

It was an outrageous prediction for February, but Sam hadn't so much as blinked. "Sounds good to me. Let's do it."

Now, two and a half months later, while winter still raged in most of the rest of the country, the temperature was already in the midseventies and climbing. The guests, which included half the police force, took up every chair that had been set up in the garden of the Lone Star Social Club, and there wasn't a coat or jacket in sight. By the time the wedding ceremony was over and the reception began, the temperature would be pushing eighty. Just as she'd predicted.

Standing at Sam's side before the minister, all their friends surrounding them as they exchanged vows, she thought the day couldn't have been more perfect. Suddenly, on the warm flower-scented air, the faint strains of an old-fashioned waltz floated down from the ballroom and gently swirled around them in approval. Startled, she glanced up at Sam and saw by the surprise in his eyes that he, too, had heard it. Her heart full of love, she squeezed his hand and couldn't help but grin. *Now* the day was perfect.

*   *   *   *   *

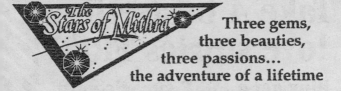

Take 4 bestselling love stories FREE

Plus get a FREE surprise gift!

Special Limited-time Offer

Mail to Silhouette Reader Service™

3010 Walden Avenue
P.O. Box 1867
Buffalo, N.Y. 14240-1867

YES! Please send me 4 free Silhouette Intimate Moments® novels and my free surprise gift. Then send me 6 brand-new novels every month, which I will receive months before they appear in bookstores. Bill me at the low price of $3.34 each plus 25¢ delivery and applicable sales tax, if any.* That's the complete price and a savings of over 10% off the cover prices—quite a bargain! I understand that accepting the books and gift places me under no obligation ever to buy any books. I can always return a shipment and cancel at any time. Even if I never buy another book from Silhouette, the 4 free books and the surprise gift are mine to keep forever.

245 BPA A3UW

Name	(PLEASE PRINT)

Address	Apt. No.

City	State	Zip

This offer is limited to one order per household and not valid to present Silhouette Intimate Moments® subscribers. *Terms and prices are subject to change without notice. Sales tax applicable in N.Y.

UMOM-696

©1990 Harlequin Enterprises Limited

As seen on TV!
Free Gift Offer

With a Free Gift proof-of-purchase from any Silhouette® book, you can receive a beautiful cubic zirconia pendant.

This gorgeous marquise-shaped stone is a genuine cubic zirconia—accented by an 18" gold tone necklace.

(Approximate retail value $19.95)

Send for yours today…
compliments of ▼ *Silhouette*®

To receive your free gift, a cubic zirconia pendant, send us one original proof-of-purchase, photocopies not accepted, from the back of any Silhouette Romance™, Silhouette Desire®, Silhouette Special Edition®, Silhouette Intimate Moments® or Silhouette Yours Truly™ title available at your favorite retail outlet, together with the Free Gift Certificate, plus a check or money order for $1.65 U.S./$2.15 CAN. (do not send cash) to cover postage and handling, payable to Silhouette Free Gift Offer. We will send you the specified gift. Allow 6 to 8 weeks for delivery. Offer good until March 31, 1998, or while quantities last. Offer valid in the U.S. and Canada only.

Free Gift Certificate

Name: _____

Address: _____

City: _____ State/Province: _____ Zip/Postal Code: _____

Mail this certificate, one proof-of-purchase and a check or money order for postage and handling to: SILHOUETTE FREE GIFT OFFER 1998. In the U.S.: 3010 Walden Avenue, P.O. Box 9077, Buffalo, NY 14269-9077. In Canada: P.O. Box 613, Fort Erie, Ontario L2Z 5X3.

FREE GIFT OFFER   084-KFD
ONE PROOF-OF-PURCHASE
To collect your fabulous FREE GIFT, a cubic zirconia pendant, you must include this original proof-of-purchase for each gift with the properly completed Free Gift Certificate.

084-KFDR2

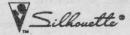

**SUSAN
MALLERY**

Continues the twelve-book
series—36 HOURS—in
January 1998 with
Book Seven

THE RANCHER AND THE
RUNAWAY BRIDE

When Randi Howell fled the altar, she'd been running for her
life! And she'd kept on running—straight into the arms of
rugged rancher Brady Jones. She knew he had his suspicions,
but how could she tell him the truth about her identity? Then
again, if she ever wanted to approach the altar in earnest, how
could she not?

For Brady and Randi and *all* the residents of Grand Springs,
Colorado, the storm-induced blackout was just the beginning
of 36 Hours that changed *everything!* You won't want to
miss a single book.

Available at your favorite retail outlet.

Welcome to the Towers!

In January
New York Times bestselling author

NORA ROBERTS

takes us to the fabulous Maine coast mansion
haunted by a generations-old secret and introduces
us to the fascinating family that lives there.

Mechanic Catherine "C.C." Calhoun and hotel magnate
Trenton St. James mix like axle grease and mineral
water—until they kiss. Efficient Amanda Calhoun finds
easygoing Sloan O'Riley insufferable—and irresistible.
And they all must race to solve the mystery
surrounding a priceless hidden emerald necklace.

Catherine and Amanda

THE Calhoun Women

**A special 2-in-1 edition containing
COURTING CATHERINE and A MAN FOR AMANDA.**

Look for the next installment of
THE CALHOUN WOMEN with Lilah and Suzanna's
stories, coming in March 1998.

Available at your favorite retail outlet.

Silhouette®